PRAISE FOR JUAN VILLORO'S *The Guilty*

"Villoro's point, punctuated by each of the stories in this powerful book, is that modern Mexico is finished, finally, trying to conform to outside notions of its tragedies.... Villoro, a contemporary of Roberto Bolaño, offers a similar style and comic tone, and much to enjoy."

—*The New York Times Book Review*

FAVORITE BOOKS OF 2015: "Magical realism is fun, but someone still has to clean up afterwards. Villoro's stories, always beleaguered but never brooding, sift soberly through the debris and extract an earthbound, workaday kind of enchantment."

—*The Believer*

"Villoro's writing, translated into English, is almost George Saundersesque: disarming, critical, and hilarious all at the same time."

—*Ploughshares*

"At last, an English translation brings his seriously funny take on identity to new audiences."

—*The Los Angeles Review of Books*

"The first collection of Villoro's short stories to be translated into English depicts the complexity of contemporary Mexico in sharp, compelling prose. In tales with fascinating protagonists and tightly crafted action, Villoro eschews stereotypes and flips common perceptions of his homeland.... Villoro rewards readers with refreshing, unforgettable stories."

—*Booklist*

"Villoro made me believe in the power of postmodernism to reflect back the multiple surfaces of our own highly constructed and often fictional lives. To do so while making the reader laugh out loud is no small feat."

—*Rain Taxi Review of Books*

"The writing is razor sharp, the satire brilliant and biting.... Villoro's English language debut presents seven expertly crafted stories that are funny and agile but also illuminating, exploring the paradox of being a Mexican in Mexico."

—*Three Percent*

TOP BOOK OF 2015: "The stories are sharp and hilarious and cut right through the (mostly) macho, male Mexican psyche. As a collection it is by turns entertaining and edifying and helped me understand our other closest neighboring country just a little bit better."

—*Publishing Perspectives*

"The recent publication of the short-story collection The Guilty is the long overdue debut in translation of Mexico's foremost author, Juan Villoro.... The prolific author of numerous novels, short stories, essays, plays, journalistic articles, and film scripts, Villoro has also become a consistent presence in Latin America and Europe, with his works widely lauded.... A fresh voice from Mexico...."

—*Review: Literature and Arts of the Americas*

THE REEF

GEORGE BRAZILLER ALSO PUBLISHES

The Guilty by Juan Villoro
Translated by Kimi Traube

THE REEF

A NOVEL BY

Juan Villoro

TRANSLATED FROM THE SPANISH BY YVETTE SIEGERT

GEORGE BRAZILLER, PUBLISHERS

George Braziller, Inc.
277 Broadway, Suite 708
New York, NY 10007

Library of Congress Cataloging-in-Publication Data

Title: The reef / Juan Villoro ; translated from the Spanish by Yvette Siegert.
Other titles: Arrecife. English
Description: First edition. I New York, NY : George Braziller, Publishers, 2017. I
    Published as Arrecife in Spanish by Editorial Anagrama (Barcelona, 2012).
Identifiers: LCCN 2016030307 (print) I LCCN 2016036380 (ebook) I ISBN
    9780807600214
Subjects: LCSH: Rock musicians—Fiction. I Seaside resorts—Fiction. I Fear—
    Fiction. I Caribbean Area—Fiction. I Psychological fiction.
Classification: LCC PQ7298.32.I55 A7713 2017 (print) I LCC PQ7298.32.I55
    (ebook) I DDC 863/.64—dc23
LC record available at https://lccn.loc.gov/2016030307

This publication was made possible with the encouragement of the Support
Program for Translation (PROTRAD) under Mexican cultural institutions.

Esta publicación fue realizada con el estímulo del Programa de Apoyo a la
Traducción (PROTRAD) dependiente de instituciones culturales mexicanas.

Designed by Rita Lascaro
Printed in the United States of America
First edition

But one day I shall find a land corrupted and depressed beyond all knowledge, where the children are starving for lack of milk, a land unhappy, although unenlightened, and cry: "I shall stay here until I have made this place good."

—MALCOLM LOWRY

I spent the first part of my life trying to wake up and the second part trying to fall asleep.
I wonder if there will be a third.

"Get out," said Sandra. But she left her door open.

A momentary paranoia made me suspect her, but my excitement was stronger than my need for safety.

I pushed on the door.

Her place seemed twice the size of mine. I passed a living room and followed the sound of a television blaring from her bedroom. I could hear panting. Did Sandra get the porn channel?

The last of the afternoon light streaked the walls of her room with a radiant violet. I turned my attention to the screen. Sandra had tuned in to a show about plastic surgery. I glanced around for the remote.

"Don't shut it off!" she yelled from the bathroom.

On TV, a doctor delicately lifted a pair of breast implants, as if handling sacred relics made of Jell-O. He spoke of "naturalness" and "self-confidence."

"You like watching this stuff?" I called in the direction of the door.

"It relaxes me," she said, entering the room.

She was wearing a terry-cloth bathrobe. The logo of The Pyramid, which shows the four corners of the heavens, was embossed over her left breast.

The walls of the room were now coated with a reddish glare from the TV. Did stuff like this calm her down? She taught some fusion of yoga and martial arts for a living, and it appeared that after eight hours at the studio, she enjoyed watching bodies get sacrificed under a scalpel.

I looked at her feet, which were bruised from exercise. The sun was already low, but its light still hurt after the five pineapple vodkas I'd just tossed back.

"Turn off the AC," Sandra said.

Her request pleased me. Switching it off made the room feel still and soundproofed.

Sandra's hand wandered to the belt of her robe, where she let it linger, like a master of suspense.

Waking up that morning, I'd stood a greater chance of doing battle with a manta ray than ever entering her bedroom. But by mid-afternoon something had changed. Maybe it was the vodka, maybe it was that terrible song which had seemed suddenly glorious: "Feelings."

Sandra and I had known each other about a year, but this was our first drink. She ordered a martini and complained about work. During her second martini, she remembered a worse job: for years she'd danced in a cage at a nightclub in Kukulcán.

On her third martini, she said, "Touch me with your finger."

The "finger" she was referring to was little more than a stump. I had lost one of the phalanges in a firecracker accident.

"Amputees," she said, "retain sensation where their missing limbs would be. My father lost one of his hands in Korea. Can you feel me with your finger?" She brought her face close to mine.

I thought back to the first erotic scene in cinema that had ever captivated me. Charlton Heston is playing El Cid and he's just slept with Sofia Loren. When she wakes up, she traces over the hero's nose and forehead with one of her gorgeous fingers. When I was twelve, that caress seemed like the ultimate erotic act: Sofia's finger sliding along the Cid as if she were drawing his form.

Forty years later here was a woman asking me to "touch" her face with my missing joint.

There was nobody else at Bar Canario. The empty stools perfected our privacy.

"Can you feel me?" she asked.

"Let's go to your room."

"What do you feel?"

"I'll tell you when we're up there," I said.

"When you're up on top of me?" She smiled, leaning back in her seat and biting a nail. Then she recited one of those annoying catch-phrases she'd picked up in her native Iowa:

"Don't shit where you eat."

I reminded her that we didn't actually work together. We *lived* at The Pyramid: the resort was representative of The City. We were isolated, living on the margins. Beyond our borders, life was detected by radar.

Luck came to my rescue. Juliancito, the 4'9" Maya bartender who had to mount a stool to mix drinks, could sense that I wanted to hear the song play on repeat. "Feelings" started again.

Certain songs possess a sentimental truth that comes to define the unspoken emotions of an era. They give voice to the things you felt but never dared to put into words. The poison you once denounced returns like the wonderful nectar of long lost days.

Back when I played bass in hotels, I could crank that sap out endlessly. I was missing half a finger, lacked the talent to be the next Jaco Pastorius, and had lost too many battles in the name of heavy metal; I accepted the night-lounge repertoire like someone reciting the periodic table of elements. I could play "Feelings" with all the neutrality with which I'd once memorized the chemical valence of chlorine.

Then, this afternoon at The Pyramid, that melody returned with a vengeance. Back when "Feelings" was in fashion, I'd still had the choice to risk ruining my life. Maybe that's what hit me: remembering what it feels like when all disaster still lies ahead of you.

"Is that your song?" Sandra said.

"Does that seem so strange to you?"

"I didn't take you for sentimental."

"I'm not sentimental," I said. "It's like pineapple juice. I don't like it, but I'm still drinking it. There are some annoyances that can get you through a bad day."

Sandra ordered another martini and became greatly interested in my bad day. I started describing the sounds of the hotel's aquarium. My friend Mario Müller had devised a novel task for me: to set the fish to music. My job was to line the sand of the aquarium with sensors that would translate the fish's movements into sounds. The resulting harmonies relaxed the guests but made the fish anxious. On full moons, the fish got particularly agitated. Stirring in a mild painkiller to seep through their gills had not been successful.

"You're a pesco-psychiatrist," Sandra said, flashing her enormous white teeth. I don't like the aggressive teeth of gringas. But there are some things, like pineapple juice, or Sandra's smile, that tend to improve with vodka.

"Your animals are neurotic," she said. "Mine are just animals. At the end of the day, what hurts most are my cheeks. Smiling that many hours is a bitch."

Sandra had been in Mexico for twenty years. She'd never lost her American accent, but she spoke better Spanish than the indigenous hotel employees. She even used more slang than me—an ex-rocker who's renounced the counterculture, that pretentious trick for turning rebelliousness into a system of profitable complaints. When I hung up my bass, I'd sworn I would kill myself before returning to pronouncements like "no way, José."

"Can't you work without smiling?" I asked.

"Exercise is a happy kind of pain," she explained. "I teach Ashtanga yoga, Tibetan kung fu, and *contact improv*. What do these things have in common? The teacher has to smile. So what happened to your finger?"

I told her that when I was sixteen a triangle firecracker went off in my hand. A girl was splattered with my blood. Her name has long escaped me, so now I called her Rebecca. The blood ran down her cheeks and she hadn't wiped it away—she was so enthralled with my injury, with this accident that was me. I'd held on to the firecracker to impress her. Sandra deserved this more complex version of the story—she did yoga. The truth is, when that firecracker went off all I could think was that the thing had cost a fortune. Five pesos down the drain.

"The firecracker was a *paloma*?" Sandra said, displaying her love of idioms.

"Yeah."

"That's fucked up, dude."

I hate slang the way you can only hate something you've spent your whole life taking intravenously. I didn't want to be *dude* or *dumbass* to Sandra, but at fifty-three, it was hard for me to imagine what else I could be to a woman of thirty-seven.

"And what about your leg?" she asked, referring to my limp.

"I got run over by a car," I said, reluctant to open another old wound.

"Was that before or after the firecracker?"

"Before."

"So you were already limping when you blew your finger off?" Her eyes were gleaming now. "You're sentimental," she decided. "I wouldn't have expected it."

This was Sandra's take on me: I had risked harming myself after I'd already done myself harm. But it wasn't self-destructive so much as it was sentimental. And Rebecca had been splattered with my blood. That would explain "Feelings."

At The Pyramid, talking about the past was unheard of. We were all there because we had screwed up somewhere else. One of the hotel's most civilized customs was that no one showed any curiosity about your previous life. Sandra had broken that protocol; she was interested in the person I'd stopped being.

Only then did I realize we were flirting.

"Do you feel anything in your finger?" she asked, returning to topic.

Sandra told me her classes usually began with ten sun salutations. The Caribbean climate had been spoiled, but not enough for my taste. There was always too much sun. But I didn't say anything; I just listened to her explain the dynamics of relaxation. She said she was sick of bodies perfected by exercise. She found my physical traumas interesting, as if my body were speaking to her in another language, in the French of injury.

I didn't answer her question about the sensation in my finger, and she went on to talk about her past. At seventeen, she came to the Caribbean with a Vietnam vet who suffered from night terrors. The two of them camped out on deserted beaches and smoked weed until the day he had a stroke.

"He went home to the United States in a body bag. Which is how he imagined he'd return from Saigon, not Mexico."

Afterward, Sandra remained on the coast and went through a period she referred to as "her misery." She got to know all the nightclubs and would show up wearing a shirt that said *Too Drunk To Fuck*, which wasn't very effective. She rehabilitated her life through an unusual form of suffering: dancing in a cage. It was like doing time. She finally got sober and discovered exercise and reliable income and hotel life. The Pyramid had been her best gig.

I had always thought of yoga as something band members took up when they got bored with success. But Sandra used complex techniques I had never heard of. She could help tourists control their aggression and get actors in touch with the visceral emotions they struggled to simulate.

"But you're tired of smiling," I said, trying to remind her that she needed a remedy of her own. Sandra was attractive, but I didn't like her so much as I liked our dynamic. She reached over and "touched" the non-existent part of my finger.

"Did you feel that?"

"Yes," I lied.

"Now you touch me," she said, extending the palm of her hand. This palmistry constituted the first physical contact between us. I traced her palm without touching her. It was almost entirely free of lines. Her skin seemed brand-new. Then I showed her my own palms, which were deeply lined.

"Your hands are like a map of Mexico City," she said. "Mine look like a map of Iowa." She took my finger and "sucked" on the invisible part.

"What do you feel?" she said.

"Let's go up to your room."

I didn't want us to go back to mine, fearing my books would kill the mood. At The Pyramid—a citadel where the beds were tended with surgical precision—a room such as mine suggested an eccentric inhabitant: a screenwriter who'd fled his life to adapt an incomprehensible novel; a voracious reader in a world where the most anyone ever read was the label on a tube of sunblock; a professor allergic to fresh air; a mentally disturbed person waiting for his chance to strike.

"Let's be reasonable," Sandra said.

"I felt something very special," I said. This was true, though I wasn't necessarily talking about my finger.

"I was sucking on air but it felt like something else," she conceded.

Then she asked for the check and insisted on paying. She wanted to give finality to our parting, in a spirit of generosity, her bills whispering kindly that I would not be getting into her bed.

"I liked talking to you," she said as she stood up.

I followed mechanically behind her.

We took the elevator up. Her room was on the fifth floor, mine on the seventh. She only pressed the 5. That was a good sign. I tried to kiss her.

"*You'd better not,*" she said, resisting. I liked that she was rejecting me in English, her native language.

I walked behind her to the room. That's when she said, "Get out."

But she left her door open.

Now she was lying on the bed, about to loosen her bathrobe.

"I have this fantasy," she said.

I felt a thrill of primal happiness—absolute, undeserved, perfect. Sandra was American and didn't like to mix business with pleasure. But she had a fantasy.

"Turn up the TV," she said.

I obeyed as she slid out of her robe. She lay down on her belly, completely naked.

"Stroke me with your finger. Just that. I don't want anything else. Agreed? I want you to feel me."

Sometimes I can sense a kind of electric current in the stump of my finger. The contractual tone of our arrangement was slightly annoying, but I was so turned on I could feel it all the way down to the tug of my shoelaces.

I proceeded to "stroke" her and then to trespass on the limits she'd imposed. *The torture of expectation,* I recalled. Where did that phrase come from? Some erudite writer of the eighteenth century? A guru? A fortune cookie? A sports commentator?

Without touching her, I admired Sandra's body, firm and toned from exercise. She parted her legs a little. I could see her bristly pubic hair, her labia, the purplish bud of her anus.

Onscreen, someone was moaning in pain. If you removed the context, the effect was erotic. *She's crazy,* I thought. The scene on TV changed. Bloody shadows glanced off Sandra's skin. Maybe in another room another couple was doing the same thing. Maybe this was normal. Caressed by these images and by the specter of my finger, Sandra began breathing heavily. Her bliss was torturing me.

I was about to interrupt the false pleasure of this ritual when the phone rang.

"You get it," she said.

"Are you sure?"

"We're adults, Antonio, you can be wherever the hell you want."

I took the receiver. It was Mario Müller. He recognized my voice.

"Tony?"

"You want to talk with Sandra?"

"No, with you."

How did he know I'd be there? I pictured a camera hidden behind Sandra's mirror. It only took a second for my paranoia to kick in: maybe the surgery channel was being used to spy on the hotel guests.

"Something's happened," Mario said urgently.

"Where are you?" I asked.

"At the aquarium."

Sandra was up and putting on her robe.

"It's Mario," I told her. "I have to go."

"Life outlasts pleasure," she said, as if reading something from a cereal box. More of her prosaic wisdom. "You'll be there soon. Good thing you didn't take your clothes off."

A practical girl, the last thing I needed.

I rushed out. In the hallway, I felt dizzy. The vodka racing to my head only added to my disappointment. I found a potted palm with large, fan-shaped leaves and reached it just in time to vomit. Now I felt better, not so much from the physical relief, but the satisfaction of having ruined the plant. I hated Mario—my lifelong best friend and manager of The Pyramid; capable of removing me from Sandra's room to go vomit in some hallway.

In the aquarium, the fish often seemed distressed. They'd swim in zigzags and collide with the glass, over and over again. So I would disconnect the tank's sensors and turn off the lights. In the dark I could make out their limp, desperately weak bodies trying to break through the glass.

I walked towards the brilliant glare of the tank where a hammerhead shark was drifting along with a total lack of urgency.

Against the crystalline turquoise, four lumpy figures appeared as if carved in relief. Three of them were standing. I could make out Mario Müller and the head of security, Leopoldo Támez, along with Ceballos the diver. I shifted my attention to the fourth figure, who was lying on the marble floor. Mario was shining a flashlight over him. The body lay in an unnatural position, as if the man were swimming, in mid-stroke. A spear was lodged in his back.

A grave silence oppressed the room, the kind only a corpse can impose. I crouched down to meet the eyes of Ginger Oldenville. Even in death, he wore the dreamy look of a man gazing up at seagulls.

There were no water tracks. He'd been murdered on that very spot, wearing his neoprene suit. I stood up and collected myself.

"Señor Tony!" Ceballos hugged me tightly. It did me good to take in the stink of plastic. Good because it kept me from thinking. I could feel Ceballos's sweaty brow against my neck. Inhaling the smell of neoprene had the soothing effect of alcohol.

My hands were shaking. I didn't want to open my eyes; I wanted to keep breathing that potent smell of plastic, to stay a safe distance from the world.

"A triple-sling speargun," Taméz informed us from behind.

"I know this is hard for you," Mario said to me.

Ginger had been one of the diving instructors. In his free time, he'd help me run the cables under the aquarium's sand. My fish bored him, they lived in what he thought of as dead water, but he was always willing to lend me a hand.

I turned to Támez, who was busy balancing two cell phones and a notepad. He was writing with a look of great discomfort and feigned concentration. All of us hated him. *He did it,* I thought. The luminous blues of the aquarium made his pockmarked face look like the surface of the moon.

I'd taken to Ginger right from the start. His name always made me think of that titan among drummers, Ginger Baker; and his face, cheerful and freckled, reminded me of a character in *Flipper*, a favorite TV show from my child-hood. Also, he enjoyed playing with dolphins and behaved like someone predisposed to having fun. Any oyster he pried open was delicious. The water temperature was always just right. To him a negative surprise was a foreign concept, as was the possibility of disappointment or the potential for an adverse outcome.

He hailed from Detroit, the "Motor City," but it was hard to imagine him on the road. This was, in fact, the first time I'd ever seen him when he wasn't soaking wet. His life at The Pyramid had played out like one long, enthusiastic dive under the sun. Who could possibly have anything against him?

Támez was still writing. *It wasn't him,* I decided. The chief of security had little respect for human life, but he lacked the imagination to commit that kind of violence, a speargun outside the water.

Diving suits worn indoors can be unbearably warm. But Ceballos was shivering.

"I'm going to get changed," he said.

Two employees entered carrying a cot. They worked for management, their uniforms pistachio-green. They stood in place for a moment, held in the stillness that comes over people contemplating cadavers. Mario ordered them to get moving. They maneuvered like they had never carried a dead body before. Ginger's face banged against the floor several times. I went to Mario's side.

"How'd you know where I was?" I asked.

"Juliancito. He saw you and Sandra leaving the bar together. Said you were both wasted—it was your room or hers."

Then, in the voice of a third-rate character actor playing the head of security, Támez announced, "I'm going to report this to the Federal Public Ministry."

Mario turned off his flashlight. The fish swam behind him.

In shadow, I mentally reconstructed my friend's face. We'd known each other since we were kids. I could visualize those features perfectly: the face of someone who can study an ant colony and never imagine getting bitten; of someone who enjoys tackling the fiercest problems but is terrified of mice; the face of a man who always knows exactly how many hotel towels are required but can never remember where he left his glasses. The face of someone whose curiosity always exceeds the facts. I knew him first as Mario, then as Chico Müller, and sometimes as Der

Meister. He was the lead singer of Los Extraditables, the rock band that had both justified and destroyed a decade of our lives.

A few years earlier, he had rescued me from a studio where it was my job to create the sound effects for dying cartoon characters.

"You remember that abandoned house?" he asked suddenly.

It had started raining. The Pyramid was an open-air atrium. Water trickled down over the plants and fed into the artificial waterfall that served as the primary decoration in the lobby below. Mario suggested we go to his office.

The Pyramid was luxury complete with a leaky roof. The hotel's waterproofing didn't work, and rain also came in obliquely through the hallways' paneless window frames. Plus, the AC units were always dripping. By the time I got to his office, my right shoe was drenched.

The disorder on Mario's desk belied the obsessive control he maintained over other parts of the hotel. He found me a mug from a local seafood place (it had a picture of a red shrimp on it) and poured me some of his favorite twelve-year-old whiskey. It smelled of coffee. Mario took his own drink in the little plastic serving cap of a cough-syrup bottle.

He rubbed his forehead, from which two small bones protruded like timid horns. His hair, too blond for the coast, had thinned everywhere except along his neck and temples, where his skin was starting to wrinkle. His thin lips, shaped for smooth insults or lazy compliments, tested the whiskey without getting wet. Then they opened.

"To the abandoned house and to Ginger!" The first toast was more enthusiastic than the second.

He drained the small cap and poured himself another finger. He wanted to sedate himself. *They're going to screw him over,* I thought. Maybe no one else knew about the crime yet, but it wouldn't be easy to keep paradise populated with a corpse on deck.

Mario rubbed his forehead again. With characteristic stubbornness, he still wore his wedding ring even though he and his wife had been separated for over seven years. He talked about the abandoned house in the neighborhood where we grew up, a mansion from the 1930s. In 1970 or '71, when we'd finally set foot in it for the first time, the place had already been vacant for more than 10 years. The electricity had been shut off, the rooms were full of leaks, and there were loose tiles all over the porch.

Being friends meant sharing our boredom. We'd get together to feed our vague need for belonging or just to escape our houses, where electronic gadgets weren't yet so interesting.

For years I'd been told that my father had died or disappeared at Tlatelolco, on October 2, 1968. My mother barely mentioned him. She was a strong woman, firm in her convictions, but sometimes she would sink—without any tantrums or hysterics—into periods of deep depression that masked this strength. She worked a double shift, at an institution and at a speech clinic for the deaf, and she'd come home each day exhausted from the struggle of trying to help people speak. She didn't want to hear any questions, so I stopped asking them. All I knew was that my father's death had affected her less than it would have affected other people, those who were capable of crying. My mother didn't cry. She never had. It's actually very strange. I wonder if there's a registry for the children of mothers who have never cried. It would make for a small and confused demographic. Not that I wanted to see her cry. It's just so hard to explain the fact she never did.

My father was an engineer and apparently not too popular among his colleagues. He had a terrifying temper, my mother would tell me. Plus, he was a genius at calculus, and who could forgive him for that?

I don't remember any drama in my early childhood, but my parents' version of getting along was co-existing in silence. You'd think this was an unusual arrangement for a speech pathologist.

It's quite possible that the rupture of my father's disappearance, which happened when I was nine, was a great relief to my mother. Had my father taken advantage of the chaos in the Plaza de las Tres Culturas as an excuse to liberate my mother from his presence? When I hear *Tlatelolco*, it still sounds like the code word for a planned separation.

The student movement hadn't been popular in either my neighborhood or at my school. The idea that my father could have died for such a cause had an air of illicit mystery. But as the years passed, the movement gained prominence and its main actors began to be seen as victims. At that point, I started to believe that this should give me certain privileges. Whenever the doorbell rang in our apartment, I'd imagine it was a bureaucrat come to present us with a brand-new color television just for having lost someone at Tlatelolco.

I only benefited from my connection to the tragedy once. Somehow, our civics teacher found out about my father's disappearance. He gave me an A+ for no reason other than that. But the reward bothered me. I didn't want an A+ in civics. I wanted the government to give me a television.

What memories do I have of my father? I know he liked bullfights and knew how to waltz. He was so tall he'd hit his head against door frames, but he never complained when it hurt. He was like a bug that keeps bumping into the window pane. His face smelled like Old Spice and his body like detergent. He could make me obey with a single glance—his eyes looked like they would explode if you didn't do what he said. He was so brilliant with measurements that he could glimpse a building and tell you exactly how high it was and how far it was from where you were standing. He never wore glasses and hated shoes without laces. That's all I remember.

We had a photo of him in the living room. He didn't look like an engineer or like a '68 militant. But he did look like something else he'd been: a cotton-candy vendor. His mouth promised a sweetness of little substance.

His family owned a snack shop where he helped out on Sundays. He met my mother in a park. He wanted to treat her to some cotton candy but she insisted on paying for it. That first disagreement was how they got together.

My mother spent her days at the speech clinic, and my father had been disappeared. As time passed, the theory behind his death faded, and I fell into the habit of imagining him back in Chihuahua, his hometown, dancing a waltz.

Mario Müller had six brothers, enough for his parents to accept one more. From them I learned that it's possible to love distractedly, without expressing it or even knowing how many other people are in the room. I was fascinated by the constant activity and disorder of his house. But Mario hated it, which may help explain why he chose to become a hotel manager, presiding like a holy tyrant over 400 impeccable rooms.

"I remember that abandoned house better than my own," he said, on the night of Ginger's murder. He took a sip from the little measuring cup. In minute detail, he could recall the mirror that covered half the living room wall, the stained glass windows in the foyer, the way the sunlight filtered through in violet and amber rhombuses. Peeking through those windows was a bad idea, because by the time we left, our sweaters were always ripped and our nondescript 13 and 14-year-old faces—subjects without stories—were completely covered in dirt. Looking at the few photos we have from that era, you'd think we'd grown up in households much poorer than our own.

Why would anyone abandon an enormous house that came with a garden and two stately palm trees; a terrace with a pergola; a semicircular staircase for the lady of the house to trail her dress across; and bathrooms with rosy mosaics fit for girls or nymphs? What crime, what curse, what spectacular misfortune could explain its emptiness?

My friends suggested zombies, ghosts, criminals. Anything that might account for these rooms where every word we spoke echoed twice. Secretly I had other ideas. Maybe the father had split, which would have meant the fast ruin of everyone else in the household. I'd become a kind of collector of absent fathers. At school, I always knew which of the kids in class had no dad.

Having such a magnificent stage at our disposal inspired all kinds of extreme ideas. One day Mario lined us up in front of the big mirror and, undeterred by our reluctant expressions, proposed we form a rock band. That was the birth of Los Extraditables. We'd rehearse in the grand, empty living room, its echoey acoustics inciting fantasies of the warehouses and concert halls we'd go on to play ten years later.

"You remember Oso Negro?" Mario asked. "Did you know there's a whole gay subculture involving bears?"

"No," I said.

"Didn't you ever discuss that with Ginger?"

"No."

"What did you guys talk about?"

"Fish. Sound. Nothing. Was I supposed to talk about bears in gay culture?"

"Ginger was gay."

"I didn't know."

"That doesn't surprise me. You live in a bubble," he said. "A bubble inside an aquarium," he added, with a hint of sadness. "Ginger didn't like effeminate men or metrosexuals. He liked athletic types and grizzly bears, big broad men with hair all over their bodies. His old-age fantasy was to have sex with Santa Claus, the ultimate polar bear."

"How do you know all this?" I asked.

"He posted it on Facebook. Intimacy is now collective. Ginger was a nice guy, maybe too nice. What kind of person murders Santa's boyfriend?" Mario looked at the floor.

"What were you going to say about the abandoned house?" I asked.

"Remember how we'd get drunk on Oso Negro? I don't know how we drank that piss."

I remembered the afternoon we'd drained a bottle of that cheap vodka, then heard a noise upstairs. Before then it had never occurred to us that someone else might be able to break in.

We were ready to get the hell out of there when from the foyer staircase we spotted a giant man, as drunk as we were. His hair was disheveled; he had a long, scraggly beard; and his face was covered with soot, or just infinite layers of filth. He wore the long overcoat of an outlaw, black and shiny, and fingerless wool gloves. A winter fugitive in a spring-time city. But the most amazing thing about him wasn't his neglected appearance or even his drunken stumbling, it was the fact that his fly was open and revealed a massive red erection.

We raced to the kitchen. The agile guys in the group managed to escape through the window. I hid in the pantry and spied through a door crack. Mario was about to slip out when the giant somehow caught him. My friend screamed, unable to get free. Those filthy hands gripped him tightly.

I crept out of the pantry and grabbed the bottle of Oso Negro, then climbed up onto the kitchen table, the only piece of furniture left in the house. The wood creaked and the bum turned toward me. I saw his grey eyes like two frozen figs. His expression terrified me. I raised the bottle and smashed it against his sweaty forehead. He landed on the table so hard that one of its legs broke off.

Whether he was dead or unconscious, his erection was preserved.

We climbed out the window. The other guys were waiting for us on the street. Mario gave me a hug I'll never forget, a calm and unemotional hug, as if survival were part of our daily routine. I didn't notice his suppressed anxiety or perceive, at the time, the lack of imagination behind such an austere gesture of friendship.

"Sometimes I dream I'm back in that house and the giant has me by the foot," Mario said. "You saved me, Tony."

"I didn't know what I was doing."

"You brought down the bear with the bottle. You were awesome." Then he added, without conviction, "You were a good bass player. The real backbone of the band."

"Don't make things up. I almost quit the group!"

"You were there," he said. "That's what counts."

Why was he bringing this up?

I remembered a guy my mother used to date. She introduced him to us as "Carlos Truyet's right hand man." Truyet was a millionaire who had built half of Acapulco. I was struck by the idea that it was possible to make a living as "a man you can trust." In some ways I had been that person for Mario. It wasn't strange that I should fill that role. What was strange was that he needed me to.

"Támez will speak with you tomorrow," he said abruptly. "Don't trust him. I didn't hire him. London handles security personnel."

"I wasn't planning on trusting him."

"Remember Meister Eckhart?"

"The Fruits of Nothingness," I replied automatically, citing the title of a famous Spanish edition by that most celebrated of thirteenth-century hippies. Mario had discovered it in the library at the Swiss School. For years it was the only book he read. This is why we all called him Der Meister. One of our songs was titled "The Fruits of Nothingness."

"The Pyramid has been my major contribution to rock and roll."

"Slow down, Mario. It's just a hotel," I said. I knew where he was going with this and wanted to curb it.... Too late. My friend continued:

"Nowadays the old hippies design software. The new ecstasy doesn't come from music or drugs, it comes from technology and entertainment. It's electronic LSD. Támez doesn't give a shit about our vision."

The word *vision* seemed a little florid for the hotel's online reservation system.

It irritated me that Mario should see himself as a kind of New Age guru. I knew him too well to find him awe-inspiring. His nickname was a form of teasing, after all: we called him Der Meister as a sign of disobedience.

Now it was time for me to play the role of "man you can trust."

"Mario," I said, "your 'vision' involves all the guest rooms having shampoo."

He made no reply.

"Are you going to talk with El Gringo?" I asked.

"I don't know. Not yet."

El Gringo Peterson was the major shareholder of The Pyramid, though the hotel belonged to the Atrium Group, which was based in London. Peterson had gone to New York for several weeks and left Mario in charge of the whole operation. Der Meister was the appointed manager and the self-appointed visionary who had designed The Pyramid's symbolic universe and the entertainment program.

The rain hadn't stopped. It reminded me of a night I'd gone out walking in the gardens. I'd been carrying one of the oversize umbrellas from valet parking. There, in some out of the way corner, I'd found Peterson, enjoying the rain.

I'm sobering up, he had said in his terse New England way. The rain served as a kind of cold shower. I'd never seen him without a glass of bourbon at arm's reach, but I hadn't noticed any genuine signs of alcoholism. Nothing but a certain calm acceptance of a world he deemed absurd. That night in the rain, though, he'd seemed lost, incapable of finding the way back to his hotel room.

After that, El Gringo would seek me out for a chat every couple of weeks. Mario wasn't jealous of him, because jealousy would look like a loss of control. Still, theirs was a tense relationship and Mario was suspicious of ours.

I never complained to Peterson about work-related issues. We had struck up the kind of friendship that only functions at a distance, as a way to avoid thinking about malaria or the heat or nature. A friendship between exiles who have resigned themselves to telling stories. Anything more than that just makes them sweat.

"What's up with Sandra?" Mario asked with no real interest.

"Nothing's up. You got me out of there."

"Don't worry," he said. "You'll get your chance. The Pyramid's not such a big place."

I wondered if Sandra might still be up. Probably not. Her body was boss. She needed a good night's sleep, free from the relatively forgettable problem of me. I yawned. Mario Müller looked at me with eyes bleary from exhaustion.

We had witnessed murder, but we still had to sleep.

The two of us parted with an awkward hug.

Walking back, I spotted a little transparent gecko. I have a certain weakness for lizards: they're great company for drug addicts. When you're high, even the presence of an insect feels intolerable and nearly all other animal species seem to pose a threat. But lizards move so gracefully, and they glow in the dark. I liked to watch them scurrying around like colorful embodiments of my ideas. Back then I rarely had any real ideas, but the lizards, electric blue, bright yellow and green, made me think that I did.

El Gringo Peterson liked to hear stories from my drug days. His best friend had died in Vietnam, gutted top to bottom by a bayonet. Deep in the napalm trenches, he'd stumbled into hand-to-hand combat, like a Cherokee. His other best friend came back addicted to heroin. *I never went to Saigon,* El Gringo would say. But he was obsessed with the place. Part of my brain had been wrecked by drugs, and he loved to hear me describe my hallucinations and the nights I half-remembered. He'd listen to my stories as if I'd just returned from Vietnam myself.

It's difficult to talk about things you've forgotten, but Peterson was just happy to be around someone who'd gone off the deep end. *You got out,* he'd say. *This ain't 'Nam, it's a fucking paradise.*

I liked hearing a hotel magnate mock the luxuries of his own hotel. Peterson wore light-colored shirts from Sears. He cut his hair very short, and his muscular arms, which were covered in a fine reddish down, suggested strenuous workouts. He carried himself like the soldier he'd never been. (They hadn't let him enlist because of some problem with his eyesight.)

The whiskey he drank was much cheaper than Mario's. During our Four Roses sessions, Peterson would ask for the details of my hard living with a noble curiosity that had little to do with compassion. He'd lost his best friends. He wasn't some anti-commie patriot. The Vietcong mattered very little to him. Simply put, his life had a tragic foundation. He'd managed to save himself.

Peterson was born in Wallingford, a drab village in the middle of the Vermont woods. His father owned a gas station. Peterson grew up filling the tanks of cars that stopped by for barely a minute. He had no plan to leave that village where nobody else stayed for long. At the local library, he would read whatever happened to be lying around, then head to Rutland, the neighboring town, to see a movie or buy spare auto parts. He swam in the cold lake, which steamed with mosquitoes in summer. When he turned eighteen, he married a girl from the neighborhood. They were the kind of people born to stay and live in harsh but endurable isolation.

Peterson had two solid pals. Together, they took apart motors and drank beer and talked endlessly about baseball. (Or at least that's what he said. I pictured him as someone who existed in his own silent satisfaction, sharing a wordless friendship as the sun fell behind dense forest.) When he turned nineteen, he had a son. Everything in his destiny pointed to an immobile life of happy stasis and pleasant continuity. But misfortune struck twice in the next few years: his son drowned in the lake, and his wife died by poison, possibly self-administered. His life suddenly became something that had already happened. Everything else—the future—now ceased to exist.

The United States, he once told me, always offers up some war to help you atone for your guilt. His best friends had left for Vietnam, but he'd been rejected by the Army. *I didn't want to kill anyone, I wanted to go die there.* He'd repeated this phrase so many times I confused it for a song by Los Extraditables. At that point in the litany, he'd take a sip of his drink then say, *I wanted to die; what I had to settle for was success.*

Everything in his town brought back memories of his wife and son. Meanwhile, his friends were cutting through humid jungles and firing their guns from inside clouds of marijuana smoke, all to the beat of Creedence Clearwater Revival.

Peterson left Wallingford and found a job at the Howard Johnson's in Rutland, where he showed an unusual talent for interacting with the people passing through. He was hired by a Holiday Inn, where he prospered in various roles, from liquor chief to head of personnel and finally to manager.

He liked to ask me about my father, the way I imagined him, my theories about why he'd walked out on us. (From the moment I mentioned it, Peterson never believed it possible my father had been riddled with bullets at Tlatelolco.) He was curious about how I'd coped with the disappearance. The uncertainty of not knowing seemed worse to him than the certainty of death. Still, he never convinced me that it would have been better to know all the details. Peterson was chained to the memory of the son he hadn't been able to save. He could recall, with maddening attention to detail, the ripped starter cord of the outboard motor on the little boat he used to cross the lake, as well as the number of minutes he had waited for the motor to cool before pulling the cord again. The transistor radio was broadcasting a Boston Red Sox game. Peterson spent the fourth and fifth innings tuning the motor. Then he rode across the lake, heading for the dock where his son was meant to be waiting for him with some friends who were throwing a party.

Nobody noticed when the two-year-old boy slipped away from the group. Nobody heard the splash when he fell into the water. There were so many people at the party that there was no one Peterson could blame. His wife was in bed with a fever. With violent insistence, Peterson would relive the exact moment when he recognized the rosy splotch in the water and then the little white dot. His son had an infection and was wearing cotton in his ears. That particular detail is what confirmed for Peterson that his son was dead. Of all Wallingford's inhabitants, only two of them were in the water, and they were father and son. In a sinister twist, the boy had appeared to the very person who'd been seeking him. Thousands of times, Peterson went over the moments it took to fix the motor. He'd always been a methodical guy. He listened to two innings of baseball while mending the cord. It didn't take long. He'd read transcripts of that baseball game trying to ascertain the extent to which he could incriminate himself. There were no runs or strike-outs in the fourth. The batters had been "retired in order," as the announcers liked to say. There were three hits in the fifth, but still no runs. The innings hadn't lasted that long—just long enough to make a difference.

He wasn't directly responsible for the boy's death. But it would have been possible to prevent it, and that was enough to sink Peterson, enough for him to pursue, with methodical effort, his own way to drown. He never spoke of it to Mario, though he did discuss it with me—with the addict who could barely remember his own father. He treated me like a war veteran, like someone who'd been fucked over in another 'Nam, like the victim he'd never gotten to be.

Peterson achieved the American Dream without wanting to attain it, and his success felt like a second annihilation. In my eyes, that alone gave him a certain dignity. *He's one scary asshole,* Mario would say, just to provoke me.

The places inhabited by nobodies—specifically, anonymous kitchens designed for industrial-scale recipes—became Peterson's new environment. He never had close relationships with anyone else again. Not even I counted as a real friend. I'd listen to the story of his aimless career and tell him about the broken world he'd never discovered for himself. That was it. Two strangers in the tropics.

But the weirdest thing about Peterson as a business man was the way he handled money. He was incurably addicted to the racetrack. He'd bet all his wages in order to absolve himself of them. But luck mistreated him time and again, forcing him to win. He followed the races, though he never gave himself the luxury of actually going to the Epsom or Kentucky Derbies. Instead, he'd place his bets over the phone, far from the spectacle of the horses, focusing solely on the names and times, like a Puritan of Fortune who distrusts everything but the results.

To me, El Gringo Peterson seemed like a great guy, the opposite of a conqueror. He had found success because he'd failed at what he was really interested in. His cold, calculating, and accurate betting had been refined by Fortune's long-term rejection.

Tell me again how lizards move when you're high, he'd ask, as a sliver of spit made its way down his chin. I didn't enjoy reliving those years I'd spent sandpapering my brain away, but given my weakness for lizards, I never passed up the chance to relate the few pleasant memories from that period.

Once I asked Peterson why he'd never tried heroin with his friend who'd survived Saigon. *I didn't want the drug,* he told me. *What I wanted was the punishment, the war. Heroin is the consolation prize of heroes. I didn't want to be consoled.* I told him I hadn't needed any wars to do drugs. He burst out laughing. *Tony,* he said, *you're Mexican. You people don't need a war to get high. Here, reality is already an altered state.*

I woke to the shrieks of seagulls. The telephone rang. It was 6 a.m., and Leopoldo Támez was talking as if there was nothing more normal than that hour paired with the sound of his voice. He wanted to meet at Tabachines, the cafeteria located on The Pyramid's south terrace.

A shower woke me up again. Under the flow of water, I decided that I'd slept well, and deeply, without memories or images. I hadn't taken a sleeping pill. Maybe all I really needed for a good night's sleep was a corpse. Ginger Oldenville was dead, and this hurt me; but I'd slept.

The chief of security was waiting at the far end of the terrace. I found him killing ants on the railing with his thumb.

His eyes had the unsettling opacity of oysters. He wore dark glasses, but it was unpleasant just to know that behind the tinted plastic skulked something so bland and vile.

It isn't hard to be dismissive of anyone who's worked in law enforcement. Leopoldo Támez had worn a uniform in order to abuse the people of Punta Fermín, the battered shantytown where all the local employees lived. Then he'd been promoted to the precinct in Kukulcán, a five-star tourist enclave. Here, dressed in plain clothes, he'd met the quota of grievances that allowed one to prosper within the ranks of private security. He belonged to that class of personal-damage expert whose great talent is the avoidance of the very injuries they're tasked to provide.

Mario Müller was his superior but not his boss. Támez had been hired by Atrium's own security office. Every month he had to send a report to London. As long as there were no casualties, his command over the tropics was acceptable. But now there was a casualty.

"What can you tell me about Señor Ginger?" he asked. His tone was as bitter as the first sip of coffee. I told him what I knew, that everyone respected Ginger Oldenville. Támez squashed an ant that was crawling up his forearm but it got tangled, and he had to tear out a knot of his own thick hair. All this was done in casual silence, as if removing dead bugs was his way of being normal.

"I need you to jog your memory just a teeny bit more," he said.

Ginger used to explore the local cenotes and the underground rivers that flowed between them. To him we owed our subaquatic "lifeline"—the cable, attached by eyebolts to rock, which guided the divers through the dark water. One time he told me of a trip he took to the Galápagos, where he saw every imaginable species and took pictures of a white shark up close. (This shot was the wallpaper on his phone). He liked controlled risk. Whenever he went on a particularly deep dive, he would leave several oxygen tanks attached to a cord, making multiple stops as he rose to the surface. At every stage he'd allow some time for decompression. I spoke of Ginger with admiration. We didn't share the same passions, but I could appreciate his dedication and his skill.

Támez wasn't interested in diving.

"He didn't have any weaknesses?" he asked.

I was familiar with some of Ginger's ways. He didn't like to eat pineapple because it made his tongue sting; he was lactose intolerant. Funny to think that a guy who could photograph a white shark from six feet away could be so sensitive to the little things. Támez didn't deserve to know this.

"Do you know Roger Bacon?" he suddenly asked.

"Who is he?"

"A friend of Señor Ginger's. He was staying in Ginger's room until the night before the murder. Roger spent two weeks at The Pyramid."

"If I saw him, I don't remember," I said.

"He wore pirate earrings and had tattoos on his arms...?"

"Most of the tourists here have tattoos."

"Señor Roger had a tattoo on his arm that was written in Arabic. I spent my early morning going over footage from the security cameras. The one in the aquarium had been turned off. Who has access to this camera?" Támez adjusted his glasses. Studying his eyes, I understood the implication.

"Any electrician could turn off the camera in the aquarium."

"The camera recording stops twenty minutes before the crime took place. There were no electricians on duty at that time."

"I wasn't there. I couldn't know who turned off the camera."

"You were with Señorita Sandra."

It annoyed me that he knew where I was, but not as much as the way he'd said *señorita*. Támez had the calm demeanor of a worldly man who tolerates the bizarre private lives of others. The civilized tone was insufferable from someone so rotten inside.

"I spoke with Sandra," he went on, smiling. "You have an alibi. That's good enough for me. It was a triple-sling speargun. Does that mean anything to you?"

"No."

"Ceballos knows the locker rooms, the aquarium, the location of the cameras; he would know how to use a speargun. According to his testimony, he was running late to meet Ginger because he was busy filling out a form for HR, who had shown up in the locker room. It's strange that they would come looking for him at that hour, but it does give him an alibi. He arrived at the scene of the crime a few minutes later. Besides, Ceballos is Ceballos! Some poor idiot! He doesn't have the imagination to murder someone." He said this with satisfaction, as if he himself had an excess of imagination. "Last night he was shitting himself."

"And why were they wearing diving gear at that hour?"

"Good question. They were going on a night expedition, to a cenote. That's one of the new entertainment itineraries: they light up a cenote and stay out diving until sunrise. Then they're brought breakfast—Yucatán-style tamales. One of Señor Mario's ideas."

He paused, as if allowing me time to evaluate the ethics of such an idea. Then he handed me a piece of paper. It was something he'd printed from the Internet. The page showed a man with a naked torso covered in spikes. This was no Saint Sebastian figure—more like the opposite: the saint's arrows were actually defensive weapons, their tips aimed at the viewer like the quills of a porcupine.

"The Cruci/Fiction group."

"What is that?"

"It's a risk club. The members are into 'ultra sports.' They parachute onto snowy mountains wearing skis—crazy stunts like that. There are no injuries, only deaths. Ginger Oldenville was a member. Read this."

He pointed to a paragraph with his sausagey finger:

"No one can predict the date of his death, and we have no desire to find out. But when that day comes, we want death to be swift, beautiful—joyful! We create legally au thorized fictions in order to live life to the fullest and to make our exit with impeccable dignity."

Támez had already finished his breakfast before I'd shown up. There were leftover scraps of egg and dry beef and bits of red sauce still on his plate. Judging by his girth, the guy must have eaten half a dozen eggs a day. As I handed the paper back to him, I grazed his plate, staining the paper red. I took a moment to study the papaya I'd ordered.

People don't accelerate to 180 miles per hour to kill themselves. They do it just to know they could. Mario had once told me this in Meister mode; this was how the great guru of The Pyramid could justify anything, from bungee-jumping to paragliding behind a boat. The staple idea for the superfast set: tourists are in love with fear.

"Señor Roger was also in Cruci/Fiction," Támez continued. "He *checked out of the hotel* two days ago. He and Señor Ginger were very close." He pressed his index fingers together. "Look, I don't care if you're a pansy, but if you kill another pansy then I do care." He paused but I refused to dignify his silence with a response.

"I found out about Cruci/Fiction from Señor Ginger's Facebook page," he went on. "We were 'friends.' I mean computer friends, don't misunderstand me. I follow many employees from The Pyramid on Facebook. It's too bad you're not on it."

"There are ants crawling on your arm," I said.

"Thank you." He brushed them off energetically, creating more arm-hair knots, which he then began to rip out. "Ginger Oldenville was a stunt double on *Jaws 3-D*. Were you aware of this?"

"No."

"He was a thrill seeker. 'Legally authorized' dangers, of course, like they say on the Cruci/Fiction web site. Have you ever gone to any of these movie *chill-out* nights?"

In the evenings, the hotel staff hosted screenings in the so-called *chill-out* room, where they'd blast techno and project a movie onto an enormous white wall. Almost all the films featured storms. A boat would set off in pursuit of a monstrous wave the surfers were willing to risk their lives for. Were those guys part of Cruci/Fiction, too?

Támez had proven himself to be surprisingly efficient. In one day he'd managed to source Ginger Oldenville's profile. *They must've sent it from London,* I thought. The security machine had been set in motion. The hotel had a dead man. And that wasn't the worst of it. Támez's speed revealed the real cause for alarm: the dead man was a gringo.

"Ginger didn't die in the water," I said. "He wasn't seeking danger."

The chief of security smiled, as if he'd been waiting to make this point himself.

"Maybe he made a pact with Señor Roger," he said. "What do you think?"

"About what?"

"Your lover stabbing you with a speargun, it makes you hard, doesn't it? That is, if you're like Señor Ginger?"

"I don't know."

Támez needed a story to pitch to London, something that would calm them down, maybe a gay suicide pact, an extreme sport that went too far, a cruci-fiction.

"If you can remember anything else, you'll be sure to let me know."

His emphasis on the word *else* was infuriating.

I stopped by Gringo Peterson's office. His secretary hadn't been able to find him. He wasn't in New York or at his place in Kentucky.

El Gringo ran The Pyramid remotely. He'd visit now and then to oversee the accounting and review Mario Müller's entertainment itineraries. He didn't want to know too much about the touristy excesses that kept the place running through periods of crisis.

Practically all of the hotels in Kukulcán were vacant. They rose up along the shore like vertical mausoleums, circled by seagulls and ravaged by plants and rats.

The cruise ships no longer pulled into the pier where an enormous statue of Sebastián, our sainted sculptor, dominated the landscape. In the distance we could see the ships passing by. Only their trash made it to the beach. In the evenings, children and old people wearing rags would emerge to sort through it. I'd seen them make off with spoons, plastic bags (their contents mysterious), and bits of soggy food.

The coastal region had entered a period of hardship. The tourist enclave hadn't heeded the warnings about building on sand: the wind beat mercilessly against the façades and then rushed out to sea, taking the beach along with it. Every day a slow boat from Santo Domingo would bring sand to fill the cavities along the shore. The coastline was slowly devouring itself.

Also, the oil rigs and city plumbing had contaminated the water, which was now threatening the second-largest coral reef in the world. Things at The Pyramid weren't so bad, especially in contrast to the thirty-story buildings of the hotel's competitors, where the only signs of life were the sudden short-circuitings of electrical appliances. Still, El Gringo never felt at ease about the business. It's possible that deep down he was still wary of success; or maybe, thanks to his Puritan heritage, he was repulsed by the idea of repackaging risk as pleasure.

Why, then, did he put so much trust in Mario? Der Meister had been Peterson's solution for avoiding total disaster. The reef's days were numbered. Under constant rainfall the hotels had been closing one by one, or operating at 10 percent occupancy. The area was moving toward decline, but Mario had found a solution: he was peddling a tropics amped on adrenaline, complete with venomous spiders, and excursions that created the illusion of miracle survival—necessitating raucous after-parties. *Fear is the best aphrodisiac,* he'd explain. *No one allows themselves more liberties than a survivor.*

In the end, Peterson had embraced my friend's ideas like science fiction. Der Meister referred to these activities as "post-tourism," to which Peterson would retort, *Watch your French.* With resigned disgust, he watched his pleasure garden transform into a Sodom with piña coladas, a Disneyland with herpes, or a 'Nam with room service.

I'd come to The Pyramid without much interest in anything. Abstinence seemed like just another kind of void. In El Gringo's eyes, I had the dignified aura of a combat veteran. He listened to my tales of addiction and endowed me with a war. His avid gaze made it clear he thought I'd been to Saigon and dodged traps lined with bamboo spikes.

I didn't always know what to tell him. The '80s and '90s were mostly a haze, a formless period of penury from which all that remained were my own unreliable memories. Had it happened, or was it just an acid flashback?

Mario also liked to relive the past with me. He liked to remind me of the things I'd forgotten. Sometimes he'd ask me to relay a message to El Gringo. In some sense, he spoke to his boss through me.

The Pyramid was divided into stratified zones. The guests wore plastic wristbands signaling different levels of membership, up to an "all-benefits-included" package.

A green wristband permitted entrance to a zone of bungalows with limited access to the beach. It was a quiet spot, hidden between clusters of bamboo, that was popular with retirees.

A silver wristband offered admission to a vast complex that extended outwards from a triangular, blue glass building known as The Ziggurat. Here you could find restaurants, bars, nightclubs, a shopping center, gyms, seven swimming pools, and a golf course, as well as an infirmary, a spa, a nursery, and a private club with every imaginable board game. For a few years now, this section had been at around 50 percent vacancy.

Inside the resort, real privilege came with a purple wristband, allowing access to all three sections. Regardless, those who wore the purple wristband spent all their time at The Pyramid, an enormous structure modeled after the Temple of the Inscriptions located in Palenque. The vertigo-defying stairways on the building's façade were merely decorative, but they, along with the triangular archways, the bas reliefs and their glyphs, the sculptures of the god Chac Mool dispersed throughout the garden, and the constant presence of the hotel logo showing a four-cornered heaven gave this citadel of relaxation the aura of an archeological site. The area was surrounded by a semitropical rain forest. Its true purpose was to hide the electric fences.

Mario Müller made sure to maintain a sharp contrast between the perks offered in the green and silver sections. Without this, the exclusivity of the purple section would have been diminished. *We need silver people,* Mario explained, *so the purple people can have the satisfaction of not belonging to that section.*

Green stood for nature, which was pleasant for obvious reasons. Silver suggested an attractive second place. Purple lacked the supremacy of gold or platinum, and its appeal was multifaceted and hard to define: it stood for summer wine, for transubstantiation, for the bishop's cloak or the matador's cape, for a royal scepter or the sacrificial dye of the Maya.

The Pyramid was governed on the principle that rest meant isolation while fun involved some form of risk. It was a place where the lights and background music created a suspended reality and the planned activities quickened your pulse. It was common to see tourists sporting minor injuries, and sometimes we looked more like a ski resort (our bars and terraces packed with splints, crutches, and slings). Evidence of harm seemed to put the guests in a jollier mood. It was proof that danger existed and had been overcome.

This conveyor belt of convincingly injured bodies had run seamlessly until the night Mario yanked me from Sandra's room with a phone call.

I had arrived at The Pyramid with my health destroyed. For years I'd suffered from extreme perspiration, gastric and cardiovascular ailments, migraines, a strange pain in my liver, difficulty passing urine, and an irregular heartbeat. All that was behind me, but now I experienced periods of incredible weakness where I could feel my pulse pounding through my temples. Walking exhausted me, and sometimes it felt like I was wearing a helmet underneath my own skull. I was in no condition to participate in the daily activities that so thrilled the other guests.

Occasionally, on nights I couldn't sleep, I'd listen to the cries of pain or pleasure that must have been part of the entertainment program. One afternoon, I was walking down the corridor when a door opened. The head of a doll rolled out into the hallway. Children were not allowed at The Pyramid. I studied the eyes and silky lashes of the severed head. I didn't pick it up, thinking it might stink or be smeared with something repugnant or bring me bad luck.

Another morning I scored notoriety points at the breakfast buffet. There were screams and a crowd of people formed behind me. A black and red spider with hairy geometrical legs was apparently wandering around the fruit section. But I helped myself to the papaya as if nothing was happening. I was brave from simple lack of information. (I had figured it was just one of Mario Müller's scare tactics; only later did I discover that the danger had been real, courtesy of the tropics.)

Children live in constant contact with their knees. They're always aware of their scabs and scrapes and the changing colors of their bruises. To grow up is to forget all about your knees.

I missed the thought of having cuts on my legs, not so much because I missed my childhood, but because for me knee scrapes meant the ability to run. From age 14, when the metal frame of a car smashed into my leg and damaged every nerve it touched, I'd been a limper. It's not severe and isn't particularly painful, but it does come to define the way you relate to the world. Even when you're sitting still, you're lame.

I found Remigio in one of the gardens. He raised his stump in greeting. We'd formed a kind of bond as fellow amputees. Even though I was only missing one of the phalanges, that was sufficient disability for him, considering my line of work.

"I wanted to see you," he explained politely in his raspy voice, "but I was scared to walk down the hallways. They film everything inside."

"There are cameras out here, too," I said, pointing to one fitted to the trunk of a palm tree.

"Yes," he said, "but it's perfectly normal for them to see me out here. And I've found something." He handed me a banana leaf wrapped around a long, thick object. I slipped it quickly into my pant pocket.

"The diver had it in his hand," Remigio said. He explained that Ginger Oldenville's body had been taken to the wharf. In the process, something had fallen onto the grass. Remigio picked it up, and now this object rested inside my pants.

I looked up at Remigio's yellowish eyes. He didn't want to say any more. He turned to look at the video camera, then raised his stump in farewell.

Remigio had told me the story of his mutilation. When he'd worked in the vanilla fields, a nuayaca viper had bitten his hand. This particular venom causes blood to rush from every body orifice, and there's no antidote. Remigio spoke of it in a tone of dull resignation, like someone faced with an inevitable transaction. He hadn't thought twice. He'd grabbed a machete and let the hand fall.

Remigio was fired from the fields without severance. He managed to survive by begging outside the Punta Fermín bus terminal. That's where he'd met Mario Müller. Remigio told him his story and my friend hired him on the spot. Mario admired decisive action. He would have done the same thing. I would have let myself die right there, bleeding through my ears, surrounded by the cloying sweetness of vanilla.

That night I dreamed of a woman who smelled of eucalyptus lying weightless across me. The only pressure I felt was her scent. She was naked, and her skin glowed as if exuding a luminous substance. I was staring at her breasts, which had nipples the color of oranges. I'd try to touch them, but she would say, "Those are for other suckling calves."

The next moment she stood, suddenly dressed and wearing high heels. She left my life at catwalk speed.

I stopped by the studio where Sandra practiced kung fu. Her movements looked gentle but were actually parodies of combat. It was an elastic, slow-motion kung fu. From an enormous window I observed her and her students in their leotards and hot pants. The room was soundproof. The students copied her moves. It looked like they were learning how to jump on a planet with a stronger gravitational pull.

I waited next to the window until Sandra came over. Her smile was overwhelming. It seemed incredible to think that we had the same number of teeth. Things improved when she closed her mouth; now she seemed warmer, knowing. She pointed to her plastic watch and signaled that she'd call me when she was done.

There wasn't much work to do at the aquarium. I went into the booth that controlled the ambient sound. At that moment the computer was translating five red snappers into music. My presence was symbolic. The machine operated entirely on its own.

For my next project, I'd been planning to musicalize the palm trees. I imagined breezes carrying their melodies like news of a shipwreck.

I was happy when the phone rang. But it was Mario.

"How did it go with Támez?" he asked. I told him about the gay suicide pact.

"He thinks you know more than you're letting on," he said. "Támez isn't the best detective, but he noticed you eat fruit for breakfast."

"So?"

"Real men eat huevos rancheros with chorizo. The ones who eat papaya can't be trusted. In his caveman's code, you're gay, or—even worse—you're secretly gay. Plus you limp, you spend hours reading books that reek of stale crackers, and you've never been seen in the brothels of Punta Fermín or the table-dance bars in Kukulcán. None of this makes you seem very masculine. Ginger Oldenville was gay. Támez needs evidence to support his gay pact theory. One piece of evidence is that you eat papaya."

Mario seemed to be enjoying himself. Here in the primitive tropics, he'd created an enclave of coded behaviors. Maybe Támez wasn't actually so different from the guests. He possessed all the backwardness of a cannibal, while the tourists belonged to a sophisticated avant garde who secretly wished to return to their cannibal roots.

I finally hung up and dialed Sandra. I left three messages on her cellphone.

Yes, I ate papaya for breakfast, but I also felt an urgent need to be with Sandra. *Touch me with your finger*, she'd said. Next to the bloody scenes on TV, her skin had seemed as unattainable as the most exclusive corner of the purple section.

Back in my room, I took out the banana leaf that Remigio had given me. Wrapped inside it was a hammock knot.

I studied it for a while. Seven floors below, the waves beat the shore with consistent, fluid sorrow: an anemic blues.

It had been a long time since I'd thought of Luciana. The knot made me think of her hands, which could do and undo things with elegant dexterity.

I remembered the feeling of her touch, like a fine rain. And then it started to pour, as if the weather could emerge from my thoughts. The window fogged and created a strange optical effect, seeming to reflect two suns.

The woman who had infiltrated each drop of my poisoned blood, promising a remedy, was now nothing more than the shadow of a caress. The drops of rain on the windowpane belonged to a world in which Luciana would never again be with me.

When it stopped raining, I went out to the wharf. The sun was shining with renewed intensity. Its heat produced threads of vapor rising from the wooden planks. A flock of seagulls floated above, angling for scraps. The boats were ringed with thick foam the color of beer. A stench of putrefaction and fermenting acid under the sun.

I didn't want to call attention to myself: it's easy to remember a cripple. I stayed there just long enough to check that none of the knots were like the one Remigio had given me. Then I returned to my room. I studied the knot; a classic butterfly loop. The cord was soft to touch.

If you're a drug addict in recovery, your private life can seem like an enigma. Studying the object that Ginger had held in his final moments, a soft noose, was a way to examine the mysteries of my everyday life. Something in me was changing. The same boarding-school regime that had helped me recuperate suddenly delivered this surprise.

When I finally spoke to Sandra, she treated me with a kind of annoying camaraderie. We weren't a couple and we weren't lovers and we weren't even dating. But we were on the same team. Suddenly I missed Luciana again. I'd originally gone to The Pyramid so that I wouldn't miss her. Being cured meant exactly that: not thinking about her at all.

Mexico is a country of enormous delusions. The current disaster is mitigated by projects that stink of excess. In the southernmost part of Kukulcán, there was a bridge, the stone embodiment of this ideal. It rose about 90 feet in the air and faced west. The idea was to connect the town's tourist zone with Punta Fermín. It was originally designed to pass across the estuary and the lagoon, but the project stalled when funding ran out and so the bridge sat there like a broken dream. At one end, its network of beams and rails resembled the oxidized entrails of a sick machine. Its columns were overgrown with vines, and a wide variety of snail shells clung to the sides like barnacles.

Kids used to beg the tourists to throw coins into the water so they could retrieve the money with their teeth. Nowadays these kids preferred to jump off the sides with the bungee cord Mario had given them. Nearby there was a car junkyard. When dusk fell, onlookers would sit on the front seats they'd dragged from a crashed sedan and watch the boys leaping, listen to their crystalline peals of laughter.

Mario saw this civic failure as a personal triumph. While residents were leaving the area, reservations at The Pyramid multiplied like sea urchins; copious that season, due to the changing pH of the water.

Mario had become my memory coach. Early mornings he would drill me on the stories my mind had misplaced. He'd look at me with the irritated eyes of an insomniac and ask me to repeat everything he said. This helped him ensure that my new memories were sticking.

Coming to The Pyramid, I had forgotten the kinds of details that drug addicts tend to forget. In other words, your most embarrassing moments, the scenes that explain the strange looks you get from other people.

Our Bajío tour might have been one of those shameful times, but I didn't remember to what extent. Mario made sure to remind me. We passed through León, Silao, Celaya and Irapuato, ending in La Piedad, which seemed to refute its own name with the unforgiving stench of pigs that spread for miles around. We rocked for farmers, seminarians, and shoemakers, all of them eager for full-blown hallucinations. I'd erased those scenes from my memory because at some point on that journey I'd pissed my pants, and because every night I had run the risk of drowning in my own vomit.

Those were the low points in a lifestyle that initially felt amazingly good. I've never had a taste for marijuana or linden tea. I hate remedies based on lethargy. But I loved coke. I'd be overjoyed to discover even an empty bag with a few flecks of powder in the corners. Just seeing the stuff gave me this pulsing pleasure. Then came the drumming, the percussion of the cosmos, the frantic assurance of being the only survivor of some atrocious event. I would talk, and talk, and talk. And I was happy, regardless of whether anyone was listening. My heartbeats were my ideas. At times like that, I felt I could pilot a jumbo jet. Even better, I felt I could run the thread through any needle. Crystal, ecstasy, quaaludes, angel dust. These were the names of my fleeting predilections. Always in counterpoint to the blazing trails of cocaine, Her White Majesty, my precise fire, my lifeblood made to measure.

My happiness would have been perfect had I only died never knowing the cost of pleasure. But I survived and ruined it for myself. I spent years trying to figure out what it had taken from me. I spoke less and less. Reality was the price for everything I'd wasted.

Mario had the delicacy not to salvage all of those memories. He was more interested in other things: anecdotes, people's names, the make of a car, a song by King Crimson, specific details that could restore some quantitative structure to my mind. Many things seemed foreign to me. As if Der Meister had spent time with a stranger who, oddly enough, went by my name. Were these the "days of future passed" the Moody Blues sang about? As the early morning stained the sky apple green, Mario brought me provisions in the form of memories, with methodical patience.

Sometimes I asked him about Luciana. He knew this could hurt me, so he answered prudently, the way stewardesses give you plastic place settings so you don't do anything crazy during the flight.

Good health meant not thinking about Luciana. When she left me, I was lost in a haze of angel dust. After that, Mario checked me into Oceánica. There I detoxed from the more potent substances, then advanced to the controlled zone of soporifics and analgesics and anxiolytics. Which was excellent preparation for working in a recording studio where it was always night, there were never any musicians, and my job was to create soundscapes for animations.

Years later, Mario went looking for me in that room, whose walls were lined with black carpeting. I had a tic in my eye from overdosing on cartoons. I knew the sound of a flying saucer, a building, a rabbit, a monster, a carrot, even a spider. My mind was a repository of cars running over purple dogs, of beavers dodging hand grenades. Mario hugged me. He smelled of coconut soap, strong as car freshener. He asked me to come to the Caribbean with him. Told me he ran this place near the sea, where he could put me in charge of all the fish I wanted and turn them into sounds.

That was my salvation, my methadone for all the drugs that failed to kill me because I hadn't been faithful to any one. I was addicted to addiction, but I could switch between substances. This is what made me different from my mother, who attended to Valium until the remedy became an advanced form of the illness itself.

I moved to The Pyramid. It was my Red Sea, my Independence Day, my Christmas in the Holy Land. No exaggerations. I learned how to chew again.

My recuperation was steady until I heard "Feelings." When Juliancito, eccentric Mayan shaman, decided to play the song a third time, I knew my moment had arrived. I wanted Sandra with every cell in my body—an organism that only a few months earlier would have been amazed to find itself awake.

I never thought that could happen, not with "Feelings."

I hadn't felt such contradictory emotions since the time I performed in Tokyo at the Budokan Theater. In 1982, I played that sanctuary of Asian pop with the Mexican singer Yoshio. I was a fan of Jaco Pastorius but had only four functioning fingers. A limited set of resources, just enough to play romantic hits.

Given the opportunity to go to Japan, I thought I could at least imitate Jaco in gesture: throwing my electric bass into Hiroshima Bay.

The Weather Report genius survived thirty-five years of decadence. He'd thrown himself into a ditch from a height of 45 feet; played basketball with the energy of Tarzan caged inside a court; changed the history of bass guitar; drove magnificent women, including Joni Mitchell, crazy; told Jimi Hendrix the two of them were the Twin Towers of musical Manhattan; composed "Three Views of a Secret;" and finally exploded in his own light. When I heard that people could die of spontaneous combustion, he was the person I thought of.

Jaco competed with his mentor Joe Zawinul almost to the point of parricide. Then he raced ahead, becoming the kind of rumor no one wanted to confirm. A legendary nuisance, a burden to everybody, the drunk who showed up at bars, bragging that he was the best bassist in the world only to ruin every concert. With desperate insistence, the virtuoso sought out his final reproach. A bouncer, kicking him out of a club, landed a parting blow that split his cranium. He died shortly after.

It wasn't easy to measure up to a role model like that. When I actually got there, I couldn't understand his sacrificial gesture at Hiroshima. That city razed by the Bomb had transformed itself into a kind of Eden where cherry blossoms bloomed, radiation survivors meditated in the parks, and young mothers pushed strollers. (The weather was wonderful and all the babies walked around barefoot.) I drank green tea and ate breaded oysters. Too many things had disappeared in that city for me to add another item to the list. Jaco had chosen the wrong place. Go sacrifice your guitar in a dirty river full of rusty cans and cadavers dumped by Mafia. Not in a garden of life risen from atomic annihilation.

The attachment I felt to my instrument was also related to the success we'd had in Tokyo. Yoshio, the Samurai of Song, was a Mexican of Japanese origin. The public embraced him as if he alone were the keeper of a sacred fire that only burned on the other side of the world. He was both local and exotic, with an aura of in-between-ness: a kind of Latin Astroboy.

At the Budokan Theater, we almost brought the house down when we played Yoshio's "Queen of Hearts." *Baby, baby,* sang Yoshio plaintively, preparing for the plunge into his deep valley of feeling. *Don't leave me. . . . No!* The crowd were well-trained to chant the monosyllables of his sentimental despair: *No. . . no. . . no!* Yoshio owned that stage. Bathed in spotlight, he worked himself up to a glorious death rattle. His hands tensed and his black mane sprayed sweat pellets like a manga character.

At the same concert, B.J. Thomas sang "Raindrops Keep Falling On My Head"—a veritable Taj Mahal of emotions. But that night, we were infinitely better than B.J. At the climactic moment, only my own instrument could be heard. My bass kept the beat, then the percussion joined in with a battery of drumming. Yoshio reached his hand out for a towel, gesturing grandly like a Kabuki performer. When someone obliged him, he caught the towel mid-air and wiped his sweat with the self-indulgent exhibitionism of a drenched hero. Then he paused, ever the disciplined samurai, until the crowd recovered its breath and began urging him on. Finally, he flung the soaked cloth into the auditorium where it met a splendid and fetishistic end.

I'd never imagined that tour would be more than a *scrap bone,* the term I had resigned myself to when discussing our thankless work. But at the Budokan, I had a sudden revelation, the elusive satori I'd never attained through heavy metal. That night we were the lords of defiance. In ecstatic synchronicity, the Japanese set off an explosion of camera flashes. Standing in front of that rushing galaxy of lights, I felt love for Yoshio, for the world, for my own electric bass.

I'd never experienced that kind of pleasure with Los Extraditables. Maybe because it's easier to accept a gift you don't deserve than participate in a voluntary kind of suffering.

Now I dreamed of Sandra under the reddish light of a Martian sun. We were melting in a warm embrace, our sensations heightened by the conditions our solar system offers far from Earth.

When we finally met up in real life, the encounter occurred on a more modest scale. She found me sitting at Bar Canario. (It was Juliancito's day off, and the bartender filling in for him had sound system illiteracy.) I showed her the knot Remigio had given me.

"It's from a hammock," Sandra said right away. "Ginger used to have one in his room. He liked to spin around with this idiotic movement he called the 'cosmic tamale.' *He was bananas!* We have to go up to his room!"

She paused, reconsidering.

"Maybe it's better if the cameras don't see us together," she said. "I'll go alone."

She stood up. This time, she let me pay the bill.

The evenings had grown warmer. I avoided the outdoors and took my walks through the air-conditioned corridors of The Pyramid. Some of the hallways had helicoidal designs I found dizzying. Sometimes I'd have to sit on one of the armchairs arranged in a circle at the elevators.

I was the only one who could justify the utility of this

furniture. To want to rest here, with a view of nothing but the elevators, you had to have leg problems.

One afternoon, I was surprised to find someone else using the sofa. His presence, already unusual, was made almost unreal by his outfit: military camouflage with a balaclava. Also, he had an AK-47 strapped across his chest. He turned to look at me, raised his hand with an out-stretched palm, and signaled for me to keep quiet. Then he glanced to his right.

Four or five hooded men were dragging two blonde tourists down another hallway. The women were gagged and their hands were tied together. They were kicking and smiling, their eyes wrinkling with pleasure, and you could hear their laughter through the bandannas covering their mouths. They were carried over to a window. Here the guerrillas pulled a rope and harnesses fell towards them. The women went out through the window, tied to harnesses, and the hooded men followed them down.

The guy in the armchair stood and walked over to me.

"You didn't see anything," he said condescendingly.

Then he reached for my throat. *He's going to strangle me*, I thought, but made no effort to resist.

I woke up in the sick ward, staring at a poster of Winnie-the-Pooh. It was hard work trying to bring Mario Müller's face into focus. I was just making out his eyebrows (blond, thinning) when he spoke.

"'The Chinese lock,'" he said, then had a coughing fit. When he recovered, his eyes teary from the effort, he told me I'd been attacked by a group of martial artists. My body showed no signs of cuts or bruises. The guerrilla fighter had applied pressure to a nerve in my neck, causing me to faint. That's what they called "the Chinese lock." Der Meister spoke about it with strange pride, then explained that these kidnappings were part of the entertainment program. The guests accepted that such attacks might happen. Even though there was an element of risk, at the end of the day the tourists got to enjoy a Tequila Sunrise, and once their panic became memory, these were accidents worth recounting.

It irritated me how easily aggression could be turned into something desirable.

"I'm not a guest," I said. "I don't want to be kidnapped. That son of a bitch beat me up!"

By way of response, Mario surrendered his spot beside me so the doctor could shine a light in my eyes. The man in the white coat took my blood pressure.

"Did you try to stop anything?" Mario asked, worrying that I might've foiled some plan.

"No."

"You must've done something." He started coughing again.

"Some guy in a hood knocked me out!" I said, directing my comment at Winnie-the-Pooh, who, I thought, looked a bit too yellow. Mario raised a fist to stifle his cough. A spasm forced his eyes shut. He held his breath.

"Are you OK?" I said.

Ever since we were teenagers, Mario had cultivated the mannerisms of a singer obsessed with the health of his throat, someone who thinks there can be no ailment worse than the flu. It was strange to see him cough. He pressed his index fingers against his temples and half-closed one of his eyes, as if the pain were seizing his optic nerve.

"What we offer is more than a sport," Mario said, as the doctor stepped out of the room. "We offer extreme tourism. We're in a guerrilla zone. Sometimes the tourists come into contact with these supposed rebels. They get a little scare, then everything goes back to normal. I'm sure many of them would want more intense contact than that."

"Who were those sons of bitches? I mean the ones with the hoods."

"Actors. They live in Punta Fermín. The National Theater Company employs 50 actors. We employ over a hundred. That's something, don't you think? Sandra helps us train them. It's not easy to perform violence like that."

"What happened to the gringas they took?"

"Nothing. They're at the nightclub."

The doctor came back in. I thought he'd say something to me, but instead he gave Mario a clear plastic bag full of pills. My pulse quickened. I deserved an explanation.

"Join me for the outdoor program," Mario said. "It'll help you understand."

"You know I hate the sun," I said.

"You were attacked by one of the actors. It's time you saw the play."

I knew The Pyramid had been built on cheap land (you'd need a small fortune to extract a drop of drinkable water from the bedrock) grabbed from a local co-op of fishermen. The rocky soil wasn't arable and was located too far from the main tourist district, but the former owners had still been reluctant to sell. They clung to a blind belief in the importance of owning that land. They couldn't afford to build anything on what was essentially a single slab of limestone, but they venerated the piece of paper that confirmed it was theirs. People tried to force them out in countless ways. The rumor went that Támez had landed his job at Atrium for threatening these local families. El Gringo arrived later, when the site was already being described as an "opportunity." The British conglomerate was looking for an investor with knowledge of the region. Peterson had hired Mario to manage the tourist resort.

It was the President's decision to put Kukulcán on the map. The biological reserve was transformed into a golf course, money flooded the area, and suddenly there were jobs for people who used to suck mango seeds to curb their hunger. Monoliths of glass and steel came to dominate the coastline.

It was easy to hate that city of extravagant geometries and easy vice. Harder, though, to understand how ruinous and unjust progress could feed children who had previously gone blind from poor nutrition. Mario Müller spoke calmly about dirty development: *Nature is good for everyone, and puppies of all breeds tug at our heartstrings, but without a little destruction, nobody eats.* He had studied hotel management in Europe and knew all about the fantasies of "civilized" countries. After centuries of carbon emissions, they asked the impoverished countries to protect their virgin beaches so they could vacation there. Everything was as complex as those unique organisms built to survive the heat. The Pyramid was the result of dispossession, and the poor continued to be poor, only now they died less often or maybe not as quickly.

That's as much as you could defend a city that had hosted both the Miss Universe pageant and the world summit on climate change. What had once been tolerably dirty development now became excessively dirty. Diseases arrived, and so did pollution and the guerrilla and rainfall every three days and the drug trafficking and beheadings. The countless churches that popped up in the region offered little consolation. In Kukulcán, the vultures lay in wait for dying cats, and Punta Fermín was a slum littered with pigs.

So who was Mario Müller? What crazy ideas was he proposing?

"You stage your little show on land stolen from the local fishermen," I told him. "I don't want to see your skits."

"Don't be that way, Tony. What happened to you was an accident. Besides, all things have their dark origins. There's fraud at the root of any business transaction. You need to stop being bitter about 'origins.' There's no point in going back to the moment your father fucked your mother so you could exist. That's where we all come from, Tony. From sweat. Secretions. Moans." He pressed his fingers to his temples.

"Have you seen a doctor," I asked, "someone who's not a part of the hotel?"

"Yes."

"What does he say?"

"You know what this country's biggest tourist problem is?"

"That it keeps you from talking about your illness?"

He ignored my sarcasm.

"This country resembles itself too much. It offers you the past, and then more of the past. Guitars, sunsets, pyramids. The new kind of tourist wants something your typical tourist has never seen. That's what we understood. I want you to get that, too, Tony. Tomorrow we're taking a field excursion."

"Where's El Gringo?"

"I don't know. The Atrium people think he's visiting a breeder of thoroughbreds. Sometimes he disconnects completely—you know how he is."

"Has he been on one of your excursions?"

"What do you think? He hates the outdoors."

Mario paused. His breathing was heavy. He looked distressed. It wasn't easy refusing to accompany him. Ever since I was a kid, I'd followed him to places that didn't interest me. He was born to arrive before the others, to clear the fence faster and without any scrapes, to go first into the abandoned house and have the most outrageous dreams. Ironically, his greatest ambition had been to find discipline: the perfectly-made beds he'd never had at home. But the absence of surprise also depleted him. His marriage had been too peaceful to make him happy. They separated due to mutual tedium. He still wore his wedding band as a sign of stubbornness and fondness for María Inés, the woman who had come with him to the Caribbean. His only true passion, though, had been The Pyramid, where he could be an orderly and capricious god, dispensing both control and fear. The worlds we'd imagined while glancing through album covers, all of them were here.

"Peterson understands this better than you think," he said suddenly.

"He doesn't like the outdoors," I countered, to provoke him.

"He doesn't have to. We have a terrific job. This country is fucked up to our advantage. You know why?"

He looked at me, his eyes bright with sickness and zeal. He didn't wait for me to answer.

"Because we don't sell tranquility," he continued. "In every newspaper in the world, you'll read bad news about Mexico. Mutilated corpses, faces splashed with acid, heads rolling, a naked woman hanging from a post, piles of bodies. This causes panic. What's strange is that people who live in peaceful places want to experience that. They're sick of life without surprises. Either you think they're a bunch

of perverted shitheads, or else they're the same human animals we've always been; the important thing is the excitement of the hunt and that they themselves are pursued. If
they're afraid, it means they're alive. They relax by feeling
fear. What is horrible to us, is luxury to them. The Third
World exists in order to rescue Europeans from their own
boredom. That's what your best friend has understood so
well. Here I am, committed to recreational paranoia."

"Recreational paranoia." It was a phrase worth repeating.

"There are other places you can get this, but you have to
be an expert. Here you don't need to be a test pilot to feel
the adrenaline. Someone can kidnap you. It's controlled
risk, but it can still make your teeth rattle."

"Some asshole gave me 'the Chinese lock,' and Ginger
is dead."

"Those are independent incidents."

"You speak like the fucking chief of police," I said.

"Come out with me tomorrow, into the field. Then
you'll know whether I'm the chief of police."

The next day we met by his Jeep. He was chewing on a leaf
and feeling much better. Even as a boy he liked to chew on
leaves and twigs and blades of grass.

We were at the head of a convoy of about ten cars.
Leaving the resort, we headed for the mangroves' deep
green stain on the horizon and, shortly after, took an off-
ramp over yellow swampland. The mosquitoes seemed to
distort the air. A putrid smell followed us for miles.

Back in the '70s, nature was a forbidden paradise. We
camped out in Lagunas de Chacahua, where the boat-
men got top-grade marijuana. We hiked to the Huautla
mountains in the Oaxaca Sierra Madre to try halluci-
nogenic mushrooms and trekked the Huichol routes to
score peyote. "Blue Deer," one of our songs, was about the

protector of the desert, the guardian angel of the Huichol people. On each of our journeys, it was important to us to feel we'd somehow transgressed. We weren't called Los Extraditables for nothing. At that time, the word *extraditable* was more popular in Colombia than Mexico, which gave us hope our music had the potential to become a crime of exportation.

One of the band's problems was we couldn't seem to keep the same four members. That may sound like a modest number, but there were always guitarists and drummers coming and going. Those revolving, interchangeable faces meant that the band was really more of an expanded duo. There were players closer to my yin and others closer to Mario's yang. In the end it was all the same. They would leave. The two of us stayed on, ever in search of extradition.

The Jeep had no roof, but the pounding wind didn't offer any relief from the heat. A hawk followed us for a while before disappearing into the swampland.

"The Earth is tilted!" Mario shouted, mimicking a slanted wingspan.

The land did in fact slope down toward the sea at an almost imperceptible angle. When it rained, the water washed away the soil that had been loosened by all the tree-felling. The mud clouded the reef, and this prevented the coral from receiving adequate sunlight. We had successfully added deforestation to the list of the region's misfortunes.

"Now this is the real Maya apocalypse!" Mario shouted. He coughed from the strain.

He had talked about this many times. The Maya had calculated that the end of the world would take place in 2012. With infallible precision, they'd predicted an alignment of planets that only happened every twenty-six thousand years. Starting from this end-date, they had organized time *in reverse.* What most impressed my friend, in his guise as Der Meister, was this organization of retroactive time. During nights of insomnia, when we left his office lights on and I was flooded with new recollections, he liked to say, *Their memories had been foreseen before they happened.*

Mario dismissed the idea that the region's ancient settlers really believed in the end of the world. According to him, it was more about putting the past behind them and starting over—a moment of self-reflection under a perfect alignment of celestial bodies. After all, the Classic Maya had disappeared before the Conquest without leaving us so much as a suicide note.

The modern-day Maya had a strange impression of their ancestors. The waiters and security guards, the day laborers and bellboys, the plumbers, electricians, maintenance workers, and gardeners of The Pyramid—all of them believed that their ancestors had been extraterrestrials. This was the only way they could account for their grandeur, for the elegant crenellations of their pyramids, their inscrutable script and exact astronomy.

The Pyramid's labor structure reflected this final period of Maya splendor. These foot soldiers were subjected to the steady destitution of the region and to executive orders handed down to them—an ancient elite who could disappear at any moment.

Mario had launched an awareness campaign called "Maya Pride," with poor results. The employees of The Pyramid didn't appreciate the culture of their ancestors. What they appreciated was that they came from outer space.

At night, the peninsula really did look like an airstrip. The flames produced by residual fumes from the oil rigs seemed to serve as guiding lights for distant aircraft.

·

An hour and a half later, we came to an ancient citadel, located in a clearing in the brush. The sun was shining brightly in a sharp, cloudless sky.

I fell back behind the group and headed for a cluster of saplings, looking for somewhere to take a piss. The fronds wove together to form a dense textile of foliage. It was hard to guess where one tree ended and another began; they were arabesques, like in the Mayan friezes. In spite of the recent rainfall, the branches were all dry.

I followed a narrow path that led to a stretch of wasteland. Here the ground felt soft; the earth was covered in ash. The present-day Maya had burned the forest to plant corn. Their best option was narcotrafficking; after that, The Pyramid; and after that, burning trees.

When I pissed, the ash on the ground turned black.

I headed back to the archeological site. There, I took off my glasses to wipe away the sweat. In the distance, some stones were moving. I put my glasses back on—it was a couple of iguanas.

The travelers had formed a semi-circle, ready to receive more information. Everyone was wearing a purple wristband. They all had self-satisfied smiles.

Der Meister took two wireless microphones held together by electrical tape. He studied them like he was performing a sound-check.

"Testing, one-two; good. Testing, one-two-three; very good." His voice echoed off the rocks and a flock of bluish birds shot away toward the sun. The heat surrounded us like a wall. My shirt was a soggy rind.

In a festive tone, Mario began to describe the Mayan apocalypse. He paused to sip from a thermos, then continued with more pop cosmology.

"They knew that we would come here. We, too, are made of stardust, and we come from the same cradle, the Big Bang." Now he was pointing to a large wall engraved with a glyph of Venus. As he spoke about the Mayan calendar, I wandered around the small archeological site, climbing up and down the narrow staircases until my leg started to hurt. Then I sat down under a triangular arch and fanned myself with the baseball cap Mario had lent me.

I was having a good time. A green fly landed on my face to drink the sweat pouring down my sideburns. Then I heard a gunshot.

I rejoined the group.

"Hunters," Mario said. "This place is good for pheasants."

"Couldn't it be the guerrillas?" a tourist asked, hopefully.

"We're very close to the line of fire, but the guerrillas respect holy cities. We're going to walk along the *sacbe*, the 'White Path' that links two ceremonial sites."

Here he paused and turned to me. What he said next caught me off guard.

"I present to you Commander Antonio Góngora, our conflict-zone expert. He negotiated the ceasefire with the guerrillas. So you're in good hands. Isn't that right, Tony?"

The visitors eyed me with respect.

"A combat wound?" a man asked, in English. He was around forty-five, with brick-red cheeks.

My limp had become proof of my experience. My hand was also being accounted for.

"What is the guerrillas' struggle?" a woman asked. She was the spitting image of Louis XIV.

"It's the struggle of all guerrillas," Mario said, smiling. "A struggle for social justice and for heroes they can print on T-shirts."

We started heading towards the "White Path." My friend came up to me.

"For someone who got screwed during the war, you look marvelous," Mario said. He handed me a machine gun. "Don't worry," he whispered. "It's made of plastic."

In this moment, he seemed far more energized than I was. Then I noticed his thermos. *Mario's high*, I thought.

"You've always been a conflict expert," he went on. "Normally, you're the one responsible for creating the drama. Does it bother you if I introduce you as an expert in conflict resolution?"

I didn't answer. The heat was a torture similar to the tourists' expectant looks. The rest of the staff carried pistols in their belts. The machine gun enhanced my importance.

We came to a path that was so white the glare burned my eyes. Along the sides was an abundance of wildflowers with yellow pistils and petals an intense shade of red. A wind came up. It brought even warmer air, heavy with sand.

Many years before, I'd gone chasing after a ball that Mario had thrown. The two of us used to play American football in the street. I had followed the projectile without noticing the car coming toward us. The driver managed to dodge me, but part of the bumper pierced my leg. The wound didn't leave me paralyzed, but it gave me the limp that would bother me for the rest of my life. Mario cried as if the whole thing had been his fault. I enjoyed his subordination for a few months. But it soon started to feel as useless as saying I had a disappeared father. Tragedy without a reward. I was lame. What fucked me up most was wondering what would've happened had the car not turned onto our street. Mario had a strong arm.

The ball had gone really far. Most likely, I would have missed it.

Who could ever trust me as a conflict mediator? Maybe these loners who two days ago had been shoveling snow in Montreal. These people who'd left their four children with the nanny in Santiago de Chile. The ones who tri- ple-locked their bungalows in New Zealand. Men and women softened by too many hours in airplanes, exotic cocktails, the scorching Caribbean humidity, the myths of crazy natives.

A young woman whose breasts were pleasantly enhanced by the sweat on her shirt asked me if I wanted some water.

I drank from her bottle.

Right then, one of the employees threw himself onto the glaring sand and started struggling with a wild ani- mal. Seconds later, he was standing, his body covered in dust. He held a coral snake.

Mario went to look at it. With a steady hand, he grabbed the creature by the head, then squeezed its fangs, studying its tongue.

"It's not a real coral," he said. "In order to survive, these guys imitate the rings of the poisonous snakes." He pointed to its black, red, and yellow bands. "Their only protection is their disguise."

Even the snakes are actors, I thought.

Another employee approached with a net. Mario explained that they would take the snake to a nature pre- serve, but it was obvious they'd just set her loose again to stage another scene. The fake coral and me, her false leader, we were members of a cast. The only authentic thing was the heat.

My head pounded. I chewed on two aspirin.

Finally we came to the unimpressive rectangular fortress.

"The Temple of the Dancers," Mario said. He headed for a stone bas-relief pocked with weeds. We could make out several blurry silhouettes, like wet stains on the stone. Our guide traced their outlines with his index finger.

"See how they're in motion?" he said. "The conquistadors thought they were dancers, that's how this temple got its name. But in fact they're figures of men wounded in battle. Their dicks have been cut off." He pointed between their legs. "They can't dance. They're doubling over in pain."

The tourists seemed fascinated by the cruelty of history.

"It's incredible that they managed to build so much in this heat!" an Argentine woman said.

"*Quite something!*" agreed a woman with hair the color of Fanta.

It was now, arbitrarily, time for lunch. In fact, we were the ones being eaten. The air was sucking us dry, squeezing our last drops of moisture while the flies drank our sweat. Far in the distance we could make out a laurel tree. I would need two more aspirin to get there.

The staff distributed lunch boxes among the guests. We bit into our sandwiches without appetite. The mayo smelled like disinfectant.

Mario took the mic and began to talk about a drought which necessitated human sacrifices in the cenotes. Who wouldn't want to exchange a loved one for a few drops of water in this deadly heat?

"Any volunteers for the sacrifice?" he joked.

After that, he talked about the Bacabs—describing them as horsemen who rode to the four corners of the heavens looking for water jugs. That land had always been dying of thirst. The Maya sacrificed their most prized possessions in the fresh-water cenotes. That's where they'd thrown their jewels and children and princesses and dwarves—all their small, adorable creatures. The Heavenly Horsemen demanded sacrifices before shattering their jugs to release the water.

It made me think of Ginger Oldenville, who'd laid his lifeline in those dark underground rivers. I thought of his body lying motionless on a marble altar. Who would have wanted his sacrifice?

"Riders of the storm..." Mario crooned, like Jim Morrison.

Glances of admiration legitimized his performance. I wondered if Mario, anointed now with the aura of a hero, would have sex with one of these tourists when we returned to the hotel. But I knew this would be less satisfying to him than holding his audience captive—with the charisma he'd never possessed as lead singer of Los Extraditables.

The visitors watched, waiting for the next strange bit of trivia. Suddenly we heard an explosion.

"Get down!" Mario cried.

A gust of wind seemed to split the air in half.

For several seemingly endless seconds, all we could do was choke on dust. Slowly, we raised ourselves from the ground. Mario, already standing, asked us to follow him.

Up on the outer wall of the fortress, we could make out ten figures holding rifles. They were wearing balaclavas with scarves around their necks.

"The guerrillas," a man said, awestruck. "They're shorter than I expected."

It took a moment to realize he was talking to me, their supposed commander.

I wondered if one of the figures was the guy who'd knocked me out.

"Help us disappear!" cried the tallest of the fighters.

Der Meister explained that the guerrilla didn't have faces. They were everyone and no one. They'd emerged from the millenarian shadows to reclaim justice, and would fade away once they were no longer needed. That's ultimately what they aspired to—oblivion. The desire to be turned into phantoms, to struggle for their own extinction. They were asking us to help them become an impossibility.

Mario was now shamelessly imitating the rhetoric of Subcomandante Marcos. His audience seemed impressed. For a few seconds, a powerful silence settled over us. Would we help these lost souls? Would we aid them in their quest to become unnecessary?

That's when the woman with Fanta-colored hair started running towards them.

"Don't you dare!" someone called after her.

Mario took off. I hadn't known he could run so fast. He caught up to the woman, spun her down to the ground, then straddled her. He slapped her, but not aggressively. A practiced move from an expert in making people snap back to reality.

The woman began laughing and crying at the same time. Mario relented, and she stood up and hugged her savior.

The fighters fired into the air, making the V for victory sign as they said goodbye.

Soon the woman found her voice:

"Thank you, thank you." She motioned to the guerillas, then muttered something about the wretched of the earth.

"She's hyperventilating," opined one of the tourists.

Even though I hadn't mobilized for Mario's contingency plan, some of the travelers still came up to thank me, if only for being there, if only for transmitting a veteran's sense of confidence.

"I'll never forget this day," said a man with a shaved head and three earrings in each ear.

We returned to the "White Path." The sun wasn't as strong now, but seemed to scorch us from the inside. It was a miracle my body could produce any moisture at all.

A man stood in front of me, swaying to his iPod. His syncopated gait made me imagine he was listening to reggae for pilgrims.

Curiously, the trip seemed shorter on the way back. Soon we approached the citadel.

"It's the hour of the bat!" Mario cried.

It was six in the afternoon, and the air was filled with black, flapping wings. The bats were looking for fruit. Maybe the employees had hidden some in the niches of the pyramid to lure them.

I climbed the citadel to the highest point. Mario followed behind me. The landscape opened up below, the earth shimmering as if light were emanating from the dust itself. Beyond a stretch of underbrush, I could see a small plane taking off.

"The military base," Mario explained. "They use it more and more lately. Now that the weather's always bad, they're constantly shutting down the Kukulcán airport."

The sunset was starting to fade. Dark stains were streaking across the land—the shadows of distant clouds. The breeze was a delayed gratification. The sky deepened. From one moment to the next, another time was intruding on our own. The Bacabs had heard the people's prayers. We were about to regain an elemental knowledge, of an age when Thunder and Storm were powerful lords, cataclysms disguised as human beings.

The rain was bewitching. I removed my hat to feel the shy, exquisite drops against my face. The rocks were so warm they produced clouds of steam.

Seconds later, it rained desperately. No one looked for shelter. The sky was collapsing; the water jars had broken.

On the way back, I asked Mario what was in his thermos.

"A liquid encyclopedia," he answered. "Otherwise, I won't make it." His pupils were grossly dilated. Now I understood the dramaturgy of his actions. The same adrenaline I felt once at the Budokan Theatre was something he now received doses of three times a week. Soaked with sweat, Mario Müller explained the moral consequences of his great vision. He spoke with fanatical frenzy. The simulation that had just been performed with such authenticity would inspire its audience to think and dream and feel and long for something different. Something in their unconscious would be altered. The excursion would have neurological effects.

"It's a rite of passage," Mario said, "like your first peyote trip. These people don't know it, but their lives can actually be changed here. If they knew that, they might not come seeking it so hard."

A while later, Mario pulled the Jeep over. He had to take a piss. We both got out of the car.

The rain had stopped and the thundering buzz of the mosquitos was a mild substitute for the storm. My friend's exhilaration—the combined effects of the trip and his beverage—had not abated.

"Remember your tour of Japan?" he said, and then added, to my surprise, "They thought you were with the yakuza! Because of your finger."

I looked at Mario Müller's exuberant face, ruddy from the outdoor expedition.

"What are you talking about?" I said.

"I can't believe you don't remember! Members of the yakuza who fuck up have to cut off one of their finger joints before they can be readmitted into the clan. You were the one who told me that! Don't you remember Japan?"

"Sure, I brought back six pounds of green tea."

"And the thing with your finger?" He pointed to my stump. "You don't remember?" He didn't wait for me to catch up. "The custom," he continued, "comes from the samurai. You played with the 'Samurai of Song.' At some party, a rumor went around that you were part of the yakuza. That bit of missing finger served as a secret password. Don't you remember? They treated you like a king. They sent you that little lacquered wooden box filled with drugs, and that Swedish woman showed up at your door. A blonde bombshell."

I closed my eyes. I saw sliding screens, a bedroom lined with tatami mats, specks of white powder, the gold outline of a tree stamped on a wall made of rice paper, blood dripping from, quite possibly, my own nose. Was it a dream or a memory? Or was it a film?

"That stuff fucked you up," Mario said. "You returned to Mexico very strange. When I came over to your place, you welcomed me wearing a kimono. You'd smoked opium in Osaka, the Yoshio tour was mind-blowing; but the best part of all of it was that you were missing some of your finger. You got the royal treatment, the kind reserved for a person with impunity—an absolved deserter. There, your stump became something significant. You gave your-self the luxury of getting bored with the blonde. After her it was Luciana. You came back with this bizarre kind of arrogance—this from a guy who'd always complained he was nothing but a rat."

"I complained about being a rat?"

"Self-esteem has never been your thing. But when I shared the best news of our lives, you didn't give a shit. You just talked about the yakuza. You thought you were some criminal mastermind. Japan made you crazy."

Mario pointed out a lagoon in the distance. A geo-graphical representation of my own mental wasteland. He remembered far too many things my own brain had obliterated.

"Don't you remember anything about the-best-news-of-our-lives?" He sounded like a teacher coaching some-one with severe learning disabilities.

I came back from Japan lost in another world. It felt like I was inside a delicate, liquid landscape. I thought I could recover my sensations, as if I'd just stepped out of an illus-tration on a piece of rice paper or the side of a porcelain cup. Japan had been too much for me, a place of perfect order and subtle harmony where I was the only disaster. At any moment, I could have ripped a tear through that fragile paradise, a place that presented a real challenge for the clumsy. I enjoyed the sentimental magic of play-ing with Yoshio, and all the inspiration of an environ-ment that harmonious and incomprehensible. But I didn't remember any of the hype surrounding my severed finger, I didn't remember the yakuza, I didn't even remember the Swede. I could imagine all of it, but maybe I was confusing these ideas with images from magazines or porn, or from someone else's fantasies—maybe Mario's own obsessions.

What I do know is I returned to Mexico in a cloud. That part I remember with tragic precision. Mario showed up at my apartment to tell me "something incredible" which I'd barely even registered: the Velvet Underground would be playing in Mexico, and we were the opening act.

Japan, Luciana, the Velvet Underground: it was too much for me. The accumulation of triumphs made me want one more. I felt I deserved a little extra. I couldn't face that much good luck unless I honored it with excess. Arid land doesn't yield good fruit. So I called up Felipe Blue— the drug dealer I'd been avoiding ever since Luciana had set me on the path to a normal life—and asked him to send some provisions.

Before stepping back into the Jeep, my friend spoke again:

"I remembered the yakuza because of something I felt on our excursion. 'The man you can trust'—that's what you've always been. And it's good to know you're there. I liked that you came with me just now. The group was also happy to have you. Some samurai somewhere would have granted you pardon."

It's possible that gaining readmission at the cost of mutilation is more important than being accepted in the first place. The man who fails and makes amends is braver than the man who has never failed. Is that what I'd been looking for in the Caribbean? Or was it what Mario hoped for my own sake?

"I don't remember any of that, I swear."

Although the story about the yakuza sounded apocryphal, I did remember one really tall building. The vertiginous fortieth or fiftieth floor of a skyscraper in Shibuya. There were lights in the distance, like frozen fireflies, and I'd wanted to step out onto the terrace. I went over to a glass door but a man blocked my way. A man of unusual girth, like a sumo wrestler, but dressed in a black shirt, black tie, and black suit. He wore a small earpiece in one ear. I tried to maneuver past him. There was no one else on the terrace. Who exactly was the giant trying to protect? I heard a voice behind me, in English: "He's protecting you. He doesn't want you to go out there. He thinks you're going to jump."

Was it a dream or some delusion emerged from fragments of memory?

I preferred to remember more distant things. The Müller family had lived in a very run-down old house. Mario was the youngest of seven brothers. When their mother called them one by one, she sometimes forgot his name. Usually she just called him *Chico*.

She was a tall woman, with hair like straw, who always wore a mustard-colored apron. Mario's father worked for the Bank of Mexico, where he performed the unfathomable role of an actuary. That vocation gave him a mythical aura, as if he were a custodian at Maracanã Stadium or Royal Albert Hall. His salary was enough to pay for seven tuitions at the Swiss School, but to judge from his threadbare suits, his ancient Opel, and their tattered furniture, he didn't exactly belong to the high-powered world of finance. Klaus Müller had caught a whiff of the gold without catching the fever.

Many years later, Los Extraditables would pay him an ironic tribute with one of our songs. We called it "The Age of the Actuary."

Right before nightfall, he would go out under the palm tree in the garden and smoke a cigar. There, surrounded by overgrown plants, he'd sink his feet into grass that hedged up around his ankles. In his mind he'd play Bach, the tempo as slow as the movement of his cigar smoke. He loved organ music but hated playing records. Sound for him only existed in a concert conducted by his memory.

Klaus Müller's father, Mario's grandfather, was born in Bern. The Müller household wasn't exactly run on Swiss discipline, but it was governed by the mind of its owner. While he undertook his orderly leisure in the garden, Mario's mother would prepare elaborate but flavorless stews. She didn't keep a maid and had never implemented a system of chores for her children. Mario would chew on a twig while watching her work, but he'd never contribute to the actual labor.

Whenever I entered that kitchen, Mrs. Müller would give me a chocolate from the stash she kept inside a ceramic crock shaped like a hen—to open it you had to pull off the head. She couldn't see me without handing me a chocolate. She had a wonderful smile, standing there next to her headless chicken.

I loved the disorder in that house, which was so different from my own, but I didn't like the acrid smell of the bedrooms or the thinness of their blankets. Maybe Klaus Müller thought feeling chilly would build his children's character, or maybe his Swiss blood helped him sleep in the cold more comfortably. But I remember I could never sleep through the night there. A real waste, in that era before my insomnia.

Mario enjoyed the neat decor at my house. He liked to stand in front of one particular photograph taken in Sacramento and later given a garish tint. It showed my mother in a desert the color of bubble gum, smiling next to a lime-green cactus, under an atomic-blue sky. But my friend ignored the picture of my father, that honest vendor of cotton candy.

Around the time our hormones started kicking in, my mother was a 33-year-old woman. She was single and attractive in a world where divorce was rare. She wore miniskirts like a TV gameshow assistant. When she crossed her legs, it was easy to see her underwear. She had a kind of casual self-confidence that I hated and Mario adored. She'd exhale her cigarette smoke with a haughty upward tilt of the chin or wiggle around in her seat when she heard a good song. My mother believed, with unwonted optimism, that all problems could be solved with Valium.

Of my father I remembered a few gestures. The way he'd press on my chest as I lay in bed, as if expelling the oxygen would help me fall asleep faster. The phone calls when he'd ask to speak to me, just to relay a few words. He was the kind of mild man who speaks only to show he's participating. I didn't miss him because I'd hardly known him. What I missed was the possibility of having a father, or the brothers he never gave me.

My mother, on the other hand, was there but never around. She worked in two clinics for the hearing-impaired and went out at night.

Growing up next to a woman whose whereabouts remained a mystery—who was private about her lovers, but had many and was openly courted—turned me into a "man you can trust" but one who, at any moment, might stop being that.

Maybe, in some calculating way, Mario had wanted to plant this false memory of the yakuza to give meaning to my severed finger, which, paradoxically, would grant me integrity. I could be trusted.

But what had he got out of it? During those periods when I'd been admitted and then readmitted into his life, I'd vowed to take his side, tolerate his whims, and come to terms with the few uncomfortable things I hadn't forgotten, like the way he idolized, and in some sense courted, my mother.

For years, she curbed her solitude with little blue pills. Maybe if she'd cried once in a while she wouldn't have needed them.

When I got back to my room at The Pyramid, I pulled across the curtains and looked out onto the mythical blues of the Caribbean. Seven shades, one after the other. I hated the third with a kind of justified animal rage. It was the color of Valium.

There are certain things that cannot happen until you've stopped caring. Sandra kept rejecting me, until one day the wind in her mind changed direction.

"We're going to put an end to this tension once and for all," she told me.

When she knocked on my door she was still in her yoga clothes, her skin flushed from exercise.

"Ginger's hammock is gone," she added, pointing to the knot above my desk.

"That's what's causing the tension for you?" My voice was groggy. I'd been busy reading, too focused to admire the amber six o'clock light—not to mention Sandra's sculpted body—now coming into my room.

"Don't be dense," she said. "I mean the tension between us." She slipped down one of the straps of her leotard. Then she peeled off the rest of her clothes, with swift locker-room dexterity. Once again I marveled at that body, so proportional and lean and supple—perfect for a sunblock ad.

"I don't feel any tension," I said.

"We have to put an end to this, Tony. Try to cooperate." She was smiling. A coach advising an athlete. Desire itself had become a kind of tension for her, a bug we had to squash before either one of us could have any peace of mind.

Gone were the protocols for showing that we liked each other. Sandra removed my clothes faster than I could've stripped them off myself. She'd brought lubricant to facilitate my erection. The condom she slid onto my cock was a brand I'd never heard of. (It was packaged in what looked like a tiny Vaseline container.) *We're animals*, I thought, remembering one of Mario's lines for justifying the strange contests that took place at The Pyramid. Sandra and I were animals, and we needed to diffuse a tension that could be potentially harmful. The downside was that we were artificial animals: the lubricant smelled like window cleaner.

Sandra climbed on top of me and started moving with a syncopated rhythm. I tried keeping up with her, to join the duet in 4/4 time that had slowly become a kind of rhythm and blues.

Watching her it seemed likely that she enjoyed the plastic surgery channel because the procedures, judging from her breasts, were not entirely foreign to her. We were living in a time of elective injuries.

I could feel something poking into my back. The spine of the book I'd been reading before Sandra had shown up. The discomfort was helping me to not think.

Sandra's eyes were closed. Her moaning was delicate and even. It was as if the disciplined breathing of yoga allowed her to dissociate from her body. We came almost at the same time, in a kind of pleasant and freeing agreement. It felt good, but that was it. One of those moments when sex seems overrated.

Sandra let her body rest on top of mine. Her hair smelled of chamomile. She placed her hand on my cheek. Then her panting gave way to sobbing.

I stroked her back and kissed her tears.

"This had to happen," she said.

And it won't happen again, I thought, feeling a mix of sadness and relief. The sex had released the tension, but had put nothing in its place.

"I don't want them to kick me out," she said. I could feel the warmth of her breath.

"Who'd ever kick you out?" I asked. "Mario is my friend."

"You don't know Támez," she said. "I'm a gringa. I don't have papers. He can get rid of me whenever he wants."

"Mario is his boss."

"Mario is ill," she said.

I stood up. Sandra wrapped the bed-sheet around her, in an unexpected show of modesty.

"He's got an inoperable tumor," she added. "In his esophagus. He's been like this for months."

I felt a tightness in my chest. *That's not true*, I thought, trying to calm myself.

"How do you know all this?" I said.

"Leopoldo told me."

It was annoying to hear her refer to the chief of security by his first name. Sandra fixed her gaze on the ceiling lamp. Her eyes filled with tears.

"He doesn't have much time left," she whispered, but it wasn't Mario she was crying about.

"What's your relationship with Támez?" I asked. The night we got drinks at Bar Canario, she'd described her methods for teaching people how to control or channel their anger. I didn't detect any of that self-discipline now.

"I'm a gringa, Tony. When I got to Kukulcán, I was drugged out. My boyfriend died and got shipped home in a body bag. I stayed and danced in nightclubs. In a cage! Leopoldo brought me here. I got better. Mario offered me work that was more spiritual. He found me a teacher from San Francisco, a disciple of Larry Schultz. This guy taught me *rocket yoga*, the express lane to nirvana. Or at least according to one of the members of the Grateful Dead—I forget his name. You must know who I'm talking about." Here she paused, expecting me to supply the information; I didn't, so she continued. "I don't have papers. Leopoldo used to be a cop. Understand? *Understand?*" She pounded my chest.

"Yes," I lied, stroking her hair. She gave me a pained look and her eyes took on a kind of liquid ferocity.

"Do you want to know the whole story?"

"No."

"Would you like to know what the police do with gringa whores?"

"No!"

Sandra sank into a deep sob. I could feel her saliva on my chest, and her skin vibrating in a way it hadn't while we were fucking. Maybe this was the real tension she wanted to get rid of. Sex had been a preamble to whatever deeper thing had been destroying her, to the opaque admission that she was at the mercy of our common enemy. To admit this, to accept her own compromised position, released her and strengthened the bond between us. We weren't *lovers* exactly—feelings played only a vague role in our connection—but we were on the same wavelength. The solitude of life at The Pyramid had brought us together for this: we were accomplices, with a clarity unspoiled by emotions.

"Is that better?" I said, stroking her neck.

"Did you feel anything in your finger?"

"I felt like a samurai. It felt like they'd cut off my finger with a sword." Again, I lied. Suddenly I remembered the book that had been poking into my spine. I reached around and showed it to her. It was *The Master of Go.*

"What's 'Go?'"

"It's a Japanese game."

"An erotic game?"

"All Japanese games are erotic," I said.

"You always stash it under your back while you screw?"

"That was an accident. Sort of like Go itself."

"Sex on the go!" Sandra smiled girlishly. Then her expression hardened, showing her age. She added, "This was a *one-timer*, never to be repeated."

"No problem."

"Better to set the record straight, Tony. This was the end-game. The end of Go." She kissed my mouth with closed lips. "We need to stick together for what comes next. I'd give anything for you to kill Leopoldo Támez! But that's not you." She sighed. "And it isn't me, either."

She got up and went to the bathroom. I could hear the water running. I love the sound of a woman showering in my bedroom, a sound I'd never thought I'd hear again. Sandra had taken her clothes in with her. When she came out, she was fully dressed.

"Sorry for pouncing on you," she said. "You were great." She opened the main door, then closed it again and said, "Did I tell you Ginger's hammock disappeared?"

"We'll have to look for the other knot."

"That's right, Go master." Sandra smiled, and then she was gone.

The thing with Sandra was depressing enough to make me think of Luciana. I'd met her on an Easter Saturday. The night before, Los Extraditables had played in an unlit hall somewhere in Atizapán, and I finally fell asleep—or finally collapsed—around five in the morning. That was the period when I'd graduated from cocaine to angel dust and the only fluid I ever consumed was beer. Once in a while, I'd eat a few Fritos or some Churrumais, not because they counted as real food, but mostly because I liked the crunching sounds they made—the way they'd stick to the roof of my mouth and the sting when they reopened an old cut. Sometimes I'd see a sandwich and think I'd eaten it. My brain couldn't always tell the difference between actions and images. I didn't know if I'd played in Puerto Vallarta or just seen a T-shirt that said "Puerto Vallarta."

That Saturday I woke up at the house of our current drummer's cousin. She'd thrown a party that resulted in many bodies passed out in the living room. On a shelf she had a collection of ceramic devils from Ocumicho. Their revelries seemed to be the inspiration for our own. I was one of the last people to wake up. When this cousin noticed my extreme pallor, she very memorably said, "What you need for breakfast is some bone-marrow soup." Maybe she suggested this concoction just to get me out of there, as her own kitchen wasn't stocked with anything nearly so potent. What matters is this: I had a sudden craving for some steaming, spicy broth.

I don't know how I managed to climb down the stairs of her building and get myself into a cab. When the driver asked me where I was going, he had to wait while an address crystalized in my mind. Where could I get some bone-marrow soup? Finally the name of a restaurant came to me: we'd go to El Venadito.

How long had it been since I'd savored some cilantro and onion? One of the walls of the place was decorated with a cheap print of a forest scene. There is no animal more melancholy than a deer. Its eyes, which already seem overwhelmed, are ringed with shapes resembling tears or question marks. This reminded me of a song my father used to sing while he shaved. *I'm just a poor little deer living on the mountain.* . . . That particular diminutive seemed to thwart any kind of aspiration—to be a deer is sad enough, but to be a "little" deer is altogether hopeless.

When the soup arrived, I suddenly felt the most productive depression of my life. A feeling of sympathy for every deer that ever roamed on royal hunting grounds, in this country where we don't even have a king. After five spoonfuls, I was full.

"Didn't you like it?" the waiter asked with extraordinary politeness. This man was old enough to be my father, yet here he was, spending his Saturday morning serving drug addicts struggling to swallow their broth. "Not feeling well, son?"

I didn't deserve his sweetness. Then and there I decided to flush all my pills down the toilet. I'd eat apples! I'd apologize to everyone I ran into for the next several months. I'd drink tea.

I left the guy an exorbitant tip, never forgetting the money was borrowed (the bittersweet aftertaste of my generosity), and crossed at the corner of Avenida Universidad in the direction of Coyoacán. I walked down Francisco Sosa, where the April jacarandas were in bloom, and observed how the mansions of the conquistadors had been turned into little fiefdoms for Mexican millionaires. It had been ages since I'd ventured anywhere. In spite of my bad leg and the giant tree roots that broke up the sidewalks, I managed a pleasant walk to Santa Catarina Plaza. A bride and groom were coming out of the yellow church under a cloud of rice. Someone was playing "No volveré" on a harmonica. Clusters of balloons and cotton candy lightened the mood, and I inhaled the elemental deliciousness of fresh tamales and enjoyed the soft caress of the warm spring sun. In the background, the jacarandas formed an archway of deep lilac.

In the midst of this commotion, I noticed a young woman dressed in black. Her face had an apocalyptic beauty. Even her fingernails were painted black. This reminded me of a small funeral home not far from there, somewhere along Miguel Ángel de Quevedo—a little house that looked like an ancient Greek palace, complete with columns and a triangular façade, suggesting that death was a transition to the classical period. The woman's black clothes and forlorn expression made me think that's where she was coming from. She was alone and seemed out of place in the cheerful plaza scene. For her, something was over. I decided I could help.

With that single false assumption, I went on to repeat the story of my parents' courtship. I walked up to Luciana and offered her some cotton candy. Later she clarified that no one had died and that she wore all black because it's the color that goes best with black. She looked sad because that's just the way her face worked. She smiled when she said that, which made her look sadder and even more beautiful.

My sex life back then was sort of like my diet. I didn't know if I'd gotten laid or just woken up next to someone.

From that first meeting, Luciana asked me strange and very specific questions, like she was trying to see if I'd recovered from brain damage. At that time, the Spanish language wasn't exactly flourishing in my organism. So I answered vaguely. She seemed to like my lack of clarity.

Luciana was studying literature because she'd failed the entrance exam for medicine. I guess she was looking for a patient, and I came along at exactly the right moment. But I'd always liked salves, so I didn't refuse her remedies. The only thing I'd ever said no to was Valium.

Detox came with a few annoying side effects. After years of never knowing where I'd slept, going to bed with someone now felt like fornicating in public.

My performance didn't live up to what you'd expect from a heavy-metal bass player. Lucky for me, she thought I was trying not to hurt her, so she forgave me this, as well as my string of tragic conquests—women with misguided tattoos who'd shaved their heads or dyed their hair red just to spite me. My sexual insecurities, she thought, were a sign that I was considerate, and she loved me more for them. Because the amazing thing is that she really did love me. She was my link to magic, an undeserved gift that came to me through sheer luck. I didn't dare ask what she saw in me, for fear she'd actually tell me and the news would hurt.

Luciana was from Guadalajara. Those eyes that had seemed so sorrowful actually belonged to a category perfected by biology and legend, known simply as "Guadalajaran."

It was hard getting used to being sober again, that state of emergency where there's too much spare time. I'd go out for a walk just to make the hours pass more quickly. One day I went to the market three times. I started reading the books Luciana lent me, hunting for lyrics for my songs.

"Poetry is one thing," she said. "Messages inside fortune cookies are another." Apparently I wrote great fortune-cookie sayings.

When I suggested we move in together, she agreed, but with one unexpected condition.

"Get a real job," she said. "Los Extraditables isn't a job."

"What is it, then?" I made the mistake of asking.

"A bad habit, a hobby. A kind of therapy. A state of being. Or maybe all of those things. But it's not a job."

She was right. The band barely turned a profit. We mostly played for young construction workers with fantasies of self-destruction. TV and radio had killed rock and roll.

It was Luciana who ultimately found the gig that helped me survive the '80s. She had lunch with one of Yoshio's cousins at the Mexican-Japanese Association.

"You guys live in parallel universes," she said. "You can join his band and keep playing in Los Extraditables, and no one will even notice. Rock in this country is a secret, not a profession."

I thought of bands I knew, groups like Mobile Hangar, Suppressed Bus-Stop, Shaking Boots, The Heavy Strawberries, The Dug Dugs, Cosmic Cheese, Impontius Pilate. Bands transcendent enough to deserve their names. Luciana was right. If any of those musicians managed to pay the rent it was because they agreed to play the standards and boleros with more commercial bands. This way they could afford to revisit the unprofitable rock they loved so much.

But when I saw a picture of Yoshio, my heart sank. His band members dressed like space cadets.

"Why don't you audition?" Luciana said. "If a finger falls off from shame you can always go back to Los Extraditables. You only need three fingers for that."

During those years of scrimping with Luciana, I missed the chaos of my life back when all my free will had to decide was which painkiller I'd take the next morning. At first, I associated Luciana's love for me with her frustrated dreams of medical school. What she wanted was to heal her patient—who, as luck would have it, was me. I worried I'd be less attractive once I recovered, but this was not the case. Luciana, it turned out, didn't love saving me, she saved me so that she could love me. *Wake up, you idiot*, Mario Müller would say. *Don't you realize what you've got there?* Of course he meant Luciana. *What can I do to repay her?* I'd ask, to which Meister Eckhart's disciple would reply, *Nothing! Isn't it great?*

I decided to speak with Yoshio's manager. When I got back to the apartment, I told Luciana I still had my doubts.

"Do whatever the hell you want," she said, licking my ear.

Which was how I agreed to start playing Yoshio's "Queen of Hearts."

Eventually, having a split personality became a kind of pleasurable new bad habit. Romantic ballads weren't exactly my thing, but they soon started to possess me, particularly in the shower. More than once I caught myself splashing around with my good leg while singing, *My sweetie pie....* And there was a new axis in my life: I shacked up with Luciana and bought a Camaro.

The night of the epiphany at the Budokan, I called her long-distance from Tokyo.

"I love you," I said, and my love felt more significant because it was coming from one day later, from the other side of the world.

Japan filled me with a special energy. . . . Luciana was a long-standing miracle. . . . They had offered the band a chance to open for the Velvet Underground. . . . Everything was going so well I couldn't resist the opportunity to screw it all up.

Lou Reed and John Cale had decided to organize a Live from the Warehouse–style concert back in Mexico City—the place where William S. Burroughs killed his wife and never saw the inside of a jail cell. The land of impunity lent itself well to the group's secret reunion. There'd be no publicity, the session would not be recorded, and admission would be limited to elite members of the avant-garde—a personnel of elegant decadence, acolytes who'd spread the cult group's legend through persistence and the seductive strategy of rumor.

I had noticed a vase of flowers, the fleshy petals heavy with dew that glistened like pearls. That's when I experienced my moment of Eastern enlightenment—when I understood the consistency of time, the fruits of nothingness. That every moment occurs in a vacuum, only acquiring consistency as anticipation or as memory. The past and the future exist, but not the present. For years I'd accepted the great existential dogma of the drug addict, which adheres to the supremacy of the Here and Now, to the eternity of the moment. Luciana dragged me out of that delirious infinite present. I'd given up drugs, which meant I'd accepted the passage of time.

But a few days before the Velvets arrived in Mexico, I again went searching for that elusive glory of the present moment. I wanted to suspend time; I was determined to make My Moment go on forever. I was going to jam with the supreme powers of glam rock; I'd be opening for the author of "Heroin," actually sharing a stage with those legendary bastards. I was going to enter the Rock Underground's Hall of Fame. I couldn't act like this was any ordinary day. The moment demanded its own kind of eternity. By which I mean Felipe Blue brought over a Blasito shoebox full of drugs.

I didn't understand the essence of happiness. Good luck makes you petty—I thought being happy entitled me to something extra, to the gratuities of the elect.

On the eve of the "Live from the Warehouse" concert, there was a full moon. I knew I wouldn't be sleeping, between the cocaine and my nerves and the celestial object that had occupied the horizon.

The next day, Lou Reed's face should have prepared me for what was about to happen. We clashed in the amp room that doubled as our greenroom. No one was smoking, on the Velvets' orders. The senior heralds of decadence had enforced a tyrannical code of wholesomeness. No alcohol, no interviews, no canned food. And there'd be no autographs or any other contact with fans. The only trace this concert would leave behind was the memory of its having happened.

A memory I couldn't erase. Impossible to forget the face of Lou the Unsinkable, his look of disdain—that incredible assurance of having returned from horror, from the grim face of death. His wasn't the arrogance of a star inflated by all his admirers. It belonged to a survivor who's risked a walk on the wild side of existence. He was still alive, like a piece of awkward news, spewing his mistrust and his poetry and his vicious vibes and rusted razor blades.

Lou Reed was a walking skull in dark sunglasses, something pulled from an altar for the Day of the Dead. He dealt the cards in the poker game of lost souls, and it looked like he was willing to give me one. Lou the Magnificent played in the major leagues of the great beyond. Incapable of reducing himself to mere singing, he would chew on the lyrics till the words sounded like extraterrestrial soda crackers. Lou the Discriminator looked at me like I was the next piece of trash, and I was stupid enough to take it as a compliment.

Luciana couldn't deal with my relapse. So she did the right thing: she went home to Guadalajara, landed a job at a recently launched newspaper called *21st Century,* and refused to be responsible for my sorry state. The ground fell out from under me. I sped up the inevitable split of Los Extraditables. And I listened in amazement when Mario Müller said he wanted to start a new life in hotel management.

I stayed in touch with him. When he moved to the Mexican Caribbean (first the Hotel Malibú, then The Pyramid), we called each other late at night and he'd walk me through his plans, until he got to his crazy idea—a pyramid made of crystal that rose from the undergrowth and looked out across the sea.

Maybe I was remembering all this because of what Sandra had said, because of the news that my friend was deathly ill. My protector, the man who'd pulled me out of so many holes, was being eaten away from the inside. But Mario was much more than his body. It was a bitter pill to know he was dying, and even harder to know he was losing his health just as I was beginning to recover my own.

I went back to find Peterson. I wanted him to look out for Mario without having to tell him about Mario's illness.

My friend didn't deserve anyone's pity. Gringos are too easily moved by disability. Only recently, at the Oscars, a movie about a stuttering king had competed for the top prize with a film about a schizophrenic ballerina. Mario shouldn't have been admired for working while sick. But he could have used Peterson's help. The death of Ginger Oldenville, which none of us wanted to talk about, loomed over The Pyramid like the black cloud of an approaching hurricane.

El Gringo's secretary told me that she'd managed to reach him. He'd be back soon, she said. She wasn't sure when exactly, but definitely soon.

"Mr. Góngora?"

In the lobby of The Pyramid, I was pulled aside by a man whose clothes were soaking wet. His business suit, made of cheap fabric, was the color of diluted coffee, and his narrow black tie gave him the look of a traveling Bible salesman. He identified himself as Inspector Ríos and mentioned one of the police bureaus in town. No one had come to question me yet about the death of Ginger Oldenville. Even *Informe K.,* the most widely read and least corrupt newspaper in Kukulcán, still hadn't mentioned the crime, though the news was sure to leak soon.

Ríos suggested we take a walk in the gardens to talk about Ginger Oldenville. The case had been assigned to his department, he said. He took out a pack of cigarettes and offered me one.

"I don't smoke," I said.

He led us over to a shaded bench under a laurel tree.

"The smoke keeps the mosquitos away," he explained, and raised the cigarette he'd just lit. "Those little shits have given me malaria, even dengue hemorrhagic fever. If I die of anything else, it'll be because I survived the damn mosquitos."

His skin bore no mark of the Caribbean sun. His nose was riddled with blackheads, as if the heat had failed to unclog his pores. In this climate, his stiff, crinkled suit inspired distrust. You'd have to be a pervert or a serial killer to wear an outfit like that in our tropical paradise. He was drenched and didn't seem to care. I asked him where he was from.

"Chihuahua."

He pulled out a notebook with a jolly-looking rabbit on the cover that read "Have a beautiful day!" He started writing down everything I told him about Ginger Oldenville: that he was a wonderful person, had no enemies, was a first-rate diver. Ríos held his cigarette between his thumb and index finger and took long, deep drags on it. Even the three fingers not involved in the procedure were stained yellow from nicotine. In the distance, on the beach in the silver section, a couple of kids were beating something with sticks.

The inspector spoke in the calm cadences of a country schoolteacher, but the words that came out of his mouth were entirely unsuitable for the classroom.

"My boss has an electric cauterizer up his ass," he said. "If they kill a gringo the guy can't sit down. I'm really a proctologist but only have one patient, see, and that's my boss. I need his ass to calm the fuck down. What else have you got for me?" The filth flowed from Ríos's thin lips in a serene, almost pleasant tone. I asked about his work in the Caribbean.

"I don't like the beach," he said, "and I can't even swim. And I detest mosquitos. But there are some interesting things that come with the job. In the touristy places, money tends to invent all kinds of novel vices. A policeman can't get bored. 'What happens in Vegas stays in Vegas,' you know?"

"I guess."

"Kukulcán's no different," he went on. "People come here to entertain themselves. Sometimes their entertainment takes on strange forms. Many crimes are really just examples of failed pleasure, like when you wake up with a vaginal fungus in your throat. This ever happen to you?"

"No."

"If you ever get this type of fungus, just gargle, don't invite the entire fucking press corps into your mouth. The key thing is to handle everything with discretion. Bad news is bad for tourism. Were you acquainted with Roger Bacon?"

"The chief of security told me he was a friend of Ginger Oldenville's," I said.

"In Chihuahua we have a saying: 'To raid one mine you need another.' If I tell you a secret, will you tell me another?"

"What would you like me to tell you?"

"Are you interested in hammocks?" I felt a chill and looked down at the inspector's feet. Street shoes, completely worn out and absurd for walking on sand. I wanted to change the subject.

"You don't talk like a cop," I said.

"No? What do I sound like?"

"You have the voice of a priest."

"I'm also an evangelical minister!" he said. His smile revealed tobacco-stained teeth. "The Caribbean is a good place for ministry. The Maya who settled on dry land built pyramids; the ones who lived along the coast and swamplands focused more on magic and faith and conspiracy. Here the politicians and the preachers are a dime a dozen. I don't make my living from this. It's voluntary work. When you see as many crimes as I do, though, you crave something else. I host a show on Radio Xtabay and give sermons on Sundays. I don't speak in obscenities there. This is my language during business hours."

"Wouldn't you prefer to take off your jacket? You're soaked!" I said.

"Oh, I'm used to it. I'm like the Irish—we live in our sweat. What else have you got for me?"

"About what?"

"We were talking about a hammock. Let me be more specific: Have you ever seen a hammock knot? We already know that what happens in Kukulcán stays in Kukulcán. Paradises are discreet places. Our Lord likes it when goodness triumphs in private. So do the police. This isn't about creating a scandal, it's about healing nether-regions—in this case my boss's ass. The crime is tearing him a new one."

At this point in the conversation, Ríos seemed dazed. He might have had a fever. In any case, craziness wasn't exactly unusual in his line of work. His tranquil tone made concealment sound like a virtue. The ruined shoes lent his voice a selfless sincerity. His boss, insulted to the point of disgrace, seemed somebody tolerable. Still, I didn't feel like answering.

"You seem nervous, Mr. Góngora. Your leg is shaking. Can you tell me why?"

"Who told you about the knot?"

"Another knot. 'To raid one mine you need another.' Are you going to tell me what you know? I don't like impunity. I like discretion, which is different. There are certain bacteria that feed on the petroleum that spills into the sea. They clean it up and nobody ever knows it was there. What else have you got for me?"

He knows I have the knot.

Ríos continued. "Yesterday they found the drowned body of Roger Bacon. Judging from the evidence, it seems he went out diving in Punta Fermín. He went very deep. And there was a knot tied to his penis. See, it's a way of reaching double ecstasy: death and orgasm. You remember that actor in all those Kung Fu movies? That's how he died, too. He strangled himself while masturbating. Like I said, strange forms of entertainment. Támez told me Bacon and Oldenville made a suicide pact. We searched for Oldenville's hammock in his room, but it had disappeared. Your friend Sandra looked for it, too; I suppose that's why she went to Oldenville's room. The security camera caught her. So tell me. Are you interested in hammocks?"

Ríos was much smarter than Támez. He'd taken his time getting to the point about the knot so he could reel me in on multiple lines. Now I had to tell him.

"Remigio, one of the gardeners, gave me a knot. It was the one Ginger Oldenville had in his hand when they killed him. How did you know I had it?"

"That Támez, he sure knows how to squeeze out the confessions. Remigio told him, Miss Sandra told him, even the mosquitos told him…"

I wondered what else Sandra had divulged. Had she really slept with me just to get even with Támez or did she do it because Támez had told her to?

"You look concerned, my friend. Are you familiar with the group Cruci/Fiction?"

"I knew Ginger," I said. "It wasn't a suicide."

"Exactly how well did you know him?"

I glanced away to the beach in the silver section. Gulls were circling over the spot where those kids had been beating something. Perhaps an animal that was still warm.

"The US consulate people are nervous," Ríos said. "Two gringos dead in only a few days. Roger Bacon had tattoos written in Arabic, did you know that?"

"Támez told me," I said.

"We don't get too many Islamists around here. But we still have to investigate everything."

Suddenly, this terrorist theory sounded much more appealing than the gay pact. I owed Ginger at least that much: his death could not have been incidental. I remembered the way he'd toss a piece of candy and catch it midair in his mouth. *I'm better than a trained seal*, he'd say, with childlike pleasure. Can someone like that commit suicide?

"They're translating the tattoos now," he said. "What happened to your leg?"

"I was chasing a ball and got run over by a car."

"See what I mean? People take risks over nothing."

I wondered if Ríos was armed. The sweaty suit clung limply to his frame, revealing no suspicious bulges.

"Can you show me the knot?" he asked.

We went to my room. I was contributing to Ginger's case in the way I had most wanted to avoid. The inspector took out a plastic bag, the kind used to store vegetables in the refrigerator. He picked up the knot using his pen and placed it in the bag.

"You really think it was a suicide pact?" I asked.

"The majority of crimes are petty. People don't kill themselves for grandiose reasons. We know Ginger and his friend divided the end knots of a hammock between them and that they both belonged to the same high risk club. They were also homosexuals. I'm not entering into any kind of judgment here. In the Green Cross I met an idiot who wanted to masturbate with a sea bass. His cock turned into a piece of ceviche. As for Ginger, I don't think he was after sea bass, per se, but I'll tell you one thing: his tastes weren't so common, either. How did the two of you get along?"

Támez told him I'm gay, I thought. It had been about forty years since that suspicion had stopped mattering to me, but suddenly it felt like I was back in the playground, confronted with the primal duty of proving my manhood. The inspector was looking at me warily.

"You haven't noticed anything unusual at the hotel?" he asked.

Had they told him about the "Chinese lock?" *He's not interested in the hotel. He's interested in Mario,* I thought.

Ríos's cellphone beeped inside his jacket. He had a new text message.

"It's the translation," he explained. "Guess what Roger Bacon had tattooed on his arm? The name Ahmad Rashad. That mean anything to you?"

"No."

"Do you have Internet?" He pointed to my computer.

I switched it on and clicked open the Google home screen. But Ríos's addiction was stronger than his curiosity. He stepped out for a smoke on the balcony while I performed a search.

I found thousands of hits for Ahmad Rashad. He had been a football receiver for the Minnesota Vikings. His real name was Bobby Moore. In 1972, while playing for the St. Louis Cardinals, he fell under the influence of Rashad Khalifa and converted to Islam. Khalifa had also overseen the conversion of other athletes. The name Ahmad Rashad means "He who is highly praised will lead you to the truth." After retiring with a slew of national records, Ahmad began a successful career as a TV sportscaster. On YouTube, I found a commercial where he is promoting a brand of popcorn. Then I came across footage of perhaps his most famous play, the so-called "Miracle Catch."

I lingered over every detail of that kick. There are five seconds left on the clock for the championship game. On the scoreboard, the Vikings are down. The quarterback throws a Hail Mary—a spectacular bomb—all the way to the end-zone of the Cleveland Browns. The ball bounces out of the defender's grasp and falls, smoothly and perfectly, into the hands of Ahmad Rashad.

Ríos re-entered the room and stood behind me, reading from over my shoulder. I could smell the tobacco on his breath.

"You see that, my friend? Bacon was obsessed with sports, he wasn't a terrorist. He worshiped this athlete. Támez is going to love this bit of news. My boss, too. A little ointment for his ass. 'He who is highly praised will lead you to the truth.' What a great name!"

"Hold on," I said. I did a search for Ahmad's mentor, Rashad Khalifa. There was a lot of conflicting data online and I found it hard to make sense of his biography. Khalifa had lived a contradictory life. He was born in Egypt, studied biochemistry in the United States then worked for the Libyan government. Back in the US, Khalifa's son had had some success as a professional baseball player while he himself presided as imam of a mosque in St. Louis. That's where he met Ahmad. Years later he was arrested on charges of sexual abuse. He was accused by a sixteen-year-old girl who said he'd promised to find her "aura." His interpretation of the Qur'an was plagued by controversy. Khalifa claimed he could prove that Allah had dictated the text through numerological code. According to his reading, every account, every Sura, every important name added up to nineteen. Not all of the passages, however, could be made to correspond to the sacred number. Khalifa said this was owing to false verses that had to be expurgated.

His campaign to "clean up" the Qur'an did not catch on. Rashad Khalifa had loyal followers in the highest ranks of professional sports, but his views were condemned by the Islamic authorities. It didn't help that he used extremely sophisticated computer software. The Prophet of the Number Nineteen fought his struggle alone. He was assassinated in 1990, in Tucson. They attributed his death to Islamic fundamentalists, but no arrests were ever made.

Ríos read the passages of Khalifa's writings, scanning calmly through the information. Suddenly his interest was stronger than mine. Khalifa was a preacher, too. Still, the more we read, the further we moved away from the Islamist theory: Khalifa had died an apostate, because his passion for numbers had led him to a baseless reading of the Qur'an.

I turned off the computer. Ríos's clothes stank of smoke and poisoned the atmosphere. I didn't wanted to hear another lurid description of his boss's anal distress ever again. I stood up to hint that he should leave.

"If there's anything else you remember, of course you'll let me know," he said, palming me his business card, which looked like it had passed through several hands.

I didn't buy the idea of the suicide pact. But the terrorist theory was even harder to swallow. Ginger's friend Roger Bacon was a diver who had admired a professional athlete. The name in Arabic script had seemed merely decorative to him.

Investigator Ríos had both ends of the hammock now. The case would soon be closed.

The "Miracle Catch" of the Vikings receiver made me think back to the ball I'd been chasing, somewhat recklessly, that day the unseen Mustang made a turn onto our block. Mario told me the ball ricocheted off the car's roof. I didn't remember that detail. He wanted to convince me I'd been close to the ball's arc and had almost caught it. Ahmad Rashad had had better luck. His most famous play was a matter of him being in the right place, with just a few seconds left and the slimmest possibility of a save, when a Hail Mary rebounded from the hands of the enemy and landed in his own. The sum of those coincidences was as random as the repetitive reoccurrence of the number nineteen in the Qur'an.

Two days after my meeting with Ríos, El Gringo Peterson returned to The Pyramid. He asked to see me in his office. There I found him in a good mood, in spite of all the bad news on his plate. He told his secretary not to forward any calls and gave her some dining coupons so she could take her family to Marina Lobster Grille. He bolted the door shut behind her, as was his custom, then made a slow, theatrical show of lighting a Cohiba. He took out a bottle of Four Roses and loosened the collar of his sky-blue shirt.

"I missed this place, Tony!" he said. "I wanted to see you sooner, but I had to make some arrangements first. The Mexican authorities aren't very efficient about shipping corpses. Oldenville's parents live in Orlando. I wanted to spend a little time with them. It's always appreciated when someone from the company shows up at the funeral."

"What's new at the horse races?" I asked.

"I can't quit my job, if that's what you mean." It was hard to tell from his expression whether he'd won or lost. The only expenditures he permitted himself involved writing checks for remote causes in places like China or Africa, as if this was just another form of gambling, or his winnings had to randomly benefit someone aside from himself.

"I haven't placed many bets in the past few days. Two dead gringos make for a lot of work."

Peterson kept his cigars in a humidor to which he'd add a few precise drops of distilled water. The Mexican Caribbean was a meeting place for Cubans from the island and those from Miami. Peterson never passed up a chance to eavesdrop on their conversations or invite them to his table to hear them compare the Havana of Batista to the Miami of Versace or to Kukulcán, that rainy layover city that the Revolution's retirees would someday adopt for their exile. *This place is going to become the red Miami!* he'd say.

El Gringo Peterson knew Mario from another of his hotels, the Malibú. One of his business partners was a Cuban guy obsessed with the idea of recreating the Tropicana Club on Mexican soil—or at least bringing over a large number of Afro-Cuban female dancers. My friend had been the manager for ten or twelve years, and had there regained his interest in singing, though his voice could no longer accommodate heavy metal. He'd lost some hair and gained a few pounds, which actually made him look more athletic, though his only exercise involved being on his feet all day, going up and down the hotel stairs. His tastes changed and he discovered his voice was perfect for romantic songs. Not the blatantly corny ballads that I was performing. Mario built a reputation crooning like Frank Sinatra and mimicking the style of Marco Antonio Muñiz. El Gringo's favorite song was "Fly Me to the Moon." Mario sang it snapping his fingers with the classic flair of Bing Crosby or Dean Martin. From here they developed a friendliness that was curiously discontinued when Mario moved to The Pyramid.

At the Malibú, they were surrounded by Caribbean dancers and were always rubbing elbows with the Governor or prominent businessmen who spun intricate tales of the Cayman Islands and other fiscal havens.

During that period of expansion the money poured in and the narco traffic flowed, leaving no dead bodies in its wake. Eventually, Peterson's Cuban business partner bought a house in Aruba (an unmistakable sign that he was about to retire) and hired some Miami lawyers who billed by the minute, then declared bankruptcy. The Cuban's shares were linked to companies no one had ever heard of: their phantasmagoric names reeked of money laundering.

Peterson recovered very little of his investment. He didn't want to confront the new owners or even find out who they were. He remained in the area, the only place where luck had ever given him the cold shoulder. He liked to go to an airless café called, rather quixotically, The Lion's Share. He'd ask Mario to meet him there. My friend had also fallen on hard times. (María José had just left him, bored of the tropics and their home among the mangroves. It felt too much like house arrest, being so far from the touristy parts.)

One afternoon, El Gringo accidentally killed a cockroach at the café. He beat his fist on the table without looking, without even seeing the thing. Then he flicked it away with the back of his hand, as if there was nothing more normal than chatting amongst cockroaches. *The Lion's Share.* If that's the lair of kings, what's the poor man's hovel like?

Maybe this was why Peterson saw an opportunity to heroically screw himself over. He enlisted Mario's help, never suspecting it would lead to unwanted triumphs. Like any decent gambler, he didn't make the vulgar choice of failing on purpose. He left fate to chance—to the same luck that had punished him with success. This helped explain why he and my friend had drifted apart.

Peterson's ties to Atrium began at the Epsom racetrack. That's where he met a group of pleasure seekers who'd once taken a Magic Bus from London to Delhi. He'd referred to each of them vaguely, confusing their surnames and resumes. He judged them as a single unit: psychedelic rich kids who couldn't be taken seriously but had a lot of money. El Gringo didn't care which of them had meditated in Tibet or tried opium in Kathmandu or who'd brought back archeological treasures from Cambodia. What mattered was that they were businessmen with unusual backgrounds who were seeking new investments and believed that tourism could satisfy the longings of a generation that in the '60s and '70s had scattered to the far ends of the earth in search of interior landscapes.

I would've given anything to listen in on some of those conversations between Mario Müller and El Gringo Peterson at The Lion's Share. It's possible that Peterson appreciated the project's theatrical element, if only because it came with the promise of such a magnificent fall.

On his desk he kept a hand towel that bore the logo of The Pyramid. Its cardinal points were embossed in the sacred colors of the Maya: black, yellow, red, and white over a field of jade green. He despised the esoteric. It didn't surprise me that the towel was used as an ashtray.

He took a deep drag then said:

"How is your friend?"

"He's got a miserable cough."

"That's because he doesn't look after himself. I keep telling him to take a vacation, go see a doctor, but the guy's a fanatic." He started fiddling with the cigar band. "Sometimes I think he brought you here just to placate me. I like you, Tony. Everyone knows that."

So Mario isn't sick, I thought. *Sandra's lying to me.*

"How is Ginger's family?" I asked.

"They're quiet. They'd already accepted his sexual orientation and now they accept his decision to die. They don't want a scandal or an investigation. For once, Támez acted fast. London had been busting his balls, no doubt. Otherwise, he'd still be swinging in his hammock."

The theory about the gay pact had become official history.

"What about Bacon's family?"

"The strangest people. Very dry. I met with them in Minnesota. They thanked me for paying for the funeral arrangements. We were generous. Roger Bacon was visiting, he didn't work here. They had a Mass and all these athlete types showed up. Bacon was a college football star who'd gotten into diving. One of the best divers in the world, they say. He'd gone to great depths, deep into blue holes. The minister said so—he knew him well. The cemetery where they buried him looked like an archive. Every urn is a little box. The parents really suffered, but they saw it coming. You can't dive that deep and not worry your family."

He finished off his whiskey and poured himself another

drink. He also refilled my glass. Peterson liked short tumblers, multifaceted.

There was something slightly crazy about him. *I'm like a Marine, you send me somewhere and I'll fight,* he liked to say. He wasn't talking about combat but about his ability to live in isolation. He'd moved from one place to the next as if he were switching naval bases. He'd arrived with a small suitcase made of old leather, something his father had brought from Germany after the Second World War. Nothing else was necessary. His office was stripped of all decoration and personal effects. There was a map of the region hanging on the wall (a red pin marked The Pyramid) and he'd framed some diplomas for staff who'd won the Employee of the Month Award. This defined his character: the decor was deliberately alien to him.

"Do you know Inspector Ríos?" I asked.

"The Good Seminarian? What's that guy doing here? I've known him since his first bout of malaria. He's OK. Did you get along with Ginger?" He looked me in the eye.

I told him how great it was to work with Ginger Oldenville. This seemed to agree with Peterson's Protestant ethics.

"Where were you when it happened?" he asked.

"Does it matter?"

"I remember where I was when they shot Kennedy. Oldenville isn't JFK: you can stay quiet."

"I was with a woman."

"You showed up at the scene of the crime right away. Támez told me."

"Mario called me."

"You don't have a cellphone, Tony."

"He knew where I was."

"You were in your room?"

"No."

"When you're in someone else's room, do you always let Mario know so he can find you?"

"Sorry, Mike, I don't know where you're going with this."

"You never call me 'Mike.'"

"I never call you 'El Gringo,' either. Or 'Peterson.' We just talk. I don't call you names."

"You seem different, Tony."

"What's your problem with Mario?"

"You tell me. What's *his* problem? He's my employee, I could fire him, but he's the only one who can fully comprehend the mess he's created. He's turned himself into God, he acts like the mayor of Paradise. Two guys are dead, both of them gringos. This is not good management of Paradise."

"It was a gay pact," I said, suddenly defending the theory I hated most.

"I guess they both let themselves fall under the spell of their environment. You can't propose all those dangers without one of them becoming a reality. And there are other things going on, too. I heard you were in the infirmary."

"Come on, The Pyramid has full occupancy," I said. "It's the only hotel people still want to visit. Does it bother you so much that Mario's business model has been a success?"

"I don't like his style, but that's not the issue. At the end of the day, there are really only two things that can divide human beings: sex and money. Mario Müller is a greedy son of a bitch. He has no integrity. *Greed is good.* Who said that? I forget, but it should definitely be your friend's motto."

It was strange to hear him talk about money. I felt an uncomfortable jolt back to reality, like coming down from a trip. For years I'd remained indifferent to the forces that both torment the world and make it run: sex and money. I earned wages that kept me afloat, I treaded the ever deepening waters of the lower middle class, I splurged on drugs whenever I could. But money had never been a problem or an end in itself for me, maybe because Mario had always been there to lend me a hand.

Peterson was looking me in the eye again.

"Mario takes care of his parents and several of his brothers, as well as a group of homeless guys in Punta Fermín. He gives money to thousands of causes. He just can't stop, it's not in his nature to do so. He's ambitious, Tony. He's not interested in money for its own sake, he's interested in using it to support people. That's how he controls them."

When they were starting out, Peterson had wanted to throw money at something, without actually throwing it away, hoping that destiny would take it from him. Mario came up with lucrative risk schemes. It made me uncomfortable, but I had come to accept the important role money played in my friend's life. And now I defended him:

"Kukulcán is a veritable cemetery of hotels. The Pyramid is the only exception."

"I'm going to tell you about something I don't think you know. Something called accident insurance. Why do you think there are hotels that go all the way down to the water? Because they're insured. They stay in business for a few years. When people stop coming, the owners close shop and bill the insurance company. I don't care about filling all these rooms so that someone can die."

"Maybe they're only full for that reason, because it's possible someone can die," I said.

"Maybe so."

"Fear is our greatest natural resource," I said. Now I was appropriating Mario's ideas; once again, I could feel him speaking through me to El Gringo. Peterson exhaled a large puff of smoke.

"I want no more corpses here," he said. "Atrium doesn't, either. There are good insurance policies out there for accidents and bankruptcy, but not for murder. A hotel closes in Kukulcán every single week. We should follow their example. We should just bill the insurance and get out of here."

"And what's in it for the insurance companies?"

"Welcome to the real world, Tony! Abandoned hotels are a fantastic racket. Have you seen all those empty buildings lining the beach? They're inhabited by rats and badgers; seagulls build their nests in the attics. But officially there are no vacancies. It's the best form of money laundering. I learn so much from the British. They're the ones who invented these so-called *offshore* paradises in their former colonies. Some figures from the *Financial Times:* Ten per cent of all money laundering happens in London. Hotels that go broke are the perfect places for simulating investments and setting up ghost accounts. Did you ever read *Dead Souls?*"

"Yes," I said.

"Well, I didn't. But I've heard about it. All this here? This is the sequel, let's call it *Dead Tourists.* In Russia, you could charge for dead servants, here you can charge for empty rooms. Money from arms sales, from white slavery and drug trafficking—none of it can just show up in a bank account. First it has to pass through a few hoops. Kukulcán is the perfect place for faking earnings that were supposedly generated here."

I stood up, took the Four Roses, and poured myself a drink.

"Go get 'em, cowboy," Peterson said, smiling.

"Your plan is to launder money?" I couldn't disguise my amused skepticism.

"That would be the easiest way out," he said. "The collection agencies buy up debts no one can pay off. You save yourself all the headaches of dealing with guests and putting up with Mario."

"Do you really hate him that much?"

"He's got no restraint," El Gringo said. "I guess that alone isn't enough to hate the guy, but he thinks he's a guru, the Messiah in a Hawaiian shirt."

"He's sick," I said.

"Yes, I'm sorry about that, Tony, really I am. And I admire what he's accomplished. He dreams up phobias, kidnappings, an entire guerrilla army to keep the guests entertained. If he could just limit himself to that, it would be fantastic, but he's after money and doesn't understand that the world works according to other rules." He paused long enough to make me wonder if he was drunk. "Did you know that 23 banks in London laundered $1.3 billion stolen by Sani Abacha, the Nigerian dictator? That money had to be legitimized somewhere. Our fate is to become a phantom hotel. I need you to help me."

"With what?"

"With Mario. His feelings are hurt. He's capable of doing something stupid. He wants to defend his territory like an alpha male. If anything else happens, Atrium will bust my balls. I'm scared of Mario's illness, I'm scared it'll make him feel omnipotent—that would be just like him. When you feel the end is near, you stop caring if the world falls to pieces. Help him, Tony. Don't let him lose his mind."

He motioned for me to get going. Then, by way of apology:

"I'm wasted, Tony. Every time I talk with you, I end up piss drunk." He smiled.

I woke up drenched in sweat. My breath was sour from the aftertaste of that smoky whiskey. I could hear the sea, which sounded choppier than usual. I stepped out onto the balcony.

When, exactly, does any disaster begin? If I had to assign some mythic origin to my own downfall, I would start with Ricardo López Ventura, that trickster who had rewritten his destiny with the moniker "Ricky Ventura." Before 1970, playing some nonspecific role at the Festival de Avándaro, he'd been known as Unlucky Rickster.

Among the many legends, it was believed he'd connected the cables, restoring the lights when they had gone out at the festival. The crowd was starting to resign itself to a night of mud and silence when suddenly the sounds of "Three Souls in My Mind" miraculously returned. Ricky had been seen on stage (one of those tiresome people always easily spotted), but nobody had ever confirmed that he was the guy responsible for bringing back the power.

The promoter frequented record stores that stank of patchouli, parks where marijuana was sold, cafeterias passing for bars, and warehouses dedicated to amplifier rentals. His great strategy, back in the days before ATMs, was to always carry a thousand pesos in fifty-peso notes. If you needed fast cash to bribe a patrol car or pay for a motel or score a joint, Ricky was your man. But his real business wasn't money-lending, it was getting you to play his venues for free.

I remember his slow way of smoking—index finger pointed out with that long fingernail he cultivated as a tribute, or so he said, to his love of the guitar (and was maybe also useful for cocaine). His greatest talent was convincing you there was nothing more normal than owing him money. *Let me invest in you,* he'd say, handing over the standard blue receipt. Then he'd make a gesture that at the time signaled pride but has since fallen out of fashion: he'd blow on his nails then rub them against the lapel of his checkered jacket.

He was so obsessed with chess, one time I saw him use that coat as an improvised chessboard. I don't know how good he was at playing. The fact is, he did his hair like Bobby Fisher and those drawn-out games served him well in a life of intermediacy, forever waiting for an auspicious occasion.

Ricky Ventura watched with the avid patience of someone scouting for reckless behavior. He drew his composure from the desperation of others. He grinned with his horse-like teeth until the smile lost its meaning. His manner was both adaptable and meticulous, like someone who doesn't make plans but is never without his hairbrush, scarf, pomade or nail clippers—in short, someone who has no expectations but is always prepared.

Ricky's participation in the rock scene was as a permanent intruder who dressed like a pool-table salesman or hawker of bowling shoes. His loans and concerts rescued us from enough sticky situations to prompt Mario Müller to this unforgettable refrain: *I hereby revoke Ricky's sentence.* Ventura deserved both the sentence and the pardon.

Back when I was playing on a beat-up Fender Precision, Ricky steered me to a Rickenbacher 40 that a salsa musician, crippled by emphysema, was selling at half price. Ricky didn't know much about music, but he always knew what musicians needed. That was the first time he talked to me about Jaco Pastorius. *He's the Jesus Christ of electric bass*, he said. *Everyone will want to follow his gospel.* He also told me that few bass players ever managed to achieve the sound of "a boat being tied to the dock." If you achieved that—that quintessential shredding of string—you had mastered your instrument.

Ricardo López Ventura trafficked in truths at a time when all of us were living at the borders of reality. He could find the info, the instrument, the plug you needed.

He resembled Dennis Hopper in the role of a travel agent. Eventually, his long-standing chess game led him to a much stranger gambit. Andy Warhol received him at Studio 54, in New York, precisely because he mistook him for Dennis Hopper. That particular mix-up led to another. Ricky introduced himself as William S. Burroughs's Mexican lawyer. The painter of soup cans was charmed to meet an evil genius. Burroughs had killed his wife in a fit of drunkenness attempting to stage the famous scene from William Tell. The accidental assassin got a free pass thanks to Bernabé Jurado, a criminal attorney who litigated with bribe money. Ricardo López Ventura was young enough to be Jurado's grandson, but Warhol took no notice of such details. They talked about the kind of inspiration that arose from the land of human sacrifice. When he pulled the trigger, Burroughs had felt possessed of some creative spirit. The painter's smooth face crinkled into a grimace—the closest approximation of emotion such a dandy could make. This was the first step towards our band's contact with Lou Reed, who was a close friend of Warhol's, and towards the "Live from the Warehouse" concert—the glory that lead to my downfall.

Most bands would've murdered one another to open for the Velvet Underground. Ricky Ventura did us the honor of suggesting Los Extraditables.

He housed us in an office someone had lent him in the Zona Rosa, an apartment that had seen better days, where plastic folding chairs comprised the furniture. Inside, he shut off the lights. Then he turned on a black lamp which made the concert poster shine garishly. On the dark purple paper, Lou Reed's face gleamed like a calavera. The name of our band didn't appear anywhere. We would either be the filler or the waste-product, but we didn't care. Under that halo of black light, I felt the horror radiating from Lou Reed's face and was captivated.

Three hours before the concert, I gave Luciana an intoxicated kiss goodbye. *You taste like chalk,* she'd murmured.

I didn't see her in the audience and didn't look for her at the exit. The next morning, I woke up far from home and far from myself, lying next to a woman who smelled like burnt yarn.

For three or four days, I stayed on a hillside below the Ajusco volcano, watching scampering lambs from behind a cloud of marijuana smoke. Down below, in the hazy distance of the Valley of Mexico, the city shimmered like an electric swamp.

When I finally had the nerve to return home, Luciana had already gone back to Guadalajara. I finished off the contents of the Blasito shoebox, cooking up some "triphase" cocktails of coke and E and Rohypnol, until Mario came to my rescue. It took me a while to even recognize him. He slapped me hard. This woke me up and I loved him more than ever; I felt that he was really there for me. I sobbed into his shoulder, missing Luciana and cursing the good luck that had sent her to me in the first place.

Like a diligent pupil of the Swiss School, Mario Müller had shown up with a packet of instant soup. While I sipped from the first hot beverage I'd had in months, he explained how I'd been paying for drugs with furniture. I'd fallen into the bartering economy of extreme junkies, unable to see what I was giving away in exchange for what I got.

He stayed with me for two weeks and made the apartment look presentable. He threw Felipe Blue out when the guy showed up with another shoebox. Meanwhile, I searched for Luciana in the underlined passages of her books, which she'd left behind, as if for a final sentimental education. I read and reread those words she'd imprinted inside her, as if that might bring her back.

Sandra would wrap a special cuff around one of her biceps to check her blood pressure. On the other she'd strap her iPod. Sometimes I'd picture her wearing nothing but devices (beeper, Walkman, cell) attached to various muscle groups.

"I'd like to have some work done." Her comment came as no surprise.

"On what?" I asked.

There was no hesitation as she listed the incisions:

"On my face and my fingertips. Enough to change my identity. I'd like to get surgery to become Mexican; then Támez might lay off."

"If we get married, you can stay here," I said.

"We live in different worlds, Tony. I love the way you drag your leg, but you're not my type."

We were in her room. Under a poster of a mandala and a photo of her teacher, Larry Schultz, the pioneer of *"power vinyasa"* and *"rocket yoga,"* a wiry man with intelligent eyes. Yes, we lived in entirely different worlds. She had learned to control her breathing as if there were waves lapping in her throat. She was a master of meditation and the specialized moves of full-contact karate. She trained tourists to control their anger, and actors to manifest theirs. One of her students had pulled the "Chinese lock" on me—only then had I fully grasped the important role Sandra played in Mario Müller's scheme.

"Ceballos found work in Mexico City," Sandra said, crouching awkwardly on one leg.

I was having trouble remembering who she meant.

"The diver, Tony! For God's sake. Where's your head? He worked with you? In the aquarium? Don't you remember?"

Ceballos. The banished diver. The sobbing, the neoprene.

"Of course I remember, it's just that there are a lot of holes in my brain."

In paradise, memory is impure, I thought. What came from a distance barely touched the present. The Pyramid existed so you could leave your former life behind.

"He's coming over to say goodbye," Sandra said. She removed her shoes so that she could rub lotion on her feet. Next she took her blood pressure, then stood up, like someone about to go on a long journey, and pointed to her closet.

"I want to show you something," she said and opened the sliding door. The shelves inside were full of miscellaneous objects. "You can touch them," she added, as if they were jewels. I found a stuffed toucan, a transparent visor, a whistle, some scrap metal, a lime-green Frisbee, a serrated knife, a cardboard camera, a compass, a Rubik's cube, a miniature Dalmatian, a pair of Zwiling scissors, an unclassifiable copper spring.

"They're things the guests leave behind," she explained. "First they're kept for six months at the Lost & Found, then they're thrown away. I managed to hold on to these."

"In Mexico," I said, "it's not called Lost & Found. It's called Lost Objects. The gringos are more optimistic—they think things can be found. "

"I keep the ones that speak to me," she said.

Her closet was like my memory. Loose pieces, fragments of something else.

What does your closet say about you? I didn't dare pose the question. The answer might be too sad. The tawny light of sunset was depressing me enough.

"What's wrong with you?" she asked.

"The sun depresses me."

"You're a *freak*," she said. "It's the darkness that's depressing."

"I'd like to be a blind black man," I said. "A blind black man in an unlit room. A blind black man from Cameroon who sits in an unlit room."

"You're completely *whack*," she said. My sadness had cheered her up.

A soft knock on the door. It was Ceballos.

"Sorry, I got caught up in paperwork for my severance package," he said.

He was never to blame for his own lateness. He'd been Ginger Oldenville's remora, the fish that follows the shark.

"Why don't you just tell Antonio," Sandra said, trying to cut the formalities short. Her Spanish was infinitely better than the variety spoken by this man who'd been born to live underwater. Somewhat awkwardly he explained that he was moving to Mexico City. Mario Müller had found him a job at Aqua Nautics. He was going to become a pool diver. It didn't sound so bad. The Caribbean had given him too many bad surprises, not just with Ginger's death, but something else from his past. He rubbed his forearms, grazing the little logo of the polo player on his shirt, and talked about the lifeline, which he'd helped to install.

He explained that Ginger Oldenville used to set up GPS for the underground rivers. Ceballos had accompanied him on many occasions—until he made an error, a minor mistake, but enough to alter their course. Ceballos's flippers had bumped the wall of a cenote, which raised a thick cloud of sand, ash, and bone dust. The water became murky, and because it was daytime the shimmer took on a brilliant viscosity. When the particles settled, they saw a halo of blue light—an underwater flashlight. They hid behind some rocks and watched the shapes of other divers passing through a tunnel. They followed these divers at a distance until they reached an underground cave where the afternoon sun was filtering through. Up ahead they could see the mouth of the river. Then they spotted a small rocky cove and started swimming towards it.

A ship had dropped anchor some two hundred meters away. Only then did they notice that the divers they'd been following were carrying black rubber packages the size of minibar fridges (Ceballos had called them "minsibars"). The ship was the gray of the Mexican Navy fleet. They were transferring the parcels there in an inflatable motorboat.

They had stumbled on the drug route. The sinkhole served as a kind of sewer that drained into the subterranean rivers, which led to a beach where they'd load the merchandise bound for Miami, all under the protection of the marina.

"Ginger told Señor Mario all about it," Ceballos said.

"You didn't speak with Mario?" I said.

"No, Señor Antonio."

"Why not?"

"I told Ginger it was none of our business." Sandra said, coming to his defense. "Ceballos didn't want to leave until we knew," she added. "He's cooperating."

Her closet door was closed now. Which was preferable. That collection of junk didn't inspire much confidence.

Now Ginger Oldenville's death made sense. He had reported the drug trafficking. Ceballos said Ginger had gone to Mario with this information, which implicated my friend. It was also suspicious that Mario would suddenly send Ceballos to Mexico City. It seemed clear Mario wanted him far away.

Ceballos said goodbye. We wished him luck with Aqua Nautics.

"He wants to be innocent," Sandra said after shutting the door. "He doesn't know if he is or not. He trusts me. He took my classes for a while. An incredible athlete. You know you had to hear this." She paused, annoyed. "Mario is your friend, and he's sick."

"So?"

"And you love him, you feel sorry for him."

"So what?"

"You love him, you feel sorry for him—and he knows all about the narco route that passes through The Pyramid."

"Everybody knows about the narco stuff. This country can't live without it! It's both horrendous and totally normal."

Sandra took a long sip of water. Then she came up to me and placed her hand on my forearm. She looked at me soberly, eyes pleading. She needed me to accept what she was saying:

"Mario is obsessed with The Pyramid," she said. "He's just gotten rid of Ceballos. Ginger telling his story all over the place wasn't very convenient."

"He didn't tell it 'all over the place,'" I said. "He didn't even tell me." I held my head in my hands. A sharp, painful idea, an idea I didn't want to have, was opening a pathway in my mind: *Mario killed him*. He wanted to keep his dream alive, at any cost; he was an obsessive piece of shit.

"You know who found the first of the hammock knots?" Sandra asked.

"It was Remigio."

"No, it was Mario," she said. "Do you really think the knot could fall from the body bag without anyone seeing it? He put it there after. He knew Remigio would find it, that's his domain, and he knew Remigio would give it to you because he respects you. He also guessed you'd hand it over to Ríos to support the gay pact theory. Mario's sharper than hunger, you know that. And you helped him. The suicide pact is a convenient story for everyone. If your son dies with a tattoo written in Arabic and a hammock noose around his dick, the news of a suicide pact comes as a blessing. Atrium is traded on the stock exchange, and Leopoldo is under a lot of pressure. . . . "

The name seeped in like venom. A poison she'd survived which I wanted to avoid.

"Do you think Mario killed Ginger?" I asked.

"Honestly, Tony, I don't know. Cross my heart."

"I don't believe it," I said, frantically, not knowing what exactly I was referring to.

"You don't believe what?"

"I don't believe anything." I got up. I'd had enough. Ceballos didn't know if he was innocent or not; he couldn't grasp the ramifications of what he'd seen. But I felt guilty—guilty of the repugnant afternoon sun, of the sweat coursing down my armpits, of the discarded objects in Sandra's closet, of everything I'd failed to do.

I left the room. Out a paneless window I saw a man floating in the sky on a hand glider.

Everything was so strange it seemed Mario Müller might even be innocent.

When evening came, I went for a walk. I lingered in the lobby before a reproduction of the central tablet from the Temple of the Foliated Cross, in Palenque.

Under the halogen lights, the exuberant fresco, framed by two opposing columns comprised of glyphs, seemed different to me now. At the center, a pair of shepherds guarded a pillar that forked into two branches: the "foliated cross." They held instruments of death and torture. Severed heads hung from the arms of the cross, irrigating the forest floor with blood.

For the (since canceled) in-house seminar series "Maya Pride," Der Meister had lectured on the first inhabitants of the region. He described how repulsed the Maya were by murder. For them nothing could be worse. That said, they readily embraced human sacrifice. This was how violence—inevitable in all human societies—had facilitated a fertile irrigation scheme: the blood quenched the thirst of the gods. The important thing, the moral choice, was knowing how to discriminate between worthy sacrificial subjects.

The Maya knew that their gods (flawed, erratic, capricious) wouldn't settle for just any offering. It might have been logical to accept the scum of society, the human surplus that no longer served any purpose. But these deities weren't known for their logic. They wanted something more. The forking branches of the Foliated Cross surged with an abundance of carefully selected bodies. To satisfy the gods' thirst you had to water the earth with the blood of children or virgins or warriors or people who displayed some worthy deformity. Only a culture disgusted by murder could value selective death.

Mario and I hadn't spoken about this again. But I'd noticed something curious in the staff's behavior: whenever they passed the Foliated Cross, the employees would cross themselves. Maybe it was just an automatic reflex, but I also wondered if they did it to guard against the kind of harm represented in the mural.

Saturated with images, the fresco required a slow, laborious contemplation. Its jungle of signs resisted being summarized or understood all at once. There were many protruding faces and masks and fruit and every kind of beast. But all of these things had the same origin—they came from spilled blood. From sacrifice.

It had been Mario's idea to commission a replica of this elaborate and fascinating hell. In another part of The Pyramid, there was a copy of the famous lid from the sarcophagus at the Temple of the Inscriptions, also in Palenque. Its image, known as "the Astronaut," depicted what appeared to be the pilot of a sophisticated (but primitive) spaceship. For some, it was proof that the Maya had been extraterrestrials.

The staff liked this image better, but they never crossed themselves in front of it.

I moved on from the Foliated Cross. If I continued staring, it would become just the trigger my insomnia needed. I decided to wander into the garden. It had stopped raining, and a deliciously earthy smell wafted up from the grass. It was an evening you could chew on.

I walked until my leg started to ache. A tourist in a closed-off corner of the garden was dancing without music, her body catching the occasional flicker of lamplight. She was barefoot. I tried to think up a melody for the movement of those arms and thighs, some fusion of incongruous rhythms—maybe swing, but very slow; or perhaps a three-note samba.

My interest in her rhythm made me stare at her somewhat brazenly. She smiled when she saw me and raised a glass of white wine in a toast. Wine served outdoors at The Pyramid always came in plastic cups. She must have wandered over from one of the local restaurants.

"I like walking around here," she said. Her accent sounded Argentine. "The ground is softer."

She was drunk. At that moment, a lightbulb went out.

"Poor little light," she said. "Do you work here? You don't look like a tourist."

"Neither do you."

"Oh, yeah? What do I look like?"

She pulled her hair back and smiled, rubbing her foot against a tuft of grass. I noticed the tattoo of a half moon on her ankle. She wore a thin, loose blouse that showed a hint of cleavage. Her breasts were browned, as if she'd been sunbathing naked all along the reef. I was still trying to come up with a response when she continued.

"What, am I breaking your balls? I know what I must look like. Someone who's about to catch the next flight to Buenos Aires. This is my last glass of wine. There were many, but this one will be my very last. You see the difference?"

"Sure," I said. "And now you're going to break the glass."

Her eyes lit up. The idea hadn't occurred to her.

"Here, feel this," she said, tapping the ground with a foot. I took off my shoes and socks and stepped into her footprint. Why did my contact with women always seem to begin with feeling the air for shadows and ghosts? First Sandra, now the Argentine.

"I'm telling you all this because I'm leaving. Everybody here is a liar. You, too, maybe? What do you do here?"

I told her about the aquarium.

"Oh, so that's you. I hate those fish."

"Who lied to you?"

"Some asshole I came here for. Never showed up. Aren't you sick of all this bullshit, all the drugs they feed us, all the porn? I used to like it. I liked the lies this country fed me. But I'm taking off in an hour. Look." She raised her wrist to the light. There was a scar. "They did this with a knife. Tied me up for three days. And guess what, sweetheart? I liked it." Her eyes filled with tears. "And that's something I hate even more than your stupid fish. Liking the lies. I liked being tied up and I liked that they lied to me."

She flung her glass away. It didn't break.

"I want to crush it with my foot. Except I don't want to show up in Buenos Aires limping all over the place. You do it."

"Me?"

"Sweetheart, you've already got a limp." She smiled. "What's a little more?"

I turned away and left her there.

"The water's poisoned, isn't it?" she called out after me. "They add drugs to the water, don't they?"

I walked all the way to the next building before looking back. When I turned around, two security guards were approaching her.

Suddenly I felt a strong desire to embrace the hotel's spirit of decadence in another way. So I went to the aquarium, my habitat for the past year. I grabbed a net and caught a red snapper. When I pulled him out of the water, I watched as he gasped for air, thrashing in my hands. I wanted to kill him. But I couldn't. I dropped him back in the water. The snapper plummeted to the bottom and paused before swimming off, as if my torture had left him stupefied.

The next day, Inspector Ríos called me at Bar Canario. I left my Bloody Mary to go talk to him. He wanted to meet me in Kukulcán.

I hailed a taxi that sounded like a pair of rattling tin cans. It had no AC, so the ride over was like being trapped inside a hot tambourine. We pulled up to a store that sold seashells. When Ríos had given me directions over the phone, the name sounded like a mix of Maya and English, something like "Síxel City." What he'd said was *Seashell City.*

I walked in and found Ríos studying the shell of a sea snail. The blast of air conditioning chilled the sweat behind my ears.

"I don't want anyone from The Pyramid to see us," he explained as we made our way down one of the store's aisles. He led us to a wall decorated with an enormous starfish. Ríos paused to touch a hairy coconut shell that now doubled as an ashtray. I saw a glazed crab, a Virgin of Guadalupe made of seashells, a blowfish converted into a lampshade. At the end of the aisle, he turned to me.

"I went over the autopsy report," he said. "I mean Roger Bacon's." Ríos was the kind of person who always had to have something in his hands. He took out a matchbook, flipped it open and rubbed his thumb along the matches as he spoke.

"His body was found by the Coast Guard. They reported it to the port authority, and the case was quickly closed. But sometimes there are loose ends. I'll leave the house and suddenly realize I forgot to put out water for the dog. This ever happen to you?"

"I don't have a dog."

"Just imagine you did," he said with a smile.

"So you went back to see if the dog had water. What did you find?"

"I was itching with curiosity, so I tracked down the Navy coroner. He didn't tell me anything. That asshole is just a piece of furniture. But I've got a few contacts in Mexico City. I was there yesterday and spoke with someone at the attorney general's office. They're the ones who called attention to the case, then filed it away. But you'd be amazed what a little rum can do."

He took out a manila envelope, removed a photograph and handed it to me. It was a picture of Roger Bacon's corpse. I was surprised by the size of the tattoo on his arm. Stranger still was the idea of having a body like that, inflated from gym workouts. You could see a blister at the base of his neck. A mosquito bite, maybe. It gave an almost human touch to his pneumatic physique.

"You know the worst thing about my job?" Ríos said. "The paperwork. With every dead guy, I have to take out the typewriter. They don't even give us computers. Bacon is making me work a double shift."

I pictured him sitting at a typewriter under a slow fan, typing late into the night. Undoubtedly this work was depressing. He laid a yellow finger on the photograph.

"Bacon's lungs," he said, "were full of fresh water. He didn't die at sea. They drowned him in a pond or a river or something. In this part of the country, we only have underground rivers. See this bite?" He pointed to Bacon's neck. "The inflamation is huge. Since I moved here, I've been interested in the mosquitoes, though the bastards seem more interested in me. They've always got me surrounded. The point is, mosquitoes don't live at high sea. But they thrive in the cenotes, the sinkholes, and all the underground caves we've got here. The most important thing, though, is that Bacon died before Ginger Oldenville. The forensic report is clear: there was no suicide pact."

"How do you know that?" I said.

"Something tells me Ginger died because Bacon did. He was going to report his friend's death so they killed him before he could."

As he spoke I contemplated a redundant SpongeBob made from actual sea sponge.

"Well," I said, "if Bacon died first, that still doesn't eliminate the possibility of a pact. Both of them died."

"You don't get what I'm saying," Ríos said. "There was a set up. Bacon didn't die in saltwater and his body wasn't discovered after Ginger's. But someone really wanted us to see it that way. Why? So we'd focus on the knot tied around the guy's dick. So we'd make the connection to Cruci/Fiction and the other knot, which we already had. Everything happened in reverse. Bacon was investigating the same thing Ginger was. Killing one diver made it necessary to kill the other."

Mario knew all of this, I thought. What Ríos said next came as a relief.

"Ginger was in touch with the consulate. He'd told them about the drug trafficking. They tipped off the DEA and that's when Bacon showed up."

Several people knew the story. Mario dropped the first knot, which was meant to be the second one. Why did he do it? I felt an urge to destroy the absurd SpongeBob still smiling at me.

Ríos put away his matchbook. He took me by the shoulders.

"Think of it this way: imagine coming home to check if your dog has water. Miami is two hours from the reef if you go by boat. Bacon was looking for a dirty route, a dangerous one. The marina reported his death two days later, when they supposedly found his body at sea. So, does your dog have water?"

"I don't have a dog, I already told you."

"Bacon had a blister on his neck the size of a bean. I wanted to talk to Ceballos but they told me he'd gone to Mexico City. The Pyramid is now without divers."

"Where are you going with all this?"

"To where Bacon ended up, and also Ginger. These are not fresh corpses. There are the Dead that never stop dying. What can you tell me about Mario Müller?"

"Nothing." *He wants me to betray Mario,* I thought. I'd given Ríos the hammock knot. I'd helped him close the case with a false clue. Now he wanted the truth.

"If the narcos are behind all this, you won't be able to do anything about it," I said. "They're the ones who own the country."

"I want to know what happened. I believe in God. I don't like the world he created, but I believe in him anyway."

"He who is highly praised will lead you to the truth," I quoted.

"The purpose of truth isn't to change the world," Ríos answered. "It's to show us that truth exists."

"I suppose that kind of thing sounds good in a church."

Ríos ignored this. He was already thinking about something else.

"Roger Bacon had gone on dives in the Bahamas, in so-called 'blue holes.' Do you know what those are?"

"Of course not."

"They're very deep pools with ancient caves. The water turns all kinds of strange, vibrant colors. Because of the bacterial organisms. Bacon worked for the University of Miami, he collected samples for them. You have to have balls of steel to dive that deep."

"What's so special about these bacteria?"

"Before the Earth had any oxygen, there were already many signs of life. Millennia ago the bacteria in the blue lagoons produced oxygen as a waste product. We're the result of bacterial trash! That's how our species has evolved." He picked up a bottle of mother-of-pearl ointment. "Will this stuff work on my boss's anus?"

"The tropical heat is getting to you. Do you go around saying this stuff at church? That we're nothing but bacterial trash?"

"Life," he said, "began with the so-called 'oxygen revolution' in these blue lagoons: a kind of deep sky, richer than the Garden of Eden. What's interesting about evolution is that it makes sense. If you can understand it, that means there's a plan. Which is where God comes in, my friend. 'The bearded guy in the sky doesn't play dice with the universe.' I'm sure you've heard the phrase. Insulting my boss makes it easier to do what he asks, but there are higher reasons to help him. The secret will. He who is highly praised will lead you to the truth."

"The will to be bacteria shit."

"A fine definition of Kukulcán," he said, smiling widely; the stench of tobacco was strong on his breath.

I left the store with a bad taste in my mouth. The air outside was searing and hit me like an insult. I wandered around for a while before heading over to the taxi line, next to an area of industrial warehouses. On the ground was the carcass of a large, ugly bird surrounded by greenish flies. Some two hundred yards away, you could see the outlines of all the abandoned hotels with their cracked facades. A neon H dangled precariously down the front of a building. Stray branches peeked through the terraced rooftops.

A little girl walked past me. She was hawking coconut soap, displayed on the board she balanced across her head. She didn't try to sell me any; clearly I wasn't the target consumer for her merchandise. I've never understood why coconut products like soap and candy are always sold with that bright, pinkish coating. Coconuts aren't pink, but you'd think it couldn't sell without the color.

The little vendor was headed for the hotel district, which was growing more deserted by the day. In a few years tourism would be over—the sand swallowed by the sea, the birds dead—but there would still be someone selling that pink-colored coconut soap.

Sandra had planned to meet me in the Solarium. You might wonder why a hotel with half a mile of beachfront would bother with a sunbathing lounge. The place was always deserted. But Mario saw its potential. Once the weather got worse, the glass solarium would be covered over and fitted with infra-red lamps. The sun would become an artificial luxury. The Caribbean of the future would be like the surface of Mars.

I found Sandra dozing on a chaise longue. Beside her, a cup of ice was sweating in the glare. A sudden gust of wind knocked over a beach umbrella, which woke her. She looked startled when she saw me, as if I were responsible for the bad weather.

Then another gust toppled her glass. An umbrella flipped inside out, forming a kind of cone. I looked down toward the garden. All along the beach, people wrapped in towels were grabbing their bags and sandals and scurrying for shelter. A bell hop was trying to drive a golf cart over the sandbank.

The sky darkened and the temperature dropped instantly. The gale was so strong that the rain came horizontally, warm at first, then icy cold moments later.

"Let's go inside!" Sandra yelled.

In the distance I saw two strangers looming over a man lying on the lawn. The two guys kicked him—what seemed like the last of many blows. The man barely moved.

I raced into the hallway, where Sandra stood shivering.

"There's been an assault," I said then ran back across the garden, dodging between all the people coming in for shelter. Ignoring the puddles, I ran like someone in desperate search of something. Far away along the beach, I saw small blobs of color: some unperturbed beachgoers staring out at the waves. Closer to me, in a sudden pool of mud, a couple received the rain, their palms raised towards the sky in a kind of ceremonial ecstasy.

The rain grew steadily colder. Maybe this was why there seemed no limit to the feeling of getting wet.

I reached the edge of the garden and approached the assaulted man. There was blood on his shirt. I wondered if he was dead. When he sensed my presence, the man rolled onto his back. It was Leopoldo Támez.

"Did you call us?" I heard a voice behind me.

It belonged to a guard. He was speaking not to me but

to his boss. Támez reached into his pocket and pulled out a cellphone.

"No. My phone accidentally dialed you when they kicked me."

I found Mario's office transformed into a kind of military conference room. Carlitos Pech, the staff manager, was there, and so was Roxana Westerwood, the PR director. My friend's expression reflected the general sense of disaster.

"The port authority, the weather channel, even the news crew from TeleCaribe, all said a hurricane was coming." He sounded desperate. "But Támez didn't do anything. He's the one in charge of contingency planning. But he didn't issue any warnings. What the fuck is going on?"

"With all due respect, Señor Müller," said Carlitos Pech in his heavy Yucatán accent. "They beat the shit out of him."

At The Pyramid I always found it difficult to make out what people were saying. The staff tended to speak in whispers, as if camaraderie was a secret. But now Carlitos Pech was making himself heard.

"They're bringing us the video from the security cameras," he said. "Támez has two broken ribs."

"We've had sixteen hurricanes so far this year. So he forgot one," Roxana said sympathetically.

Aren't you sick of all this bullshit, I almost felt like telling her, *sick of all the drugs they feed us, all the porn?* We were living in a fortress full of mentally disturbed holiday-makers.

When the video arrived, Mario tossed it to Pech like a hot potato. Roxana sat down beside me. She smelled of organic strawberries, of deliciously synthetic shampoo.

The footage revealed a detail I hadn't noticed from the Solarium terrace: Leopoldo Támez's assailants had been none other than Vicente Fox and George W. Bush.

"Masks," Roxana explained.

The chief of security took the blows in total stillness. It was as if he looked down on his assailants too much to dignify their punches with resistance. The attackers reduced him to a motionless heap, then grabbed his wallet. When they kicked him the final time, Roxana yelled "Ouch!" and dug her nails—not so unpleasantly—into my shoulder.

Roxana Westerwood belonged to a world completely removed from my routine or dealings with Der Meister. She was married to an oceanographer from Punta Fermín. When the sea was calm, she'd come to The Pyramid on a boat captained by her husband. She spoke four languages and could find agreeable solutions for everything. She saw any problem as an excuse to spend a night at the hotel.

"Look at this," Mario said, switching to another camera angle. The assailants were getting into a Tsuru. He paused the image.

"A rental car, from Tours Mayab," Carlitos Pech said. He pointed to a decal on the rear window.

The theft is just a pretext, I thought. *They were after Támez.*

It pleased me that Roxana seemed to be following my train of thought:

"They were taking an enormous risk by attacking him at The Pyramid. They could've made off with his wallet on any other street."

"It's an invasion," Mario said. "They want to show us how vulnerable we are. 'Look! The chief of security, beaten up in his own garden!'"

Carlitos Pech had always looked at me with narrowed, distrustful eyes. He was suspicious of my closeness with Mario and the obvious pointlessness of my job. So it seemed only logical he should question me now.

"What's your opinion about all this, Señor Tony?" He had the tone of an oracle who knows his question has no answer.

"The same thing as you."

"Támez got careless, that's all we know," Roxana interjected, trying to keep the peace. "We have this magnificent workplace. In paradise."

Her husband doesn't want her to keep working here, I thought.

Mario gave Roxana and Pech their instructions. Then he told me to meet him later. I left his office with nothing to do. *He just wants me to listen,* I thought. The man you can trust.

I went to Sandra's room. I'd found myself missing that perfect moment when she'd said *Get out* and left her door open.

Now she opened the door but not before asking, twice, who it was. She fell into my arms.

"I'm sorry, Tony. Forgive me." She sobbed into my shoulder. "I wanted to talk to you." Her words were choked. "Out on the terrace. But then the hurricane..."

She handed me a document on letterhead from the SEGOB, Mexico's ministry of the interior.

"The fucking cunt!" she said, biting her lip.

I read the letter. Sandra had thirty business days to leave the country. Her papers weren't in order. They never had been. The notice cited an irregularity on page 281 of some official document, which pointed to a long paper trail of various legal breaches.

"I told you Támez had friends," she said. Her mascara was smudged. A box of Kleenex sat on the table in the middle of the room. I handed her a tissue.

"Why didn't you ever get your papers straightened out?" I said.

"So you think this is my fault?"

"I'm just asking. Mario could've given you a hand. You're not the only gringa here. Peterson's got good connections. Even Támez could've helped you earlier, since he takes such an interest in you."

"Yes: it's my fault. I just never thought I'd have to get my papers in order. I've been here forever. I was playing Russian roulette. 'Recreational paranoia.' You must be familiar with the term. Security is boring, and besides, I trusted Leopoldo! That's the most fucked up thing about it. I trusted that son of a bitch. I took it up the ass so much that I actually trusted him. Do you understand what I'm saying?"

"Yes," I said.

Sandra covered her face with her hands. Then she looked into her compact mirror.

"I look like Alice Cooper," she said. "Thank you for being here, Tony. What I just told you isn't even the worst of it."

"What's the worst of it?"

"Forgive me."

"I forgive you. Now tell me what for."

"Támez told me to stall you. That day we were listening to 'Feelings.' He needed some time to disconnect the security system in the aquarium. So I lured you back here."

"I followed you even though you didn't want me to."

"*Bullshit.* You were trashed and horny. You would've followed me even if I'd punched you in the face. Don't get me wrong, I had a good time, too. I enjoyed your imaginary finger. What's fucked up is that Támez would ask me to do that. I had no idea what was going to happen, I swear. I never dreamed they'd kill Ginger. When Támez was a cop, he was one of the officers who investigated my ex's case. You know, the guy I came with from the States."

"He died of an overdose?"

"An overdose I gave him."

Her answer made me shudder. My voice faltered:

"You killed him?"

"I helped him die, which is different. He had horrible nightmares where he screamed like a dying man. He confused the sound of the sea with helicopters and the Maya waiters with Vietcong. He was sick, and he was twenty years older than me. His paranoia wasn't recreational. He asked me to increase his dose. I did it. And you know what?"

"What?" I said.

"I felt the hugest relief when he died. I wasn't worried about injecting him. What worried me was how good I felt about his death. It's fucked up to be so at peace with the death of someone you love. Because I did love him, Tony. I've never loved anyone so much in my life, swear to God. I didn't straighten out my papers because it felt like my life was over. Besides, Támez knew about the overdose and could blackmail me. In fact, that's exactly what he did. 'Visa stamps'. That's what he called it when he fucked me up the ass. *No pain, no gain,* like they tell you at the gym. Am I horrifying you?"

"No," I lied.

"Forgive me. You know I'm garbage. *White trash.*"

"There's nothing for me to forgive," I answered, weakly.

She inhaled deeply and hugged me again. She'd made my chest damp. Her hands were trembling.

"I'm not a whore, Tony. I'm a survivor. My life may be strange, but I'm not, I swear. Do you believe me?"

"I believe you," I said. It was a relief to speak the truth. With vindictive pleasure, I thought of the video in which Támez was beaten up by Vicente Fox and George W. Bush.

"I have to leave. It's for the best," she said, pointing to the letterhead, which was now watermarked with tears. "This way they'll let me go without any trouble." She stroked the soggy paper. "Mexicans are a sentimental bunch."

"If you were doing what Támez said, why did he have you kicked out?"

"That's what's so *weird* about this whole thing." She raised her hands and reached for another Kleenex, then sat down on her leg. The next thing she said baffled me.

"He's kicking me out because he loves me." She gazed at me like a cornered animal, one I didn't want to get closer to.

"He loves me, in his own fucked up way. *He's a fucking maniac, and he loves me.* He wants to protect me. He's always protected me. Why do you think I have a room twice the size of yours? Leopoldo can get things Mario Müller can't. *He thinks the world of me,*" she said in English, as if it were open to interpretation.

"If he loves you so much, why doesn't he go with you?"

"He can't enter the United States. He's been under investigation. The DEA would snatch him up in a second. It hurts him to see me go, it hurts him more than the beating he got today."

"He could take you somewhere else along the coast. Would you go with him?"

"No. I don't love him. Maybe I'm more of a jerk than he is. He wants to get me out of here before it's too late. He wants to protect me."

"From what?"

"From whatever. But also from himself. Leopoldo loves me enough not to want to kill me, but he's already killed people he loved. If things here get worse, he's going to lose it. . . ."

"Did he kill Ginger?"

"He doesn't have the balls for that. He's got enough balls to fuck a gringa up the ass and kill his own flesh and blood. He's, you know, *a regular guy.* I didn't want to use you, Tony."

"You didn't."

"You're kind of strange and you know how to play Go."

"Wait, I'm the strange one?"

"You need to understand. I can handle physical pain," she said. "I got used to it. It's my job. 'What doesn't kill you makes you stronger.' The best job I've ever had. They're giving me thirty days, but it's better to limit my goodbyes. I'm going to send my stuff by freight," she said, pointing to her closet full of lost-and-found objects.

I could hear the rain. At that moment, the water falling from the sky was "Oklahoma"—or "Nebraska," or "Indiana," or whichever stupid place she'd eventually settle.

"A penny for your thoughts," she said.

"I'm tired of thinking."

"Come here." She hugged me. I could feel the tension in her back, a back injured to the point of perfection, and wondered what it would be like having to rely on owning a strong body. Sandra had had to live on a different plane of existence. Maybe that's why it seemed even more humiliating that a body sculpted by will should have to yield to Támez. Her mastery over pain couldn't eliminate the horror she'd endured. Sandra had wanted to screw herself over, and she'd succeeded.

"You started thinking again," she said, concerned.

I pressed my fingers against my temples to prevent the formation of further thoughts.

"Here," Sandra said. She handed me a rusty compass. "It's from my collection."

I took comfort in the fact that the compass was broken. It wouldn't have to endure the uncertainty of finding its own way. The needle, ruined by rust, pointed east.

I went back to Mario's office so shaken I couldn't figure out what anyone was talking about.

"'Variable cloud cover,'" Roxana said, reading from a document. The person in charge of tracking the weather reports had recorded this token observation. Then he spent the night partying. Two women came to visit him at The Pyramid. They'd been caught on camera.

"They're from an agency. Level C," Roxana was saying. "They're prepaid workers. I have a copy of the *voucher*. Their agency gave me the information and I've passed it along to the police."

"What's Level C?" I asked, intrigued by the cool objectivity with which Roxana discussed prostitution.

"It means full service. I'm guessing this is not the first time they've come to The Pyramid. But it's the first time they've visited an employee during business hours."

"Támez gave his secretary the day off," Carlitos Pech said. "That's why she didn't relay the weather report, which was incorrect anyway. She had to deliver some donations to a church in Tizimín. She took a car there with Filiberto, one of the guards."

"So who was at the front gate?" Mario asked Carlitos.

"Just some slacker who normally works as a waiter. Filiberto gave the guy a hundred pesos to cover for him. The assailants who showed up in the Tsuru ID'd themselves with a card from Blockbuster! No one asked them for picture ID. And it wasn't even their card! It belonged to an English guy who'd long since left Kukulcán. I spoke with Tours Mayab. The driver was paid in cash. We're not going to be able to link him to the credit cards that bought the hookers."

My friend scratched his temples, then made a sudden lurch, like he was about to throw up. He managed to collect himself.

"How do you read all this?" Roxana asked. I didn't like her question. People who "read" reality tend not to read anything else.

"If someone wanted to prove that The Pyramid is a disaster area, they got what they wanted," Mario said.

He had probably been sick for months. His reflexes weren't sharp. We had a hurricane. That wasn't news, they happened all the time. But Mario was losing his control. It was only normal for others to fail. What was strangest was he didn't seem that concerned.

Roxana gave him a patronizing smile. Cheerfully, almost enthusiastically, she suggested that they organize a black and white ball to entertain the guests. To forget bad weather, you need indoor amusements.

Carlitos Pech said he'd gather his staff in the Izamal Room to enforce discipline.

The meeting adjourned in a mood of uncustomary calm.

I couldn't sleep, but it didn't bother me. At that moment, insomnia was a kind of obligation. I needed to keep watch over my room, my disordered memories, the ideas that hadn't yet occurred to me. I thought about Sandra and wondered if she was up packing her things in the red suitcase I'd once seen in a corner of her room. At 2 a.m., Mario called me.

"You have to come over, there's been a plane crash," he said, as if the news had something to do with us.

I made my way through various hallways, which all seemed less deserted than usual. The new curfew had inspired the guests to enjoy the building in different ways. On the couch where I'd seen the actor with his AK-47, three guys with shaved heads were typing furiously on their laptops, as if in competition with one another.

At the far end of one of the corridors, a man was pacing in an S-figure. He wasn't drunk. His movements seemed deliberate. Maybe he was some kind of surfer recluse.

Getting to Mario's office always gave me a slight pain in my bad leg. The distance from my room was at the upper limit of what I could walk. It lay just below my pain threshold. I found him hunched in front of his computer screen. He turned to me with white lips. He'd been drinking milk.

Mario opened his mouth into a perfect O shape but didn't make a sound. It reminded me of the way he used to build tension before singing "Accomplices of Silence," one of our band's loudest hits. After a few seconds, he began the explanation for his call.

"An Air France jet just went down," he said. "It was flying to Paris from Rio carrying three hundred and nineteen passengers. No one knows what happened. It flew into some bad turbulence—an air mass the size of Spain!—then disappeared. Have you got any idea what a storm that big even means?"

"Did you know anyone on board?"

"Tony, for God's sake. Don't get all literal. A year ago, you had no idea who you were. You made cellophane sound effects for candy commercials. Don't turn into Mr. Rational on me."

I peered around for his thermos. My guess was Mario had downed a milkshake loaded with amphetamines.

"What did you drink?"

"My words aren't a product of pills! Don't be so simplistic. An addict's real vice is believing that all the bizarre stuff comes from the drugs. It's time for you to wake up, Tony. Here in the tropics normal means 'delirium tremens.' You think my words were produced in a Swiss lab?" He opened his mouth and pointed at it with his index finger. His tongue looked pasty, coated in a whitish film.

"What's this you're telling me about the plane?" I asked, making my voice as gentle as possible.

"You don't need to know someone personally to be moved by a tragedy," he said. "Do you know the word 'empathy?' It's easier to identify with tragedy when you're sick, but that can also make it easier to enjoy. When you're dying, the deaths of others can be like vitamins. But I'll tell you something: what happened to those passengers terrifies me. I want them to live. I feel like death and I want them to live!" His eyes had a manic glow.

"Go back to María José," I said. "Check yourself into a hospital."

"And what's this? You become normal here and now you want me to be normal, too?" He smiled, then went on about the accident, as if it were all the same thing:

"The plane lost contact with air traffic control in Europe and Africa and was still off the American grid. Did you know there are areas you have to fly without radar coverage?" He raised his hand to his brow. His bloodshot eyes shone with a feverish intensity.

"It's amazing to think," he went on, "that radar has these black spots. The plane entered a dead zone. The last bit of information we have is that it achieved 'vertical velocity.' You know what that means? It went into free fall! That plane was really in for a beating! It took a nosedive into a region they call the 'Underwater Andes.' A mountain range in the Atlantic. You want some milk?"

He doesn't want to talk about The Pyramid. He needs some other drama, I thought.

"I'd prefer whiskey," I said.

"Me, too." Mario poured some whiskey into the white liquid. He passed me the bottle. He took a large gulp, seeming to enjoy his concoction.

"What's going on with you, Mario?" I said.

He ignored my question and continued down the track of his derailing thoughts.

"Back when we were kids, there was nothing better than flying. They made me wear a tie the first time I got on a plane, the kind that came with a knot and all you had to do was fasten the clip. I was fourteen. I went to Acapulco. These days flying is a shit-show. Like a deportation. In the future, only the poor will fly!"

"Are they going to close down The Pyramid?"

Again he ignored me.

"Getting around cities will become a job for specialists: for chauffeurs, beggars, and pizza delivery guys. Same thing with traveling. The rich will buy their thrills online. Only poor people will go to unpleasantly real places. The airplanes of the future will be infested with rats!"

I didn't say anything, just sat and drank my whiskey.

"It was an Air France jet, Tony! And I'm a fucking control freak." He pointed to his desk. The mess proved that in other parts of the building the beds were impeccably made. "Someone like me inspected that plane!"

"And someone like you inspects The Pyramid," I said. "A car with two assailants managed to get in here undetected. Did you fire Ceballos so that he wouldn't talk to the consulate?"

"I fired him so that he wouldn't talk, period. To protect the Spanish language. Ceballos is an oaf with a middle-ear infection. He's got fungus in his cochlea and seaweed in his brain. He can't survive in the Caribbean." He paused. "Three hundred and nineteen people are sitting at the bottom of the ocean and you're asking me about Ceballos! You're so insensitive, Tony. You've always been insensitive. Maybe the only sensible thing you ever did was get high."

"You're wasted, Mario."

A lock of hair fell across his brow. He tilted his head as if he were experiencing some kind of chest pain. I looked him in the eye, waiting for his gaze to meet mine. Finally, I confronted him:

"There are three hundred and nineteen people at the bottom of the ocean, and that's fucked up. But here *you* are, dying right in front of me. What have you got?"

"The ancient visitor," he said with a theatrical voice. "I'm sure you already knew that. There are no secrets in this piece of shit hotel; rumor is our most efficient room service. The Pyramid has full occupancy. This guest couldn't get his own room. He arrived without a reservation. Cancer, Tony. Of the esophagus. Inoperable. The size of a baseball."

"Have you seen good doctors?"

"I didn't bring you here to take care of me."

"Why did you bring me here?"

"You don't have the faintest goddamn idea."

"I've spent weeks trying to talk to you. There's radiation therapy, chemo, alternative—"

"Fuck you! A year ago you were a life-loving junkie! And who are you now, my mom?"

"I loved your mom."

"And *your* mom? I wanted to go to bed with her! She was so incredibly hot. That can't offend you, can it, Tony? First of all, because it was obvious and you knew it, and secondly, because I'm dying."

"And that gives you the right to do whatever the hell you want? How much time have you got left?"

"Western medicine isn't as exact as astrology. Nobody knows. But I'm not going to sit around waiting for that moment. I'm going to die here," he said, waving his hand around vaguely. "Right around here.... It'd be a little much to die *inside* The Pyramid, like some goddamn Maya king." He covered his mouth, trying to hide a spasm. It took him a few seconds to get a hold of himself.

"Are you OK?" I said.

"Apart from this whole dying business, I feel marvelous." He smiled and took a sip from his absurd cocktail of milk and whiskey.

"I don't think that's good for you."

"Of course not. Nothing is good for me." He drank aggressively, as if it might hurt me, then wiped his mouth with the back of his hand. "Did you think I brought you here to fuck Sandra and drag your leg in the sand? They're closing in on me, Tony. A flight without radar. Here I am. With the screen blacked out."

He shut off the computer monitor with his fist then turned to face me.

"We're going to have company," he continued. "Some idiot from Atrium is coming to check on us. They're not satisfied with the reports from Támez."

"Ginger reported the drug traffic. Ceballos knew about it, too." I tried to hold his gaze, but he started shuffling through the papers and coupons and invoices scattered all over his desk.

"Any taxi driver in Kukulcán could tell you we're floating in a sea of drugs. Have you never taken a cab?"

"Ginger wasn't killed by a taxi driver. Did you kill him?"

I stood up. Mario tried to join me, but his body failed him. He fell back into his chair, gasping. He looked at the floor.

"I'd love to tell you I did it, just so you could regret having rescued me in the old abandoned house. But I've got bad news for you. Your best friend. . . your only friend. . . is not a murderer. Are you disappointed?"

"You threw the hammock knot in the garden. Then Roger Bacon turned up with the other end."

"Am I a suspect, Mr. Inspector? Should I call my lawyer?" he said. "The thing about the knot was a nice touch, wasn't it?" His mocking tone annoyed me.

"What, so they wouldn't know you killed Ginger?"

"They called me from the port authority to tell me they had Bacon. He'd been drowned. Then Ginger turned up dead in the aquarium. I remembered that mess he made of the hammock, that thing he called the 'Cosmic Tamale.' So I cut off both the knots and got the idea for the suicide pact. It has a kind of beauty to it, no?"

"No," I said.

"You're so boring, Tony. Bacon had Arabic on his arm.

They couldn't send over a whole squad as if they were hunting down Bin Laden in Islamabad."

"It was the name of a football player."

"There wasn't going to be enough time to fact-check all that. It couldn't help Bacon or Ginger. They were already dead. The thing about the gay pact saved all our asses," he said, coughing. His eyes were watery. "And it worked. Ceballos left, too. We had to get rid of all the people who could report a problem that had no solution. Aren't you proud of me?"

"Does Atrium know about the narco stuff?"

"Of course. Those English asses are out of their diapers. They speak with the DEA every day, and with Interpol and Scotland Yard and the attorney general and even Disney Latino, who'll probably make a fucking movie about us someday. We're under strict surveillance. They know the size of our dicks. The guy from Atrium isn't coming here to unravel any mysteries."

"Why's he coming then?"

"To see you."

"Me?"

"He's going to offer you a job."

"What are you talking about?"

"El Gringo loves you. I do, too. Though that's beside the point. What matters is that El Gringo and I hate each other. We love you but can't stand each other. That kind of dynamic is priceless. You became useful by sheer accident."

"Who killed Ginger?"

"What, you think I know the answer?"

"You say everyone around here knows everything."

"Everything except the stuff that matters."

Mario closed his eyes. It was easier to look at him like this, without that fanatical intensity. *He who is highly praised will lead you to the truth.* At that moment, I saw Rashad Khalifa's story in a very different light. The sports guru lived to spiritualize his athlete's records. NFL stats had acquired sacred meaning. On his best day, Khalifa's star disciple pulled off his "Miracle Catch." Then, after inspiring athletes with the Qur'an, Khalifa started looking for statistics in the Qur'an itself. He became obsessed with the number nineteen and got sucked into a one-man religion of his own making.

Maybe that kind of fanaticism came from misinterpreting miracles. The ball fell into the hands of his disciple and Rashad Khalifa felt a new sense of command confronted with his great good fortune.

Mario and I were united by a failed pass of our own. The ball hadn't bounced out of our opponent's hands to fall into mine; it had bounced off the roof of the car that had run me over. Mario felt guilty about that unfortunate turn of events. We'd been brought together by accident, so that he could protect the injured friend and I could be his confidante.

Like Khalifa, my friend believed that chaos was a kind of red zone, and he sought to control it with a faith that reflected the force of his imagination. But, unlike Khalifa, his second act was better than his first. Rashad Khalifa failed because he thought he'd performed a miracle. Mario Müller still had faith in his own miracle—that he could save The Pyramid.

As I reflected on all this, I studied Mario's gaunt face. The life was being ravished from his body. I felt, with an almost physical sadness, that I'd never get to know him completely.

Sitting in silence was becoming unbearable. I needed to hear him say something.

"So did Támez kill Ginger?" I asked. "Was it him?"

"My head is killing me, Tony. So are my ears. Please don't mention that name to me." He closed his eyes again, carefully, as if the pain extended to his eyelids.

"You have any idea," he continued, "what it's like to wake up in Punta Fermín in a little room with a dirt floor next to five other people and three pigs? Do you know what it's like seeing your little girl in bed with a fever and not being able to afford a fucking aspirin?" He opened his eyes. "We offer work here. We're keeping these people from eating each other alive. This is the region's only real ecosystem. All these plastic hotels. The destruction of the coast. It's saved thousands of people. The root of it is completely fucked up. But look at the Louvre! It wouldn't exist without looting. Don't you talk to me about green utopias. Organic jam isn't going to save the poor. We need real food! We sell fear in exchange for food!"

Indignation had revived him.

"You're delirious, Mario."

"Europe and the United States pumped the world with shit so that they themselves could develop, but now they don't want us to do the same thing. They want to preserve endangered plants and animals in far-off places. Our lack of development is the ecosystem they depend on."

"And what's your solution to all this? A Disneyland with kidnappings?"

"'A Disneyland with kidnappings,'" he said mockingly. "You surprise me sometimes, Tony. That would've been a dope song title for Los Extraditables. Jesus! I said 'dope' again. I get very coloquial when you're around."

"Maybe it's because we're, you know, talking."

"You're the one making me delirious," he said. "I suppose that's what childhood friends are for. You're like an IV solution that drips memories I don't want to remember. The things that always rise to the surface. That's ecology. Our species needs to share secrets. Would you like me to confess, Your Honor?" Here he opened one of his desk drawers and pulled out a fistful of pills—I couldn't tell how many—and shoved them all into his mouth. The gesture seemed almost spontaneous.

He'd watched over me for decades and now I couldn't save him. His wasn't a treatable kind of addiction. Mario Müller was in a tailspin. Vertical velocity.

"What did you just swallow?" I moved towards him.

"Pain killers. Sleeping pills. A piece of candy," he said. "My quarter's run out. You remember the old-school pay phones? Remember that wonderful voice? 'To continue, please deposit 50 cents.' I was so in love with her. But I'm out of quarters. Just stay on the line till we get disconnected."

"That's what I'm trying to do."

"That's why I love you so much...I love you very much," he said, and started sobbing.

He remained seated, while I stood. Now I hugged him awkwardly. I moved my head close to his. He didn't smell of coconut milk. My dear friend smelled of vomit.

He sobbed a little more, then asked that I leave him alone.

"Are you going to sleep here?"

"It doesn't matter. I have to leave at 7 a.m. anyway. I'll wait for you here."

"What for?"

"We're going to pick up the guy from Atrium. The unwelcome guest. The other esophageal cancer. He couldn't get a flight to Kukulcán because of the weather. And he was delayed in Campeche, so he had to hire a private plane. He's landing at the military base. Támez must be thrilled."

"Why's that?"

"They're going to see him all beaten up, like a fucking Catholic martyr. They'll think he's a hero."

I remembered how passive Támez had been that day in the garden as the two men tore at him. That strange sense of superiority that made him refuse to put up a fight.

"I'm dead," Mario said. His expression was ironic but bitter. "See you tomorrow. Don't flake on me."

"I won't," I said, and turned off the light.

At 7 o'clock the next morning, my friend had the formidable look of a man who has walked away from his own operating table. His gait was unsteady, but he knew where he was going.

Mario asked me to drive. He handed me the keys and shot me one of his meaningful looks, as if he were turning in his sword. He'd accepted his weakness—a striking gesture from a control freak.

The airport in Kukulcán was still closed when we arrived. But in the distance, the sky had cleared a path of lapis lazuli. The little plane would be able to land at the military base.

The storm had created many potholes and upended road signs. It was as if the landscape were already anticipating the region's ultimate desolation. In a few years, there wouldn't be any billboards left. The empty rooms would house iguanas who'd feed on bed-sheets, and London and New York would keep accounts for all their imaginary guests.

"Last night," Mario said, "I was being crazy. Forgive me. You know what I thought about this morning? The day you nearly died in Ecatepec. You remember that?"

Sometimes I preferred his delirium to the real events that had, disturbingly, left no mark on my memory. I told him I didn't remember.

"You had one of your classic blackouts. We carried you to a back room. Some girl took care of you, this beautiful blonde girl, the daughter of the bass player I'd called as backup. When you came to, you thought you were dead and that the girl was an angel. You don't remember?"

"No," I said.

"You died and don't even remember? I hope it's the same for me. That girl took good care of you. She cried like she'd known you her whole life; she wouldn't stop caressing you and wetting your lips with a damp cloth. She saved you. I wish you could take care of me like that, but you're not a beautiful blonde. I'm stuck with my crippled angel!" He opened his leather backpack and took out the chrome thermos. Judging from the tone of his voice, he'd probably had several swigs from it already.

We drove into a clearing that cut through the mangroves, then passed the yellow swampland, with its rancid smell. In the distance, the air shimmered with heat and clouds and mosquitoes.

Half an hour later, the rain started. The sky's promising patch of lapis lazuli had disappeared. The windshield fogged up; the AC was now barely functioning. I opened one of the windows and felt a few surprisingly cold raindrops slide down my neck. As we drove, the paved road got increasingly worse. The flatness of the Yucatán landscape contrasted sharply with the cracks and ravines we had to navigate.

"Talk about 'Heavy Weather,'" Mario said, citing a Jaco Pastorius album. In the back of the truck, the air had condensed into a thick, grayish-blue vapor. Behind the windshield wipers, the blurred vegetation made me think of the aquarium. It was like driving through seaweed. I didn't care about the rain coming in on my side. Adjusting to the climate meant you didn't mind getting wet. The water fell on the peninsula with oppressive sluggishness.

Suddenly, in the middle of the road, several blue and yellow shapes came into view. The windshield trembled like a watercolor. I slowed down, braking a few yards away from them.

Six people were blocking the road. Two women and four girls. They were trying to shield themselves from the rain with useless plastic tarps that clung to their bodies. One of the tarps was yellow, another blue, and the rest were black and looked like trash bags. They placed their hands above their eyebrows like visors. I turned off the fog lights but left the others on.

"They're from the shelter," Mario said. He honked. The colored silhouettes didn't move.

"Which shelter?"

"The one for battered women. It's around here somewhere," he said, pointing vaguely into the brush.

"What do they want?"

"A donation, I guess."

I got out of the truck and walked through the rain to a heavyset woman in the blue tarp. I could tell she was their leader. From far away, she seemed to be scowling hatefully. Up close, there was no doubt about it. The little girls dragged tiny cars filled with toys.

The fat woman's age was hard to guess, anywhere between 28 and 50. Behind me, Mario turned off the truck's brake lights.

"That's better," the woman said. Her lumpy pink gums covered parts of her teeth. One of the other women, wrapped in yellow plastic, stood shivering next to her. She held her makeshift hood closed with her hand. Stray blonde hairs clung damply to her brow. *They're insane,* I thought.

"How can I help you?" I said.

"Tell him." The leader elbowed the blonde, who came forward and loosened her hood. She had a stunningly beautiful face with a scar at the corner of her mouth.

"You have to pay us, señor," she said haltingly.

"What for?"

"It's a toll," she said.

I'd never heard a demand made with such a broken voice. A "donation," Mario had called it. The other woman was growing impatient.

"Did you hear what she said, buddy? You give us $50 and then you can go fuck yourself. Get to it, asshole, I don't have all day. You think we like standing out here getting wet? We've been waiting for you for ages."

"You were expecting us?"

"You or any other idiot. You're here with Mario Müller, aren't you?" She pronounced it "Mew-yer." "Tell him to pay up or I'll go over and piss in his pool."

I took out a five hundred peso note and handed it to the woman in yellow.

"Nice try, sweetie pie, but you owe me six hundred, that's the current exchange rate," said the woman in blue.

"That's all I have," I said, reaching into both pockets and fishing out a few wet coins. I handed them to the fat woman.

"Fucking cheapskate!" she said.

"What happened to your leg?" asked the one in yellow.

"A woman broke it on a road somewhere, when I didn't have enough money for the toll."

She smiled, slightly—barely enough to strain the scab on her face.

"Did it hurt?" she asked, suddenly chummy.

"A little."

"Did it hurt enough?" There was a glint of madness in her eyes. She smiled like she was savoring the word *enough*. Her face lit up—a slightly demented excitement with a trace of cunning.

I was starting to get cold. Water was seeping in through my shoes.

"It hurts when it rains," I said.

"Welcome to my world." Her expression changed. "You remember?"

"The pain? I remember when it rains."

"So you don't remember?" she asked with insistence. Her look was making me more uncomfortable than the rain. *Remember what?*

"What about your hand?" the fat woman asked.

"What's wrong with my hand?"

"You're missing a chunk of your finger."

"A firecracker exploded in it," I said.

"Ah, so that's why you're so good at cooperating. Cripples always break their bills!" She grimaced with satisfaction, as if the humid air tasted sweet. "I've enjoyed doing business with you."

The women continued on their way. When they'd crossed the road, I was still standing there.

Mario honked the horn. I turned back and got into the warm truck.

"How much did you give them?"

"Fifty pesos," I lied. I felt defeated, ripped off.

"You should've given them more. They really need it."

"Sorry, I had no idea."

"Don't worry, I always send them money. Candy, the fat one? She seems scary, but she's a sweetheart. You have no idea what those women have been through."

"Why didn't you warn me?"

"I wasn't sure we'd see them. They stop the cars sometimes, but you never know when."

"Did they know we were headed for the base?"

Mario took another gulp from the thermos, then screwed the cap on slowly. He changed the subject:

"James Mallett, that's the jerk from Atrium."

"Anyone ever tell you you're nuts?"

"I only hope I'll have time to go crazy before I die!"

We came to a fork in the road. One arrow pointed towards the military base, the other: inland. The sign read "Refugee Hangar."

"It's for the people who lose their homes after hurricanes," Mario explained. "One day all of Kukulcán will end up here. They'll just get used to it, Tony. Our ability to adapt is more powerful than any storm."

Just before the base, we ran into a military squad. I saw an Army sign: "PRECAUTION, REACTION, DISTRUST." The first two words were standard. But the third one reminded me which country I was in. I lowered the window.

A soldier approached us. A cap hid half his face. Still, I could see his yellow eyes.

"Wheah?" he asked, as if his tongue was missing.

There was only one possible destination, but I still had to tell him we were headed for the base. The soldier wanted my name.

"Sir Antonio Góngora," I said, trying some old-fashioned charm.

The soldier flipped open a notebook, fattened by the humidity. He jotted down my name and our plates and asked me to spell "sir." I said it wasn't a name, just an hon-orific. He glared at me with the distrust of his station. I gave in and spelled out "sir."

The soldier was shivering. He looked feverish. In another context, he could've been a malaria patient. In the glory days of the Maya, he would have been lined up for sacrifice. In my country, he was a soldier. Only in a land conquered by magical thinking could a bloated notebook, filled with the scribblings of an illiterate soldier, count as an instrument of federal security.

Reconciling myself to the absurdity of living there, I thought of other nonsense I'd heard those past few days: *We're basically bacterial trash; he's turned himself into God, he acts like the mayor of Paradise; we sell fear in exchange for food.* Inspector Ríos, El Gringo Peterson, Mario Müller. Each of them had his own way of defining the things that were difficult to understand.

You remember? the blonde woman had asked, and with such intensity. I was struck by her particular kind of madness. It made me feel like we had something in common.

Mario started coughing next to me. The day he died, my past would be over.

The military base was nothing but a shed with an airstrip that led to an embankment, beyond which lay the sea. The rain had stopped.

At the front gate, we were met by a guard who seemed to belong not merely to another regiment, but another civ-ilization. His questions were clear and efficient. Then he got into the truck and gave us directions to the base.

We parked in front of a rectangular structure made of

wooden planks with shoddy partitions. It looked like a makeshift headquarters for construction workers.

We went into an office that smelled of coffee. Two soldiers were studying a computer and a small radar screen. We stepped into another room. Outside the window, stained with saltpeter, lay the thin black strip of the runway and the sea behind, a lead line.

They served me coffee in a mug sponsored by the Rayados, Punta Fermín's soccer team. Mario's cup was emblazoned with the official logo of the PRI, which may have lost in the last regional election but had not lost the race for coffee-mug distribution. To my surprise, the coffee was delicious.

We sat in silence for awhile. The window looked like it had never been washed. Against the backdrop of this grimy, fogged view, Mario said the most unexpected thing I'd ever heard come out of his mouth.

"I have to tell you something, Tony." He coughed for dramatic effect, like a singer clearing his throat before the next number. "I have a daughter. She lives at the shelter."

I thought of the women standing in the rain. I started to say something, but Mario held up his hand:

"She's 6. I found out a few months ago. She's Camila's daughter," he said, as if I already knew who that was. "I don't want to talk about it."

"You're already talking about it."

He gave a resigned smile.

"That's why you're here, Tony. Welcome to Kukulcán."

"I'm here because you have a daughter?"

"You're here because I have a daughter and I'm about to die."

"What's her name?"

"I don't want to say it. It'll just make me cry."

"You're already crying. You've been crying since yesterday."

He wiped his eyes with desperate clumsiness, as if the tears were ants crawling on his face.

"Who is Camila?"

"You mean who *was* she. She was killed about a year ago. She was one of the dancers at the Malibú, one of the Cuban women hired by Peterson's guy. María José was already bored with me. Isn't it strange how someone can get bored with you for *not* being home enough? María José was fed up with my absence. What she didn't get was that my presence would've been even worse. None of that matters, Tony. With Camila, I was helpless as a dog."

"Do you see your daughter?"

"I've seen her, but she doesn't know who I am. There's no point. I don't want to fuck her up with a father who appears one day then dies on her. You know what it's like when a father disappears on you. She needs someone who will stick around, who knows everything about me— someone who could *be* Mario Müller." He looked at me intensely.

"What are you talking about?"

"About my best friend, the one who saved my life in the old house, the one who had the wildest, sexiest mom; the one who played in a band with me, screwed up his life, and sits here now in possession of all my memories."

"Mario, I barely remember my own!"

"Don't underestimate yourself. This year you've become a memory collector. To my daughter you could be both Antonio Góngora and Mario Müller. I told you I wanted to lose my mind before I died. Well, this is my madness. You're going to adopt my daughter. You're as close as she will ever get to me. You don't have to start chewing on leaves, but you remember that I used to do it, and that's enough. You've got no family. I've got money put aside. You two will be able to live well. She can't stay at the shelter forever."

"And the adoption papers?"

"That's easy. Her mother is dead. She got killed. It was a narco shootout. A drug boss never leaves a woman once she's been tagged. Camila had been tagged; she was one of Two-Tone's women."

"Who was this asshole?"

"Some local hero and international villain. The usual character. I never would've got involved with her if I'd known who she ran with. Sometimes Camila mentioned these ordeals of hers, the crises and the threats, things that had gotten her into trouble. But she never went into any details. The whole thing made me feel good, like the great redeemer of the land! I stood for something better, I'd saved her—but I didn't know from what or whom. This Two-Tone guy only bothered to show interest in her when he found out she had another lover. Camila was his property, his piece of meat; she'd been branded. He kidnapped her and took her to join his harem of prostitutes. Six years later her body turned up, hanging from a bridge. Before she died, Camila called me and told me the girl was mine."

"Well, is she?"

"Does it matter?"

"Did you get a DNA test?"

"It's the only medical test I haven't taken. Two-Tone wanted to kill her. If she's not mine then she's nobody's. The shelter saved her life."

I was perplexed. Life was like smudged glass, a stained window. The news that Mario had a daughter was not nearly as wild as the idea that I should adopt her as my own. I pictured the blonde woman in the yellow plastic, and the larger one under the blue tarp. Mario's daughter lived with them. I couldn't be made responsible. My friend was dying, but that didn't mean he could impose such a demand on me.

"I don't understand." It's all I could say.

"You don't understand what?"

"Why Two-Tone kidnapped Camila and didn't do anything to you."

"Because Peterson handled it. He paid the 'right of the soil.' For years, El Gringo sent a monthly ransom just to keep me alive. Then luck turned in our favor. Two-Tone got the 'Colombian necktie:' they slit his throat and ripped his tongue out through the gash. That got him out of our hair, but I still owed a debt to Peterson. I couldn't work with anyone else. It sentenced us to each other for life. Things started looking up and that's what ruined our friendship. That's people for you, right?"

"Peterson knows you've got a kid?"

"No."

"Did he ever meet Camila?"

"Of course. And he took a gamble on me, like I was a thoroughbred."

"I don't want any kids. Never have."

"You're missing out. I am, too. But I only realize this now that I'm dying. I don't want you to go through the same thing."

"She could be Two-Tone's kid."

"You're not in a position to make excuses. You're just some druggie who used to hallucinate Technicolor lizards. This place saved your ass. Now you can save a little girl. Your life, my dear Tony, finally has a purpose."

"That's not my purpose." I felt an emptiness gnawing at me from inside. Like I'd felt when I knew my mother was dying. But it wasn't just another step down the ladder; it was the final descent. Mario was taking me to the outer limit, to the extreme edge of nonsense in a life dedicated to setting fish to music.

He interrupted our conversation, signaling me over to the window. Through the fogged glass, we could make out the headlights of a plane coming into focus. Two beams of white suddenly lit up the airstrip.

We stepped outside. The paleness of the tropical sky was producing an atemporal effect. The brightness bore no relation to the actual time—too weak for morning or late afternoon. It was an anemic, in-between light that required a strong wind to give it definition.

Mario walked ahead of me. His words had been a shock—like another nerve snapped in my leg. He'd always been a master manipulator. Most of the time, this quality served him well. He'd put himself in charge of even the most minor details: on our first tour with Los Extraditables, he made sure to pack plenty of sugar calaveras, because we were going to be together for the Day of the Dead. Anyone who thinks of such insignificant things knows exactly what he's doing. We'd mocked Der Meister while still appreciating the bug spray he'd packed for our concert in humid Veracruz.

My stay in the Caribbean now took on new meaning. Had Mario looked for me in Mexico because he was terminally ill? Because he knew he had a daughter? After all these years, the strangest thing was that he still needed me. He had plenty of relatives. He could have asked one of his brothers, but instead he'd chosen me. Had he done this to refill the lagoons of my mind with remembered scenes of his achievements? Had he prompted these memories so I could pass them on to his daughter?

While the small plane maneuvered its way along the far end of the strip, I kept wondering about Mario. He hadn't tracked me down on account of my virtues. He'd chosen me for what I lacked. I didn't have anything else to do other than take care of his daughter. The best contender for establishing ties was a loner. The fact I didn't have a father made me the ideal candidate to become one.

Mario lingered on the tarmac. We could see a silhouette descending from the plane.

"An 'unwanted guest,'" said Mario. "Take care of her, Tony. The concert's over. There won't be any encores." He patted my back.

We were approached by a gringo in a caftan. He was carrying a leather suitcase that seemed a little small for an international flight.

"James Mallett," he said. He shook my hand energetically. His skin was rough, and he was sporting a three-day beard. This wasn't a mark of fatigue from his journey, but rather a calculated look of dishevelment. He wore a Mickey Mouse watch on his left wrist and a few leather bands and colorful handmade bracelets (camel or elephant hair) on his right.

He spoke Spanish with a Colombian accent, and explained that his father had been a diplomat in Bogotá.

"He worked for the Foreign Office, as the spies like to say." He smiled. "Care for a lolly?"

He offered us some eucalyptus drops, but Mario and I

turned them down. He had the look of a hipster explorer or else a freshly-minted magnate, the kind of guy who donates a fortune to some African cause then volunteers to sleep in a mud hut.

When we got into the truck, he took off his caftan. Underneath he was wearing an Indian shirt the pinkish color of mamey. Through his V-neck collar, you could see the top of a tattoo.

I started the car. Meanwhile, Mario was briefing him on the latest: the hurricane, the assault of Leopoldo Támez, the disappearance (this I didn't know) of two employees from a Laundromat. He rattled off the bad news first to give it a sense of normalcy. I could've added another brief: DRUNK ARGENTINE BOMBSHELL GOT TIED UP AND CLAIMED SHE LIKED IT. Maybe the real disaster wasn't that wine glasses were being broken, but that someone wanted to cut themselves with the pieces. I'd always seen The Pyramid's guests merely as figures to be avoided. But the more I thought about them, the more they frightened me.

"How's your health?" Mallett asked.

"Better," Mario said.

"We're publicly traded, you know. If the director gets sick, it affects share prices. Have the 'guerrillas' surrendered yet?"

During previous trips, Mallett had tagged along for hikes through the jungle. He spoke enthusiastically now about Mario's war play, then transitioned seamlessly to a news story from London.

"I just saw that video of the old woman who found a cat in the street. *Your perfect granny.* The neighbors adored her. She always wore a smile and baked the best cookies. You know what she did to the cat? She lured him with a bowl of milk, grabbed him, then threw him down the garbage chute. The cat stayed there for fourteen hours. It was caught on a security camera. Video is tenacious; it's always watching. Making a cat suffer in London is like pissing on the flame at the Tomb of the Unknown Soldier. The granny gave no excuse. All she said was, 'I had to do it!' She should come to The Pyramid! If you experience a fear safari, you don't need to go and abuse a cat.'"

Mallett's cheerfulness belied the seriousness of the crisis he'd come to resolve. He'd somehow managed to dig up an old article online, "Mexico's Rock and Roll Hole of Fame," in which the writer describes the "unfulfilled promise of heavy metal, an achievement of sorts for national rock." Mallett knew all about my obsession with Jaco Pastorius and had heard Weather Report and Return to Forever play live. I admired this insider access to music that for us in the '70s had taken on mythical proportions. Then, to my surprise, he said:

"I envy the importance you people assign to things. *I'm not patronizing.* I tell you this with my heart on my sleeve." His language skills suffered with his sincerity. He tried to explain himself—telling us he'd partied with David Bowie, Bono, Robert Smith, and many other luminaries. He said that that sense of familiarity destroyed the mystique.

"Geniuses," Der Meister quipped, "can never just be your neighbors."

"*Brilliant,*" Mallett said. He pointed to the blue horizon with the flames from the oil rigs. Perhaps he was more struck by this sight than my friend's idea.

The Englishman's arrival had an unusual effect on me. For years, the past just seemed like *that period when my hands shook.* Our failure had not been an interesting tragedy. The band broke up, honoring the national habit of undramatic endings for that which had never really happened. I didn't dwell on this, and it was better to remember the time I'd had strange eye spasms or when my stomach shrank. These things confirmed that sobriety was worth the trouble.

I was intrigued by the way James Mallett's presence completely altered the mood in the car. In London, everything happened, but nothing mattered; in Mexico, nothing happened, but everything mattered. Mallett had stood among music legends and felt none of their greatness. I suppose that being on a first-name basis with posterity is one way to dismiss it. *Geniuses can never just be your neighbors.*

Sitting at the wheel of that truck, I felt an unexpected thrill of pride. I had been part of Los Extraditables. Once there was a broken country that a pair of naive guys had tried to set alight with music. We'd had a brief but shared dream, a devoted following keen for pleasure and suffering, a girl like paradise who vanished as an undeserved gift, a crazy investor who judged us creditworthy, an endless output of low-budget recordings that made us feel we were igniting the fire of an idea—a time and place we could call our own.

I felt like the driver of a Magic Bus heading for India or Kathmandu. Mario and I had watched each other through that enormous mirror in the abandoned house, and where others might have seen blank faces devoid of history, we dared to desire something greater. We were young and on an empty stage. Perfect candidates for changing the world. We had never managed to do that, but there had been a day when we'd dreamed it. Standing next to Mario Müller, James Mallett had no idea who he was dealing with.

I thought about all this as the sky transitioned from its aquarium blue to a majestic purple. Mallett was scrolling through his iPhone. He started telling us about his background, about growing up in the British public school system, reading Latin at Oxford, getting a master's in business administration at the University of Chicago. Jobs with Atrium in six different countries.

"I'm the *trouble-shooter* in the family," he said, pulling an imaginary trigger. Then, out of nowhere, "Los Extraditables. What a great name!"

When we made it back to the hotel, Mario stayed with the Englishman while he finished checking in, then handed him a purple wristband. He knew Mallett would be having dinner with El Gringo Peterson and suggested he try a new dish: shrimp in a tamarind sauce with guajillo chili.

"I'm reachable," he said noncommittally by way of goodbye.

"That shrimp sounds tempting," Mallett said with a smile.

"I'll have dinner in my room. And you'll eat with me." Mario was looking at me. "We have to take care of a few things."

I could tell he wasn't talking about The Pyramid.

At 9 p.m., Mario was floating in the pool of his two-story suite. The living room lights were off. The only bit of illumination came from the bulbs at the bottom of the pool. The red mosaic tiles created the illusion of flowing blood. Mario had handpicked the color, his own "purple section." It reminded me of the surgery channel Sandra liked to watch.

I didn't care for the music he was playing, maybe because I'd composed it myself. "Compose" is a generous verb in this case. I'd tinkered with some variations on a computer program. A sinister E-flat kept slicing the air like a knife blade.

Mario's gaunt, pale body floated with what seemed like enormous effort. His hair stretched out behind him like strands of yellow rope.

"The water is delicious." It was strange to hear him say that.

I reached down to touch the surface. Cold, just as I'd imagined. Like the pool at the Swiss School. I left him floating there and went into the living room. Sandra liked to collect lost and found objects; Mario, on the other hand, didn't want to leave a trace. Nothing—no keys on the table, no half-empty glass, no magazine lying open on the sofa. There were no decorations or souvenirs. His rooms were the opposite of his office desk.

He lived as if he weren't there, the most discreet guest at the hotel.

"I love these sounds," he said, coming up behind me in a terry-cloth robe. His wet flip-flops had left tracks on the tiles.

"They drive me nuts," I said.

"You wrote it."

"I arranged the sonic foundation. A robot did the rest," I said. "A robot that never attended conservatory."

"I've lost 5 pounds," he said, stroking his ribs. "I'm a waning man."

He went into the kitchen and came out with a pottery dish full of fruit, each piece still wrapped in supermarket plastic. I took a cold, almost frozen piece of mamey and unwrapped it. I took a bite. It was flavorless.

Mario was obsessed with sanitization. The type-A flu epidemic had finally given him the perfect excuse to install antibacterial gel dispensers all over the hotel.

"Aren't you meeting up with Mallett?" I asked.

"It's too late for that. The die has been cast. I'm leaving, Tony. But this is where you come in. They're going over the options right now—looking for ways to recruit you."

"Can I turn off the music?"

"It's yours."

I walked to the sound system. Behind me, Mario spoke.

"They need you, Tony."

"What for?"

I found the Goldberg Variations and hit play just as he started to explain:

"They need new entertainment programming. My ideas don't seem to work anymore. The narco is perfect at turning people's fears into realities. All the news of decapitated bodies travels around the world. And that helped us think up dangers. Controlled ones, of course. But everything fell apart with Ginger."

It was the first time he'd talked this way about the diver. He picked up a knife and, with great effort, managed to peel the skin off a green apple.

"He meddled where he didn't belong," he said. "He talked to the consulate and got everybody worked up. He spoke to the DEA, brought in his friend Roger . . . a huge pain in the ass. With him, the violence became real—suddenly there was a diver floating dead in the river next to a cocaine shipment. Then another diver at the aquarium."

"Why didn't you call the police when Roger died?"

"You think they didn't know about it? They're up to their ears in this mess. The best way to protect Ginger was to keep him quiet. I tried to persuade him, Tony. The drugs aren't our problem. I told him this, maybe a million times. But he believed in what was right. He'd watched too much television."

I poured myself some water. The glass smelled like disinfectant. I thought of Sandra's body wrapped around my own, the two of us reeking of window cleaner. It was hard to focus on what Mario was saying.

"There's a legend that when the Spaniards came here, the Maya king Juan Tutul Xiu went east, to the sacred place of origin. He traveled along an underwater sacbe that has its source in Tulum. His tribe waited for his return. The narco took the same path. Thanks to them we now know where that sacbe leads: Miami. Los Conchos always let us go about our business."

"Los Conchos?"

"The local cartel. We used to have ZIP codes. Now we have cartels."

"Did Two-Tone work for them?"

"Stop asking for all the specifics! This isn't the House of Orleans . . . though Two-Tone did die in high style. They gave him the 'Colombian necktie,' after all." Mario wasn't chewing his fruit, only sucking the flesh and then discarding it on his plate. "Los Conchos want to subdue our operation. We're bad publicity for them. They don't like our kind of violence."

He smiled, then continued.

"Please Tony, don't look at me like that. We need them for our own credibility, but they're not happy with all the noise we're making. Someone is bound to catch on. They've sent us warnings. Every day we lose more and more forks at The Pyramid."

"How serious can that be?"

"Losing one fork each day is more dangerous than a

fire," he said, spitting out a piece of apple. "You want to know what happened to Támez? The guys who beat him up left the Tsuru near the swamp. Those Fox and Bush masks were in the trunk. There's only one store in Kukulcán that sells them. Ríos went there. The clerk remembered exactly what the customer who bought the masks looked like. He wore six earrings in each ear. Easy person to recognize. Ríos found him at the Keops, that *table-dance* joint. He was celebrating with some Solera brandy. There are thousands of guys lining up to beat the shit out of Támez.... But there's some poetic justice. You know what it is?" Here he paused. A piece of apple was stuck in his throat—or maybe it was his illness, now throttling him relentlessly.

"What is just pure poetry about all of this," he went on, "is the fact that Támez hired those guys to beat him up! They were released immediately. There's no law that says you can't hire someone to beat you up. Támez sacrificed his own ribcage just so we would trust in him again. Getting kicked around in public makes you trustworthy. He didn't hire professionals, either. No, he found two actors who work at The Pyramid!" He laughed so hard he started coughing again. He pounded his chest. "Two of my actors! The idiots over-acted and left quite a trail."

He combed his hand through his wet hair. More than a few strands came out, clumping between his fingers. He frowned and brushed them onto his plate, next to what was left of the apple.

That's all we were having for dinner, what Mario Müller's diet had become.

"I have something for you," he said. "Something from another era, from a lost world when people still wrote letters. We belong to the last generation that knows what it means to wait, to recognize that something could be delayed, to anticipate a beloved's penmanship. . . "

"Are these letters yours?"

"No. In some sense, they're yours, or for you. At least they are now."

Mario raced upstairs to his room. When he came back, his breath was short. He fell into a chair. "I've got to get all these things in order before I go. Here are the girl's papers."

He pointed to an envelope, then handed me a bundle of letters tied together with twine. I noticed the careful cursive, coldly geometrical. My father's handwriting.

"We Müllers were too many. My mother loved you like a son—she had so many of us she probably loved you as much as she loved me. Your mother, on the other hand. . . her way of showing love was very different. I'm guessing that wasn't great for you."

"I didn't care that you were in love with her," I said. "That was normal. What bothered me was her interest in you. Luciana helped me see that. I'd never thought of it that way before."

"Luciana's very smart."

"Of course she's smart—she left me."

"The Swiss School had an unconventional schedule."

"So?"

"Sometimes I'd go over to your house when you weren't there."

"I knew that. I'd find plates smeared with marmalade. You loved orange marmalade with bits of rind."

"Your mom worked a double shift but sometimes she'd go home to change. She treated me strangely."

"It's not that strange. She let you worship her."

"I'm dying, Tony. Forgive me for telling you this. She used to let me watch her come out of the shower wrapped in a towel. She'd let it slip down a bit, never as much as I wanted, but enough for me to catch a glimpse of her breasts. One time she let me rub in her body lotion. She asked me if she had any stretch marks from when she'd nursed you. She was very depressed—there were tears in her eyes. Her tongue was chalky, like she'd taken sedatives. Maybe she'd just suffered some kind of disappointment or was feeling old or lonely. But the fact is, she asked me if she had any stretch marks then let me rub cream on her body. Forgive me. I'm dying."

"So die already."

"Every man has his first goddess, his perfect muse. She was mine. The fucked up part is that you existed."

"You touched her tits!"

"Just once. I don't know why I'm telling you this. She really wasn't well. She told me she wanted to kill herself."

"She said that every Tuesday and Thursday."

"And then she did it. Twenty years later, Tuesday and Thursday had become every day of the week."

Mario grew quiet. Glenn Gould's playing sounded as sinister as my own compositions.

"Can you hand me that?" he said, pointing to a blanket on the couch. "I'm cold."

"Should I turn off the AC?"

"No, I'm good like this." He wrapped himself in the blanket.

I touched the bundle of letters. *Now I have them,* I thought. *A piece of paper my father wrote on. A memory that isn't mine. A message from a lost time.*

I didn't want to know what was in them. I already hated whatever they might say. There was no relief hearing more from Mario:

"One day, while your mother was in the bathroom, I

looked through her drawers. I found a key—one of those old-fashioned hollow keys. In the closet I'd noticed a little wooden box with a lock. The key opened it and in that box is where I found the letters. I took them. They don't contain anything too personal. They're a kind of farewell. Your father didn't die at Tlatelolco."

"We knew that already," I said, though for years I'd continued to fool myself into believing the story.

"He left her because your mother loved some other asshole. He didn't want to stand in her way. She made up the thing about Tlatelolco so she wouldn't have to explain anything else to you."

"I don't want the letters."

"They're sitting there."

"They don't interest me. You've told me everything." I hated that there should be anything left of my father. He'd disappeared so that he wouldn't have to be responsible.

"So, did she have any?" I asked.

"What?"

"My mother, you idiot. Did she have any stretch marks?"

"Are you crazy?"

"You fondled my mother's tits and *I'm* crazy? I want to know. I don't want any bullshit. Just the goddamn truth, for once."

"No, she didn't have any stretch marks. She was the most beautiful woman in the world and she felt worthless."

"Why did you keep the letters?"

"I regretted stealing them. Eventually I had to confess to your mother. I guess I did it so she'd hate me, and refuse to let me see her again. I needed her to kick me out. I couldn't sleep. I loved her, Tony. My love was unreal. Enormously unreal. Don't look at me like that. Even what's unreal is true."

"And what did she tell you?"

"She reacted in the worst way possible. 'I'm giving them to you,' she said. She wanted me to keep them so that I could give them to you when the time was right—when they couldn't hurt you anymore. It was a way of guaranteeing you and I would stay friends. The letters incriminated her. They mentioned her lover who also disappeared in the end. But all of this would've shattered you when we were fifteen. Your father doesn't go into any details. He accepted that he had lost. . . . "

"A sore loser."

"Reading all of that couldn't be good for you. Not back then."

"Or even now."

"You need to know your dad split. Maybe he's in Chihuahua. You're not the son of a Disappeared. You're just the son of someone who left. That's it. An ordinary story. Knowing this is depressing, but it's also comforting."

"Why did you wait so long to comfort me?"

"You were set on self-destruction, idiot! I didn't want you to read those letters and respond with an overdose. The only thing keeping you alive was the story that made you take drugs in the first place. Your mother had invented a martyr: the absent father figure. She offered you a narrative—the drama of a man who was felled at Tlatelolco—so you wouldn't completely annihilate yourself when you got fucked up. Just like her and her sedatives. You wouldn't have survived her betrayal back then. She betrayed both your father and herself. You wanted to rescue her. That's how she made you feel. But all of you were on your own, because she took a lover and your father couldn't deal with it. Luciana was going to tell you."

"She knew all this?"

"I told her. While you were in Japan. You were back on your feet. You could handle difficult news. But then you returned to Mexico in raptures, some samurai-fuck-ing-cretin. After that came all the madness of playing with the Velvet Underground. Everything you'd built with Luciana you tossed overboard. At that point there was no way to break it to you."

I took the letters into the kitchen. I turned on Mario Müller's pristine gas stove and set fire to the bundle he'd given me, all with a kind of fumbling slowness. My fingers stung. The air filled with smoke. I don't know what kind of paper my father had used, but it seemed to be coated with natural resin, a substance from another era.

"I'm going to die of smoke inhalation," Mario joked. "Cancer is the least of my worries compared to friendship with you. Parents are always absurd, Tony. But remember, for some period of time, yours happened to love each other."

"How do you know that?"

"It's better you see things that way. It's good to believe we love our parents. Our love for children is different."

He reached into his robe, took out a photo, and set it on the table. A girl looked back at us.

"That's her, Tony."

Investigator Ríos was examining the tip of a spear. He'd arranged a meeting with me at Captain Bubbles, a local diving-goods store.

The shop was located inside an American-style mall that was largely empty. Most of the businesses were closed, and their windows had been covered up with large X's of masking tape, to protect against the hurricane.

There was a jewelry store that had managed to stay in business. It was strange to think there were still people willing to spend lavishly on rings and necklaces. In the window display was a board of blue felt, persistently revolving its arrangement of sapphires and diamonds.

I entered the diving store. The setting was perfect for discussing Ginger Oldenville. Instead Ríos said:

"Now the actors from The Pyramid have two gigs: scaring the tourists, and beating up heads of security. Do you know what a 'godmother' is?"

I figured he wasn't talking about infant baptism.

"It's a police officer's assistant. He's not on the payroll, but he helps with everything—he's always packing heat. He does the dirty work, brings the guy a Coke, whatever he wants. The public prosecutors in this country all put up with 'godmothers.' In the Middle Ages, you had squires. Here we have slaves who take out the trash, so you don't scuff your shoes. Támez had several 'godmothers' while he was on the police force. He could've asked anyone to beat him up. Do you know why he didn't?"

"No."

"If they found out who his assailants were, people would know they were actors, that they were Mario Müller's guys. Támez wouldn't be the only one responsible. Everything would stay 'in the family,' so to speak: another strange group activity." Ríos then confirmed everything Mario had already told me about the easy capture of Vicente Fox and George W. Bush.

"They're free already. 'Lack of evidence.' If someone beats the shit out of you because you asked for it, the case has no merit. Now, I want to ask you for a favor." He smiled. "Mr. Peterson isn't taking my calls. I figured you could help."

I thought about the documents Mario had given me. My crazy responsibility of fatherhood. I was supposed to go to the shelter, meet his daughter, get the paperwork started...

"I've got a lot on my plate," I said.

"Of course, with your new job. Congratulations."

Ríos's answer surprised me. It also reassured me. *He doesn't know about the girl,* I thought with a kind of violent, jittery happiness. It was a secret I wasn't about to share with him.

"Thank you." I walked over to an assortment of neoprene wetsuits. I could smell them from several feet away. A smell that seemed to fortify me. Nothing organic could please me more than that synthetic stink of newness, the way it triggers a certain feeling of readiness before a journey to the depths. I wanted to convince Ríos.

"Leopoldo Támez is the one who shut off the security cameras," I said. "They killed Ginger while Ceballos was answering that stupid survey. Támez hired some thugs to make himself look innocent and prove that there's no managerial control at The Pyramid. Where does all of this leave us? At the beginning. Who asked Támez to disconnect the cameras? The killer did."

"Támez could've disconnected the surveillance camera *and* killed Ginger."

"I doubt it."

"Why?"

"Támez is incompetent. If he's got a gun, he'll injure you, but that's about it. From someone so useless, all you can expect is a few disconnected cameras, nothing more. He prepared the scene of the crime so that someone else could act. Who is he answering to? And if he forgets his saintliness and rips somebody's balls out so the guy will confess—what then?" I asked. "How's your boss's ass doing these days?"

"The crime agrees with him." Ríos smiled.

Returning to The Pyramid I looked out to sea and spotted a cruise ship on the horizon. It was the size of a floating city. The best that could happen to one of the beggars asking for alms along the coast was a shipwreck. That's the only way that those hands, wrinkled by humidity, would ever come into contact with the highest-quality trash. For them, no shop item could compete with the value of a broken, waterlogged piece of electronics salvaged from disaster.

My mother had worked at institutes dedicated to studying the problems of language. Her job had never interested me because it left her too exhausted to hold a conversation.

The Pyramid had been a linguistic landscape that was as unfamiliar to me as the clinics where my mother had been employed. The Maya staff would whisper their inaudible niceties, and the tourists would exclaim in ecstasy, astonishment, pain or numbness, which to my ears was all incomprehensible.

I lived there, at the borders of language, with Mario and Peterson and Sandra as my only points of contact.

Now I was regaining my focus. Cellphones were ringing everywhere; conversations that didn't interest me but which I could understand:

"That's more toxic than your foot," said a guest into his Bluetooth.

That afternoon, the guests were gathered in The Pyramid's Katún auditorium. Roxana Westerwood was in her element now, wandering up and down the aisles, enquiring after free seats. When she saw a towel lying across a chair, she'd move it aside so someone could sit. It was like being at a movie premiere where everyone is wearing sandals.

I sat down next to a tourist who spent the whole time typing on his BlackBerry. Traveling for him meant writing messages to Finland or Philadelphia, Caracas or St. Petersburg.

I scanned the room for Mario. He wasn't there. It was a relief when they dimmed the overheads. Another revelation that comes with age: bright lights are for the young.

Mallett went up to the podium and placed his caftan on the back of a chair. Roxana followed after him. She was wearing high heels and leaned against the front table where the Englishman fiddled with his water bottle. The curve of her hips conveyed both a classic sensuality and efficiency. Beauty in a tailored suit.

The English have an unusual flair for being both spontaneous and familiar in their public speeches. This talent, in the end, may account for their ability to keep their private lives private. When Mallett spoke, he became best friend to all of us.

He apologized for the inconveniences caused by the hurricane and invited the guests to an evening buffet where they'd be served a thematic new margarita called "High Tide." He also announced a masked ball, themed "Black and White." Outdoor activities were suspended to avoid unnecessary risk: the guerrillas had taken advantage of the bad weather to gain political standing, but they sent a cordial greeting to their "brothers" at The Pyramid. The guests received this news about risk and solidarity with reverence.

Then the representative from Atrium asked a pilot to come up on stage. A man wearing a WWII-era leather jacket rose and greeted the auditorium. He had a bandanna around his neck. He smiled with that likable innocence unique to high-risk athletes who believe danger exists as a source of amusement, an expression ignorant of consequences. The expression of Ginger Oldenville.

Now the Englishman was speaking about African bees. He explained we had some nuisance visitors. A real plague. The restrictions on outdoor activity presented the perfect opportunity for fumigation. A small plane would be flying overhead and releasing purple smoke. The poison wasn't toxic to humans, but it was better not to inhale it. The only accessible outdoor area would be the main beach. To make up for all these inconveniences, each guest would receive discount coupons towards their next visit.

People started filing out of the auditorium. They'd come to terms with the bad news. Mallett had managed to paint the extenuating circumstances in tones of exclusivity. Their vacations would no longer proceed as planned, but guests were guaranteed more stories to share once they got home.

Roxana came up to me.

"Mallett is a genius," she said. "He organized a fumigator so the guests wouldn't go outside. But it's not poison he'll be spreading—it's just purple smoke! Did you see their reactions? Being trapped indoors becomes a novel kind of luxury. Have you heard anything from Mario?" Her voice suddenly lost its energy.

"I'm seeing him soon," I said, uncertain of whether that was true.

"Tell him I miss him." Roxana Westerwood lowered her eyes. It made me sad to watch her wrapping a curl around her finger, not knowing how to leave in an efficient, neutral way. What made me even sadder was thinking my friend had remained ignorant of how much she admired him. Roxana continued:

"I also miss Sandra. She taught me how to breathe. If it weren't for her, I'd be dead. She has this incredible inner calm." It surprised me to hear her talk like this about a woman who'd sobbed against me, defeated by her own pain. "Do you believe in auras?"

"Yes," I said quickly.

Which meant I believed in Sandra, in the way she breathed, in the techniques I dismissed but had been life-saving for people like Roxana.

Two hours later, I saw the first explosion of purple smoke in the sky. I was in the Solarium. Dozens of digital cameras snapped pictures of the plane.

Back in my room, I found a note penciled in an elegant hand. It was from Mallett, inviting me to dinner at Xibalbá restaurant.

The air was now violet. I went out on the balcony and breathed in the sweet smell of hibiscus. The fake fumigation reminded me of an afternoon I'd gone to Peterson's office right as a fumigator was leaving, hooked up to his tank of poison.

"He's the best one we've ever had," El Gringo had said. "You know why? Because he admires his enemies."

The fumigator's respect for cockroaches meant he could fight them better than anyone else. The abandoned hotels in Kukulcán had become sanctuaries for wasps and black butterflies. Mice chewed on the electricity cables, and rats hid in any pipe that contained even a drop of moisture. The Pyramid, meanwhile, was free of pests, at least as free as one could expect in the pressure cooker of the tropics. All thanks to a man who took his opponents seriously.

"Never trust a fumigator who doesn't talk your ear off about how marvelous the insects are," El Gringo had said. Then, he'd gone back to discussing the napalm jungles of Indochina. He'd talked about fumigation as warfare— that hell he'd so wanted to be worthy of. The strangest part of my conversations with Peterson was the joy conveyed through his complaining. In a way, he'd adopted a puritanical view of success: work was a highly productive personal Calvary. He was resigned to winning without enjoying it, and this made him pleasant to be around. He had the decency to win without being abusive, or at least to win with only minimal pleasure. *Even if you don't want to be,* he'd once said to me, *you're a man condemned to being happy.* As if happiness was an obstacle.

That afternoon, he'd also spoken of another obsession. Because he hadn't been to Vietnam, Peterson subscribed to every conceivable kind of military magazine. In combat strategies, he sought inspiration for how to live his life.

Ever since September 11, 2001, he had been trying to conceive of a world without the traditional firing line. He reflected on ideas like the "front" and "back" guards, on newly obsolete oppositions and the lack of verifiable enemies.

Like the fumigator, Peterson admired the terrorist enemy's resistance tactics. How many times had I heard him go on about "solitary responsibility?" His whole life could be summed up by that term. At the heart of it was the idea that to avoid endangering an operation, each participant could only know a minimal part of the larger plan. The strength of the collective was dependent on the individual work of each member. If one was captured, they wouldn't put everyone else at risk.

As he spoke, he'd pointed to the Employee of the Month certificates decorating his office walls. He'd built up The Pyramid on the organizing principle that assignments were allocated so that no single error could disrupt the hotel's overall functioning.

Enclosed spaces exist so we can say things that would sound nonsensical anywhere else. I'd start talking about Jaco Pastorius; Peterson would ramble about military strategies applicable to personnel management.

"The greatest virtue of the Maya," he liked to say over a glass of Four Roses, "is their capacity for obedience. They come from a long line of tyrants. The high priests dominated the sciences and agriculture and writing and ritual. The rest of the population didn't know how to count to ten. When the priests disappeared, all hell broke loose. Only the slaves were left, Tony. Don't ask them for motivation or initiative, ask them to obey. Here the employees of the month are like Al-Qaeda operatives. No one can ever answer for the guy standing next to him."

There were two lit torches at the entrance to the Xibalbá, and it bore a thatched palm roof. I spotted Mallett sitting at a table towards the back of the room. He raised both arms when he saw me. The place was packed. I could feel the diners' admiring gazes as I made my way to the man who'd just managed the storm crisis with such panache.

"Cheers, Captain!" a man said as he walked past. I was reminded that I'd also been taken for a military expert.

Mallett ordered a plate of grasshoppers because the kitchen was out of scorpion. He was obsessed with those BBC shows that featured dishes from remote corners of the Earth. England had gone from the country with the world's worst cuisine to an intrepid explorer of exotic gastronomy, boasting the inquisitive appetite of a pirate or castaway.

Atrium's conflict top-gun looked tired. But his fatigue and sloppiness were derivatives of energy. The bags under his bloodshot eyes, the film of sweat and road-dust on his skin, his wind-tousled hair, the grasshopper leg stuck between his teeth—these were the features of a man who could walk out of here and win the Paris-Dakar.

Mallett ordered fish *a la talla* with a side of *chiles toreados*. He switched between his tequila and his travel stories and a bottle of Corona. At one point, he looked out at the horizon. A small vessel dotted the landscape with a delicate triangle of lights.

"Mario's history now," he said. "Don't get me wrong, he's tenacious, a prize bull. He invented the ecology of fear and even got it to work. But sooner or later our clients are going to want more authentic dangers, and the narcos get nervous when you interfere in their world. Which is genuinely dangerous. I don't need to tell you about your own country, Tony."

"Why don't you guys close the hotel? If it goes out of business, can't you just bill the insurance company?"

"This baby has a few miles in her yet." He shook some salt into his hand and rubbed it along his gums like cocaine. The Englishman had the quick movements and muscular tension of someone in need of constant stimulation.

"It rains almost every day," I said, sucking on a lemon rind. "And the narcos are in charge. Who's going to want to come here?"

"The same idiots who are coming here now," he said. "Tourism has always been a way of screwing yourself over. It's punishment you accept as a form of entertainment. If you stayed home all the time, you'd murder your own mother. That's the only way to explain how on the same day John Doe can pee in Amarillo, Texas, the Persian Gulf, and Cambodia, with a rubber sandwich in his stomach and his head exploding from jet lag. People aren't masochists for nothing, they're masochists for the pleasure of survival, and to unite with the holy masses."

It seemed Atrium only hired motormouths. Back in my coke days, I'd been a wretched marvel of that species myself.

"Have you ever seen Spencer Tunick's photographs of naked crowds? It's not hard to round up 50,000 people willing to stand outside at dawn and let their genitals shrink in the cold. Everyone wants to be part of something." He paused, as if waiting for my mind to process the image of 50,000 unappealingly naked bodies. Satisfied that he had a captive audience, Mallett continued:

"Every species has its own cure for despair. Horses stampede through canyons, whales wash up on beaches. Human beings just pack their bags. In the future there won't be any wars. There'll be tourists—exhausted invaders. Euthanasia in slow motion. Am I right?" He smiled with satisfaction, as if life held no other alternatives.

"I guess so," I said.

"I'm impressed with Roxana," he said, as if continuing on the same topic. "She's incredibly efficient. Poor thing: she fell in love with Mario Müller. She got tired of her husband. A plankton researcher—can you imagine anything more boring? But your friend didn't give her the time of day. Zealots are too preoccupied to let themselves fall in love. Did he ever let himself be loved?"

"By Roxana?"

"By anyone," he said with intense curiosity.

I worried he might know something about Camila

or the shelter or the girl. It was unsettling how quickly Mallett could get inside people's lives.

"Mario," he went on, "is emotionally autistic. *It's quite intriguing*! Doesn't he need anyone?"

His confident way of stating these opinions, his complete assurance about my friend's indifference to other people, all of it filled me with quiet joy. I knew something I wasn't going to confess: Mario needed me.

"But I didn't call you here to talk about that," the Englishman continued. "I want to make you an offer, Tony—a designer job, something specialized we've created just for you. No responsibilities aside from those that you propose. *No strings attached.*"

Here it came.

"Atrium donates to NGOs and has its own non-profit organization. *We are global players*," he added in English. "We're interested in your country, Tony. The Pyramid is the ideal setting for our new project."

He raised his hand and ordered a single malt whiskey. Glenfiddich. A competent drinker. Alcohol lent him even more poise.

"There's a word that until recently," he said, "used to be very vulgar. A word used questionably by politicians, but one that still has relevance. The Pyramid was never your average resort, it was never the standard five-star *vomitorium*, if you will, with whores and cocaine included in the *room service*. We're a little more ambitious than that. The word I'm referring to is 'culture.' How does that sound to you?"

"Like nothing."

"Tony, you're a musician! We have major connections. The British Council has expressed interest. The tropics and the Maya make for an excellent backdrop to the drama, but we need to give it a new script. English writers only read and talk about one another; they like to be among their own. They'll be very happy to come here. And the rest of the world loves listening to them and assuring themselves they didn't learn their language in vain."

Mallett gave me a sly smile, bracing himself for criticism.

"Let's call it 'sustainable colonialism' shall we? Or 'soft imperialism.' The whole scheme—it's not only safer than Mario Müller's, it's also more marketable. We could open a children's center with a Harry Potter Pavilion! The only thing more commercial than culture is ecology."

He took out some tobacco paper. We were in the no-smoking section, but a man in a guayabera shirt came up to offer him an ashtray. Mallett was well-positioned within the hierarchy. He had the grace to ignore the reverential treatment, handling his privilege with elegant obliviousness.

"Guilt," he said, as he licked the rice paper, "is a lucrative business. The people who pollute the most are the same ones who invest the most in organic food and eco-tourism. All we need now is someone to play the background music."

They're afraid of Mario, I thought. They didn't need me, they needed Mario's best friend around to make sure he didn't do anything reckless.

"Another thing, and more importantly: with this plan we qualify for funding from Development Assistance. Do you have any idea how much money they've got lying around?" He shot back some whiskey. "And this is something I know you care about—we're going to look after Mario. The best way to guarantee that, Tony, is to stay on the team."

I'd fallen into Mallett's trap. He was presenting the offer as a way to protect Mario. He gave me a sympathetic look.

THE REEF

"I have to think about it," I said.

"I'll give you two days, but that's it. I'm leaving on Thursday. I'm really excited about this project. There's some chauvinism there, I'm aware of that. We Brits are very patriotic. It doesn't matter if you're a *hooligan* or a *punk* or a lord, we all love *the good old Union Jack*. We're an island people who export symbols: Peter Pan, the Beatles, Shakespeare, Mary Poppins, Harry Potter. We're the greatest promoters of culture in a world we know the least about. Isn't it a marvelous paradox? Art can purify The Pyramid, Tony. How would you like to meet Brian Eno?"

I was awake until 6 a.m. The sky was overcast. When the clouds parted the sea was covered with small luminous circles. Little navels of light.

I studied the picture of Mario's daughter. She didn't look like him. A gentle face the color of cinnamon. A half smile probably interrupted by someone telling her to behave. The kind of photo you put on an ID card.

She would be my responsibility. What kind of life would she have? What kinds of pain and dreams and lovers and jobs, what kinds of desire would beat behind those eyes staring into the lens? I'd accompany her through all of it. For her, I'd be Mario Müller.

Mallett had been surprisingly deferential, as if I were something more than a conductor of fish. Which could only mean that Mario was still a threat to him.

It was in my best interest to delay my decision. No one could know that I was leaving and taking Mario's daughter with me. I had two days left.

In the end, everything was falling into place. I couldn't sleep, but everything was falling into place.

•

The adoption papers had an X penciled at all the places I needed to sign. The girl's name was Irene. She had both of Mario's last names: Müller Soares.

I signed the final page then dialed the phone number Mario had given me. The director of the shelter answered in the tone of someone trying to be polite but afraid of being recorded.

"You must be familiar with us," she said. A few moments later I received a text message from an unknown number, asking that I come to the shelter the next day.

Mario called me soon after that. I went over to his suite. Not even illness had cluttered those scrupulous rooms.

I found him lying across a gray sofa, chewing on a piece of bamboo.

"A woman from the shelter will accompany you and the girl to Mexico City," he said without preamble.

"A flight? How'd you manage that?"

"Friends of friends. It's important you don't leave a paper trail. Of course, the woman already knows you."

"Who is she?"

"Laura Ribas. You met her a long time ago, at a concert for Los Extraditables. You were having a rough night."

"That could've been any night."

"She was a kid."

"I'm supposed to remember this?" I said with what had become the refrain of my stay in the Caribbean.

"I don't know. She remembers you. She was very little when she saw you, but you left a lasting impression."

"I doubt it was my virtuoso bass-playing."

"She's been through a lot shittier things than you. Things

only a woman can endure. She's been living at the shelter for months. She used to be the wife of an arms dealer. She showed up very badly battered. And she's grown attached to Irene. It's strange to say it. I never thought I'd have a daughter with that name."

"What did you think her name would be?"

"I never even thought I'd have a daughter. It's good that the girl—" He hesitated, as if saying her name were a struggle, an appropriation he didn't want. "—it's good that she's traveling with Laura."

He pointed to a cardboard box resting on a wide dresser.

"A gift," he said. I stood and went to inspect it. Mario seemed unable to move from the couch. I opened the box.

"It's the sounds of The Pyramid," he explained. "I recorded all kinds of things. Sometimes I loop them back to the guest rooms at an FM wavelength. It's very disconcerting to hear a dog barking when there's no dog. Sounds can impact your ideas. The sensations we provoke all have their consequences. You know, the 'butterfly effect.' Maybe one day someone will invent a cure for cancer and the idea will have struck them in a moment on some beach, when a dog that wasn't there was barking. I like that chain of possibilities, though it's also possible the guy who hears the dog barking thinks about killing his wife or his neighbor with the horrible dog. We can control the causes, but not their effects."

"Did you record inside the guest rooms?"

"I'm not morbid, Tony. These sounds are like Mayan deities. The Ocean God, the Wind God, the Door God, the Bell God, the Bird God, the Dog God. There are coughs, too. That's what the tourists leave behind—acoustic gratuities. I'm guessing you'll go back to recording? You remember what Eric Clapton used to say? The virtuoso isn't the person who plays a lot of notes, it's the person who plays *the* note. You can do amazing things with these sounds. You're in good shape."

At that moment the last thing I wanted to think about was music.

"Who's taking us to Mexico City?" I said.

"I've done my share of favors. There are people who like us and care about the women at the shelter. People of extraordinary courage. Everything's going to be fine. I recorded these sounds so that you and Irene can remember me."

"They offered me work here," I said. "A new cultural project."

"You're not going to take it."

"How do you know?"

"Are you going to take it?"

"Obviously not."

"They offered it to you because I asked them to. It was one of the terms I gave them before agreeing to give notice. I want them to think I'm resigning and leaving an heir."

"You're not resigning?"

He smiled.

"I'll take one final little trip. With Cruci/Fiction. I want to throw myself into an ocean that deserves its reputation, a real son of a bitch, a sea mad as hell. I've sent word to London. To the *Independent,* the *Guardian,* the *Times.* Every man and his dog will know how The Pyramid operates. I'm throwing enough breadcrumbs to get them to the witch's cottage. Off-shore investments in Jamaica, the Cayman Islands; protection money paid to Los Conchos . . . I have copies of the money transfers. What are your extraditables for anyway? To denounce from a distance."

"Who gave you the photocopies?"

"Someone who stopped being my friend."

"Peterson?"

"The very same."

"Why? That kind of trail will screw him."

"People are breathing down his neck, and he needs a traitor. If I point the finger publicly, he can blame me all he wants when I'm dead. No skin off my nose. I'll be his accomplice from the bottom of the sea. He'll cause trouble for Atrium without having to get directly involved. He'll bill the insurance company and he'll disappear somewhere to enjoy the races."

I could hear a noise in the distance. Maybe the sound of the fumigator plane.

"The Bacabs, shattering their water jugs," he said. "Good topic for a song."

"What exactly does El Gringo get out of all this?"

"To cover up the scandal, the Brits will agree to his terms, which have been the same for a long time. Bankruptcy, an insurance claim. He hates Atrium as much as he hates me. He hates having depended on them. He hates that they're English. He hates having been successful in a scheme that originally seemed uncertain. He wants to get out of here and settle down by some racetrack, alone, for the rest of his life. We're all leaving, Tony. A toothless Eskimo retreats from his igloo to die in the ice. Natural history."

It started to rain. The window overlooking the swimming pool rattled in the wind.

"I'm getting on a helicopter," Mario continued. "And letting it take me to some fantastically disastrous climate. Picture an aerial shot of turbulent water. The storm sewer of the Earth! You release the cord and the rest is free fall.

It's a narcissistic dream, and very expensive. Did you expect anything less from your favorite singer?"

He rapped his knuckles on the table in 4/4 time. Then he got up, moving towards me with great difficulty. He spread his arms. It was upsetting to inhale the smell of his skin. Upsetting to feel his bones, to touch him and know—body against body—that he was finished.

I closed my eyes and resisted my best friend's show of affection.

I took a taxi out to the junction where a small road veered off the highway. From here it was only two hundred yards to the shelter. The director had advised me to walk the rest of the way in case the car got stuck.

The road was filled with potholes from the previous days' storm. A sign said, "Church of the Seventh Day." *They can't just advertise themselves as a "refuge for perse-cuted women,"* Der Meister had explained.

I heard an exploding sound in the sky and looked up to see the fumigator plane spewing pinkish smoke. The purple dye must have run out. A farce like that couldn't last long.

I followed the dirt path toward a white building dec-orated with blue crosses. There were so many denomi-nations in the area that some of the churches resembled video stores. This one made its adherents seem like a per-secuted sect. The roof was adorned with three layers of barbed wire and two security cameras.

I rang the bell. The door—a solid sheet of metal—was buzzed open. I walked into a small room with a one-way mirror.

"ID, please?" The voice came through a microphone.

A screen slid open to reveal a deep tray. I handed over my voter registration card.

"I've come to speak to the director about Irene Müller," I said to my own reflection.

"Place all metal objects in the tray."

Now I was taken through a metal detector and then an imposing electronic door.

I'd had a bleak notion of the shelter as a place for ruined lives. So it surprised me to hear laughter and the echoes of a ball bouncing in the courtyard. I saw a colorful mural, toy cars, a table with glasses half-full of juice.

My arrival was causing a stir. I was the only adult male in the building. The children stopped in the middle of their games. A blonde woman turned toward me to see what everyone else was looking at.

"Oh, it's you," she said listlessly. "I'm Laura. Laura Ribas." She was the woman I had met on the road in the rain a few days before.

Three other women were eyeing me from afar with stony expressions. I was an intruder, so they could stare shamelessly without appearing rude or betraying their obvious curiosity. All three were wearing very tight jeans, plastic flip-flops, and body suits with wild prints (a spider web, jaguar spots, psychedelic cells). They were attractive in a vulgar way. A despicable thing to think, but I couldn't help it. They'd been tortured by men who thought like I did.

Laura, on the other hand, was wearing a dark blue smock like hospital scrubs. She still had the scab on the corner of her lip, but a piece of it had flaked off. The new skin, very pink, looked irritated.

"Come," she said.

We went up to the second floor. On the landing, we made a detour around three mattresses.

"They're going to be burned," she explained. "Whenever a woman is taken away, they burn her bed to erase all her suffering. No one could sleep on it anyway."

We came to a door with a cardboard sign that said "ACUPUNCTURE."

I looked around the scantly furnished room. A bed beside some electrical equipment, a cupboard with various medical instruments, a wooden chair. I sat in the chair while Laura sat on the bed. The walls were postered with diagrams of male and female bodies, each one mapped with the nervous system and all the pressure points. Lines in red, blue, and yellow.

Laura traced her gums with her tongue. *She has sores,* I thought. Our consultation began, but she was the one asking the questions:

"What happened to your hand?"

"It was a firecracker, I told you."

My explanation left her indifferent. She had a red dot on the sclera of an eye, and a scar at the top of her neck. It was my turn to say: "What happened?" I pointed to the scar to show which one I meant.

"It's not something you want to know about," she answered, sounding more weary than aggressive. She crossed her legs and I noticed her feet inside the plastic sandals. The nails were cracked in a way I'd never seen before.

"Do you have a cigarette?" I asked.

"I don't smoke."

Those deep brown eyes watched me carefully.

"Did Mario say I was coming with you?"

"Yes."

"Do you have kids?"

"No."

"Do you know why I'm here?"

"No."

Had I asked ten more questions, I sensed she would have given similar answers.

A strand of hair fell across her forehead. When she brushed it aside, I thought I saw a fresh scar along her scalp.

"I met Tristán," she said.

"Who is he?"

"Was. They killed him. People called him Two-Tone." She studied me—trying to figure out how much of this I knew from Mario. Her expression was becoming guarded. She didn't want to tell me more than that.

"What about Camila, Irene's mother. Did you know her?"

"Yes," she said.

"Are you also a dancer?"

"Do I look like a dancer?"

"No."

"What do I look like?"

"A person living in a shelter."

"Come on, don't be an idiot. What do I look like? Be honest." She gave me a hard stare with her dark eyes. Again I noticed the red dot. Was it a birth-mark? A burst capillary? Some kind of injury?

"Unwell," I said. "Because of your shirt."

"It's from a hospital. I was there for six months."

I looked away to the pictures of the human body. The nerves formed a colorful circuit. A map of my body. Maybe Laura's was different, her circuits broken.

"So how did you meet Two-Tone?"

"The less you know, the better."

"OK, I don't want to know anything. I came to help."

"Well, don't get all defensive. It's true, I haven't been well. And you really don't remember?"

"Remember what?"

"About me."

"Yes, we met the other day. On the road?"

"You think I care about that? I'm talking about something else."

She's nuts, I thought. *Mario's nuts. He wants me to travel with a nutcase.* Was this hospital she'd mentioned a psychiatric ward?

"How good is your memory?" she asked.

"Bad."

"How bad?"

"I lost half of it."

"How do you know it was half?"

"That's what it feels like. Half is a lot, don't you think?"

"Did you quit doing drugs?"

Mario told her about me.

"A long time ago. Drugs took half my memory. Or something like half."

"I was a little girl." When she looked at me, her eyes were glistening.

"When was that?"

"When you fainted. At a concert. My dad was a bass player. He played with you guys once." She started telling me everything Mario had said. "They'd called him in case you couldn't get it together. My dad didn't have anyone to look after me, so I went with him to the concert. You guys really sucked." She smiled but not to soften the insult.

"The walls were vibrating," she continued. "I thought they were going to collapse. I stayed in a room behind the stage, playing with a stuffed animal—I remember, it was a rabbit I lost not long after. They brought you backstage. You'd fainted or had some kind of attack. They laid you out on a table. The rest of the band kept playing, each song a disaster worse than the one before. They should have all fainted. You looked like you'd died. Then suddenly you opened your eyes and asked me if you had."

"You're sure it was me?"

She rubbed her wrist. "You only had four fingers," she said. "You still only have four fingers. And I don't forget faces. I want to but I can't. You remember what I said? 'Yes, you're dead.' Then you thanked me. Like I'd given you good news. You *wanted* to be dead. You don't remember?"

"No. I also have no recollection of the other times I've died."

"Your playing really sucked."

"What happened to your dad?"

"He got involved with a cult. In Tabasco." She rubbed her wrist again. "It's a nervous tic," she explained. "I was tied up for a long time."

Laura seemed to remember everything. Maybe this was what tortured her most. Her gaze was disconcertingly steady. Her expression seemed comprised of all the things she'd seen.

"Mario is dying," she said. "He's been dying for months."

"Have you seen him?"

Her answer surprised me.

"He stopped by yesterday. Looks like a skeleton. He didn't want to say hello to Irene. He told me about you and reminded me of the concert where they laid you out on the table. He said you'd lost your memory. You've no idea how much I envy you. And Mario loves you. Very much. I guess you know that, right? Though I don't think you appreciate what it means. The jerk who loved me tried to skin me alive. People show their love in strange ways."

I thought of Leopoldo Támez protecting Sandra from

his own rage. Laura gave me a sad smile. One of her teeth was chipped.

"So you don't sleep, either?"

"Mario told you he doesn't sleep?"

"I was talking about myself. I have trouble sleeping."

"Did you live with a narco?" I looked her in the eye. She rubbed her wrist.

"Why do you care?"

"I'll be traveling with you. I'd like to know if you're going to see me die for real this time."

"I used to live with one of his suppliers. He buys weapons in Israel, Brazil, South Africa..."

"Can he find you here?"

Laura stared down at her cracked toenails as if looking for the answer there.

"Of course he can."

"That sounds reassuring."

"Irene's not leaving without me," she said. Her tone was threatening. "She needs me. She doesn't know you."

Laura fiddled with a button. It came loose and fell to the floor. When she kneeled down to hunt for it, she winced in pain and pressed her hands over her kidney. Then she turned to me, still kneeling, hair hanging over her face.

"How did you expect me to recognize you?" I said.

"What do you mean?"

"I met you as a kid. A million years later, we meet again on a roadside in the rain. There was no way I was going to recognize you."

"Mario told me about you. I figured he'd told you about me as well."

Mario had been playing with my memory. He'd selected everything he wanted me to know.

"Besides," Laura said, "you told me you wouldn't forget

me. You said it was nice dying next to an angel. You called me Cherub."

"I forgot," I said. It made me feel awful.

Laura found the button. "Do you want me to go with you?"

"Yes," I said.

"Why, because I'm kneeling, and it turns you on that they tortured me?"

"I have other reasons."

"Give me one that matters."

"Because I shouldn't have forgotten you."

Laura grew quiet, as if waiting for my words to crash to the floor.

"What happened to your leg?"

"I got run over when I was a kid."

"So now you run off with battered women?" Again, she traced over her gums with her tongue. Then she stood up. We were the same height. I turned back to the anatomy diagrams, with their trails of yellow nerves. I made myself take a small step toward her. She seemed oblivious to me now, distracted by her toothache. She had a sugary smell, cloying, like fruit fermenting in the sun.

"Did it hurt?" she said, pointing to my finger.

"No."

"Do you get turned on by other people's pain?"

"You already asked me. I'm not excited by torture."

"Do you still want to be dead?"

"Not right now."

Laura led us to the door.

We crossed the shelter's patio. The children were gone, and the discarded balls shone in the harsh glare of sun.

I looked through one of the windows. It was a classroom, and inside the children were drawing.

"All the way at the back, sitting on the chair in the corner," Laura whispered to me.

A brown-skinned girl was sketching with a purple crayon.

"Irene Müller," Laura said. "The director is waiting for you. I can't go beyond that door." She pointed to a part of the building that housed the offices. An area with less security.

I positioned myself in front of a camera and the door opened. I handed over the documents Mario had given me to a slender middle-aged woman. The secretary interrupted to let her know they had finished painting the truck.

"Last week we had a car chase here with gun-fire," the director said, by way of explanation. "They tried to make off with one of the women. We painted our truck so they won't recognize it." She was composed, as if describing a common problem.

You needed incredible presence of mind to live this way. How did they endure it? I asked her this, and she gave a tiny, almost imperceptible smile. Her answer was not what I expected.

"When we see someone's gaining weight, we scold them. If a woman lets herself go, she could end up somewhere very bad. No one here gets fat."

Her words sounded like a moral judgment, a modest form of heroic resistance. In a place meant for lost causes, here was some specific conduct for saving the world.

"Irene and Laura have completed their time here," she said. "It's not good for people to stay too long. They must learn to fly on their own."

The verb "to fly," which I would never have used in this context, revealed the optimism of someone who overcame crisis for a living.

"Who is Laura going to live with?" I said.

"She knows people in Mexico City. They'll help her start a new life. Mario Müller has done a lot for us. He's just made a very generous donation. Lastly, I ask that you be prepared for the operation. They could summon you at any time. Thank you for your help. Your taxi is waiting."

I didn't realize they'd called me a taxi. The shelter functioned with precision. She said the word "operation" in the same tone she'd used to discuss the importance of not getting too heavy. *The weight of the world.* For the women at the shelter, this was less a pat phrase than a test of their mettle. The place had impressed me first for its lack of squalor, now for its discipline. A fortress of self-control. Defeating the horror demanded another kind of suffering—valid, necessary, and completely beyond my own capabilities. I thought of Irene. Did she need a person with four fingers, someone with a lame leg and only half his memory? I remembered the moment I'd chased after the ball Mario Müller had thrown. As if I'd been running blind. I'd missed it because the car ran me over, but maybe I could've caught it under different circumstances. I wasn't going to abandon Irene Müller.

At 1 a.m., I went over to Mario's suite. He'd left his door unlocked. I found him in bed. I wanted to turn on the light, but he stopped me.

"I don't want you to see me," he said. "I'm a yellow monster."

I told him about my visit to the shelter. Then I asked about Laura.

"Her dad filled in for you once. Now you're subbing for me," he said. "Were you happy when you were in Los Extraditables?"

"I guess so."

"Those were some glorious years. We were so optimistic, we made a hobby of destroying ourselves. But by the time we got sober, there was no point being lucid. The country had gone to hell. Our insomnia is generational. It's better to live at night."

Mario turned over in his bed. I couldn't see him clearly. Was he looking for a pillow, a hot-water bottle? He settled back down with difficulty. Something gleamed on his dresser, maybe a glass of water. *Still life,* I thought. Mario continued:

"During the Maya's Classic Period, it rained a shitload. The water would run down the pyramids; you'd think they were magnets for attracting rain. Then the droughts came, and it was all sun and lizards until the tourists arrived! Now it rains again. Did you know that 'hurricane' is a Mayan word...?"

His digressions were making me uneasy. I started pacing his room, trying not to trip on anything.

"Sit still," he said. "Your moving around makes me nervous. It's like being with a caged jaguar. Are you sitting down now?"

"Yes." I sat on the edge of the bed.

"Are you telling me the truth?"

"Can't you feel that I'm sitting here?"

"You think I can feel the bed? I can barely feel my own fucking bones and you expect me to feel the fucking mattress?"

"We need to call the doctor."

"He's coming later. He's going to take me on vacation.

'Vertical velocity.' That's what they call it when you take a direct flight."

It was impossible to imagine him climbing into a helicopter. The idea of a trip with Cruci/Fiction sounded like a megalomaniac's fantasy.

"What time is the doctor coming?"

"In a little while. Now be quiet and listen. I want to speak. Can you do one final thing?"

"Speak."

"Laura Ribas used to live with a highly educated man. He spoke several languages. He endured her whims and beat the shit out of her. Apart from that, she's more reliable than Ginger Oldenville."

I didn't say anything, just waited for him to continue. Mario tried to clear his throat. I poured him a glass of water but I couldn't see so it overflowed. I wet the sheets. Neither of us cared. Nothing mattered anymore. He took a small sip and continued.

"Ginger was a crazy piece of shit, a white guy with a freckled face like rye bread. Sometimes the devil has a freckled face like rye bread—it's time for you to accept that! I don't want to die thinking you were stupid enough to believe him. Ginger wasn't innocent. He was a stunt double on *Jaws III*—a perfect job for him. But here the dangers aren't a game. Thinking you're the good guy can make you very aggressive."

"What are you talking about? They stuck a spear in his back!"

"They stabbed him for nosing around. He broke all the rules, with everyone. A messiah with the face of an angel. He saw himself as an aquatic sheriff, a vengeful cherub. He thought he was the good guy. It's something I can't stand, this Hollywood-style happiness. He wanted to do the right thing and fucked everybody up."

"Who killed him?"

"Ginger being dead was convenient for all of us. He was too good not to end up causing someone harm."

"I worked with him—I can't see it that way. You're going to die a cynic."

"Fear is the greatest thing about this place. Ginger killed the fantasy. He wanted reality, that was his vice. He was a truth fanatic. He gave the DEA the GPS coordinates for the rivers. He gave them to the Attorney-General, to the consulate...he ended the dream. The only fiction left is those planes hovering over us like mosquitoes with diarrhea. There are queers who behave like fucking Quakers. Ginger was one of those. I don't give a shit that they killed him. I'm telling you about his death so that you know why I do care. His death only hurt me because it was pointless. If I thought his death could've done something, I would've skinned him alive myself. His *do-good-ism* put an end to everything. You've no idea how many people I've watched enjoying themselves here. This hotel achieved a fucking incredible thing. For Los Extraditables, this hotel was the performance of a lifetime. Children die of dehydration in this area. We built a dream where there'd been only insects. Does that seem like nothing to you?"

"Who killed Ginger?"

"If the question concerns you so much, Inspector," Mario said with the melodramatic intonation of a radio soap star, "then blame me. I can go down with one more sin to my name." He coughed. His chest was completely congested with mucus. He hocked some up into a handkerchief and asked for a Kleenex. It was difficult to locate the dresser. Finally I found him some tissues and he hurled up a huge gob of phlegm.

"That's my legacy, Tony. Phlegm. But don't leave with a bad impression of me. Don't think I didn't want to kill Ginger Oldenville. I would've strangled him, but certain things can only happen in dreams. I also never got to be with your mom."

He buried his face in the pillow and started sobbing. I sat beside him and placed a hand on his back. It was damp. Strange that a body that ravished could produce any sweat.

"It's all right," I said.

"I'm an asshole. I wanted to be a bigger asshole but I couldn't. Forgive me, Tony, I couldn't do it. Can you forgive me?"

"I forgive you." I stroked his neck and when I pulled my hand away, a tuft of hair came with it. He was running a fever.

I waited until the doctor arrived. The man stayed an hour. My friend was now delirious.

"Less butter, please," he said, his voice soft, humble.

"It's all right," the doctor said in a tone of professional kindness, responding to nothing in particular. I didn't recognize him. We were still sitting in the dark, but I could tell this man was a stranger. Probably from Kukulcán. He'd brought a square briefcase that looked like a toolbox. I wondered if he would take Mario to a hospital.

"I'll keep you company," I said to my friend.

Mario gestured "no" with his hand. The smile frozen on his face. Only then did I notice the doctor was administering an injection.

"It's all right," he repeated. A phrase to show that the difference between life and death was simply a procedure.

It was 2 a.m., but even so I was detained three times on the way back to my room. Security staff I didn't recognize kept halting me to check my purple wristband. At every inspection, I had to explain who I was. At the last stop, I ran into Leopoldo Támez, whose face was still swollen and covered in bruises. For the first time, his dark lenses were functional.

"How good to see you," he said insincerely, taking me aside.

"What's going on?"

"New security measures. We've been noticing phony wristbands. I'm sorry about Señor Müller. They retired him. So it goes. They've pulled us all out. I'm leaving, too. Things have become dangerous here."

Támez gestured to his bruises, then grinned. The guy deserved stained teeth full of cavities; it was irritating that he had such a perfect smile. "I'm switching to another private police unit. Luckily, there are three hundred of these outfits in Kukulcán. The hotels are closing and every day there's a higher demand for vigilantes."

"Send my regards to Bush and Fox," I said.

"I see someone's been talking shit about me. You can pass along a message: If they don't like the taste of my cock, they shouldn't suck it."

A perfect sentence for rotten teeth. I was full of loathing for the impeccable orthodontics of Leopoldo Támez.

He used to fuck Sandra. I thought this both to hurt and to steel myself. I could've pushed him out the hallway window. He deserved to die. Picturing his thick fingers parting Sandra's legs was enough to make me want to kill him. But I didn't do it.

Mario wasn't the only one who would regret not having murdered someone.

The encounter with Támez, the filth he represented, the rotting face of justice, made me think of Inspector Ríos. I needed to replace the sordid image of the head of security.

I slept from five to seven, took a cold shower and read a little (or rather reread the passages Luciana had underlined in *The Master of Go*). Then I called Ríos. I had to see him as soon as possible.

"Any news?"

"Yes," I lied. What I really wanted was for him to tell *me* something, anything—give me some scrap of information so I could forget Támez and believe that there were crimes out there that could in fact be solved. I knew justice wasn't possible, but I kept hoping for some unexpected logic to emerge.

"Come by the church," he suggested. Only then did I realize I had called him at 7 a.m. on a Sunday. I hated people who called at that hour. Now I was one of them.

Ríos's church was a small, wooden structure painted white. A place for low-budget dreams. I didn't even have to go inside to hear the sermon. A loudspeaker was blaring his words from the roof.

His preacher's tone was confident, convincing—the tone of someone who's seen many corpses, held the hand of a drowning man, salvaged a woman's bloody bracelet and given it to her daughter. It was the voice of someone who knows that things can tremble and tear but still hold together. His gospel sounded like an extreme form of resignation. Hearing it didn't do me any good. At that moment, what I needed was an inflamed prophet, full of fury, or a divine chief of police, or even just a vengeful cop who could conclude the disaster set in motion by Ginger Oldenville's kindness.

After twenty minutes, the sun began to feel oppressive. (It had been oppressive from the start, as it always is on that coastline punished by light, but only now did the idea sink into my thoughts.) I entered the church just as a black man began improvising on an electric keyboard, accompanied by three girls (one played maracas, another guitar, the third on tambourine).

I was forced to endure the gospel's musical supplement: the space filled up with the prayers of Roberto Carlos. The parishioners looked like shopkeepers, electricians, plumbers, and mechanics. Specialists in practical matters. A flock of artisans that would've fascinated Christ himself. Oddly enough, there weren't any sailors or fishermen in their ranks. Ríos's fold was the small urban community of Punta Fermín: people without roots, people willing to accept an alternative version of the Christian faith.

That the ceremony should include a Roberto Carlos song was annoying, especially when my right foot started tapping to the beat. A sure sign of my musical "calling" is this inability to stop my foot from keeping time with the rhythm. You can always tell a bass player by his shoe-tapping. This might explain why the paradise Felipe Blue had brought me was always stashed inside a shoebox.

What Roberto Carlos wanted was a "chorus of birds." For this he needed "a million friends," an enormous flock to help him sing. My foot provided percussion for the Brazilian's pleas. How I longed to usher in the dark blasphemy of Black Sabbath.

Just as I was fine-tuning the terms of my heresy, a man hugged me warmly and called me "brother." The service was over. There was silence again.

Ríos was wearing a black suit, different from the one he used for work (which had been a dull shade of brown, the color of tree bark). He said hello, that he was pleased to see me there, and suggested we go for lunch.

"I have a surprise for you," he said.

We walked along an esplanade where the local government had left sprawling deposits of mango-colored trash bags. As if the ability to store waste was the greatest proof of development.

Ríos smoked two cigars in the time it took us to find a tavern. The place was painted twenty shades of blue. If the sea suffered from dermatitis, that's what it would look like. Surprisingly, the tavern's name didn't sound in any way maritime. It was called The Crafty Bishop. The words were written across a sign painted like a chessboard.

As soon as we stepped inside, a voice called out:

"Turn off the TVs! The Inspector's here."

"You know I hate all that gossip," Ríos said, as the television screens were switched off in quick succession. From the ceiling a net sagged with many curious objects.

"Things that come in with the tide," Ríos said. It wasn't so different from Sandra's collection—the whole room was covered with beach balls, broken toys, several diving flippers. I thought of the plane that crashed into the Underwater Andes. Maybe an emergency life vest would one day wind up in that net.

"A campechana?" a waitress said to Ríos.

"Yes," Ríos said, turning to me. "I haven't had breakfast yet. You want something? It's on me."

I ordered a fish taco to be polite, and a beer. It had been a long time since I'd enjoyed alcohol before eleven o'clock. But this was a special occasion.

Ríos paired his shrimp cocktail with an enormous glass

of café con leche. It seemed like an abusive combination for his small frame. He probably wouldn't be eating again until the following day. *The missionary's diet*, I thought.

"What's on your mind?" he asked.

"You."

"I noticed you were interested in my sermon."

The beer was lukewarm. I drank quickly.

"And I hear you're going to be running The Pyramid." Ríos lit another cigar before touching his food. "Is it true?" he said.

"They offered me a job."

"You'll fill Müller's position. A great honor. You loved your friend very much."

"I still do. He isn't dead."

"Forgive me. I see dead bodies from Monday to Saturday, and on Sundays I preach about them."

At the back of the room, two men were struggling to keep their balance. They hugged each other to stay upright then stumbled together towards the jukebox. When they reached it, they lost their footing and fell to the dirt floor. They lay there in a calm embrace.

"The guy who owns this place is a chess player," Ríos said. "That's why he called it the Crafty Bishop."

He pointed with his long cocktail spoon to the photos lining the walls.

"Spasky, Fisher, Capablanca, Kasparov, Karpov...." His voice trailed off. The combination of a nautical theme with the chess legends was bizarre.

A man walked in hauling a block of ice with enormous tongs. It was too late to chill my Sol, so I ordered another one. Living in the Caribbean I'd started to hate that brand, sponsored by the sun. But I was getting used to the things I hated.

"Támez is leaving The Pyramid," I said.

Ríos muttered something about private corporations recruiting corrupt police officers. Leopoldo Támez would fit right in.

"In this country," Ríos said, "failing at your job helps you land another one. No one ever checks to see if you were fired. There are hundreds of jobs Támez could take. He'll die before he can be fired from all of them."

A street dog had wandered into the tavern. It walked over to the fallen men and started licking their faces and wagging its tail.

"Támez was the one who disconnected the security camera," I said. "He's an accessory to murder."

"The bad news has revived you, my friend," Ríos said approvingly.

I told him about Ginger. What it was like to arrive at The Pyramid like the survivor of my own shipwreck and encounter his unbridled optimism, his willingness to help everybody and see each day as a miracle. A biologically happy person. Such a thing can sound simple-minded or tedious, but not to someone who's been holed up in recording studios where all the technicians mysteriously suffer from PTSD. Ginger didn't visit the aquarium to train dolphins; he came to cheer me up. He'd praised the musical notes of each fish like points scored in a basketball game.

According to Mario, Ginger's inherent goodness caused him to make a serious miscalculation. He saw something he shouldn't have, then tried to fix it. But he didn't pick up the signs of reticence, or the wariness of a centuries-old culture founded on distrust. He didn't understand that Eden is a very discreet place.

Years earlier, I'd been guilty of acting with an even worse naïveté. I thought you could get in tune with the universe by combining music and the perfect dose. I was zealous in my belief that altering the mind was an art that would change your life, the country, the cosmos itself. I didn't regret my addiction so much as the optimism I had initially brought to it. "Chilling out" had been my noble cause, but that led to something very different: narcotrafficking, bodies floating in the underground rivers explored by Ginger. I wasn't sure that *do-goodism,* as Mario called it, had been Ginger's great sin, but it was certainly mine. I shared a similarly destructive enthusiasm with the diver. He'd acted on his faith in goodness and ultimately hurt everyone. He believed in those idiotic stories where the heroes won.

"Mario hated Ginger," I told Ríos.

"Enough to kill him?"

"It would be convenient to have the killer at death's door. An open-casket confession. The case would be closed with the lid."

"You've grown fond of metaphor, my friend," Ríos said, smiling. "Welcome to the club. Ginger Oldenville should've worked in the aquarium at Disneyworld."

I glanced up at the hanging net. It made me wonder whether Mario's body would be dragged along a beach by the tide or sink into an abyss. Would he throw himself from a helicopter, strapped with weights, and plummet to the ocean floor? Obviously he wanted to be remembered in grand style.

"Mario didn't kill Ginger," I insisted. "I've known him all my life. Támez disconnected the video cameras. Didn't you question him?"

"Of course I did."

"So what else you got for me?" I said, mockingly.

"A little surprise." He gestured to the back of the room.

I thought he was going to reveal more about the case, but he was referring to something completely unrelated.

A man with an ash-blonde ponytail was walking to the jukebox. He kicked the drunks aside and stood watching as they struggled to get up, then shoved them towards the door. He pressed play.

The warm air of the bar rang with the unforgettable, achingly sentimental notes of "Queen of Hearts."

"Remember me?" a voice called out from the dimness. For a second I panicked that it was Yoshio, the Samurai of Song.

But no: a potbellied man approached; the buttons of his Hawaiian shirt had popped open to reveal a thick, dark scar. It was the bygone band-promoting loan shark, Ricky Ventura. I stood, a little dazed.

"Been a long time, guy!" He hugged me with love I hadn't known he'd felt.

All the time that had passed since we'd last seen each other, the things we'd each gone on to do—all of it filled us with affection. I remembered the checkered jacket he'd used as an extravagant chessboard in his large waiting room; all his cryptic references to defensive plays—the castling and gambits that had justified his risky career as a promoter.

He sat down between us and quickly quit the small talk.

"I fell into a hole, my friend," he said. "I lent money to the wrong kinds of people. Well, that wasn't really my mistake. I've always loved investing in other people's talent. I sure gave you enough breaks, didn't I? The problem was I wanted to collect my money. I became tiresome, Tony. You know I'm insistent, that's how I got gigs for everybody. You should've seen him—" He turned to Ríos and pointed at me. "Tony was a fiend on the electric bass. This guy you're looking at, he got to be better than Jaco Pastorius." Now he was lying for my benefit with blithe recklessness. "But in this country, all our big exploits remain a secret. John Cale wanted Tony to play backup, but that piece-of-shit Lou Reed threw a hissy fit. Tony here would've upstaged him. You shoulda heard Lou bitch about it!"

"What happened to the guys you were chasing?" I said. His charade was making me uncomfortable.

"They owed me serious money and weren't paying up. I'd appear every place you could imagine. Ricky Ventura is persistent as a retrovirus."

Had he always talked about himself in the third person? I couldn't remember.

"One day," he continued, "they sent me a message: if I kept bugging them, there'd be trouble." He mimed slitting his own throat, and I noticed he still kept the nail long on his right index finger—his signature style. "But Ricky Ventura is sticky as glue, you know that. I was relentless until they set fire to the Caveman—a club I handled acts for. I was arrested for it. They had friends at the precinct. I got locked up. Five years at Reclusorio Oriente. Which is even worse than listening to Yoshio! So good to see you, guy!"

All the strangeness of this Sunday—from the church visit to the breakfast beer and the sight of those drunks getting licked by a dog—converged onto the face of Ricky Ventura: the extravagant promoter who could fool Andy Warhol; the moneylender in the days before ATMs; the madman who'd dragged us into the prestigious hell of opening for the Velvet Underground. The same mythomaniac who now ran a seaside tavern called the Crafty Bishop.

"You still play chess?" I said.

"I was penitentiary champion. I'm the Reclusorio Grandmaster!" He smiled, with teeth that suggested prison fights. "I defended my title more times than you played with Los Extraditables. What a band, Tony! Never anything better in Mexico—in the world of Aztec *heavy metal*. It's a pity nobody knows that. I worshipped you guys. Mario never forgot it, he never forgets anything. He's the boss, that guy, only one I've ever had." He brought his hands to his face; his eyes had filled with tears. "Sorry, Tony, I've gotten sentimental over the years. I still hate Yoshio but I've gotten sentimental." He took some rough paper napkins from the dispenser—the color of ham— and wiped his tears. His skin was so dry the napkins must've felt like sandpaper. "Mario got this place off the ground. He gave me a nice sum as payback for some old loans. This place isn't Maxim's or anything, but I give it all I've got." His chest expanded as he leaned back in his seat. "The Inspector here is one of our best clients," he said. Then he pointed to a large, burly man, coming in from the glare of the road. "So's Carnitas."

"How long have you been here?" I said.

"Five years. Mario saved every last one of us. You remember Carnitas?"

"Nice to meet you," I said as the guy pulled a chair up to our table. He was wearing a T-shirt from Señor Frog's. The frog was pulled taut across the extensive surface of his belly.

"I was the P.A. for Mobile Hangar, Shaking Boots, and The Heavy Strawberries," he said. "Now I'm M.P."

"*Member of Parliament!*" Ricky joked.

"Ministry of Public Affairs," Carnitas said.

"We do good barbecue," said Ricky proudly. "We're a seafood place but on Sundays we're all about the feast of the goat. People from the coast get sick of shrimp."

"They get sick of the prices," Ríos said.

"The Sunday sermon! I don't take advantage of any-body. I'm a money lender, a music promoter, a seafood vendor. . . . " Ricky shook his head proudly. "I have to earn a living!"

I asked him about his scar.

"Cancer. They took out a chain of lymph nodes. I swear to you—" he said, crossing his chest then kissing his fingers. "I'd give my life for Mario Müller. Tell him, Carnitas."

The fat man was ordering a slab of barbecued shoulder. He mentioned various people who'd abandoned the rock scene and then come to Mario for help.

"The sound guy from Toncho Pilatos? He lives here. He owns three taxis! And you remember Chito Mendoza? Mario hooked him up at Pemex. He works as a supplier for the oil rigs."

"A supplier of what?" I said, just to keep the conversation going.

"Not barbecue, that's for sure," said Ricky Ventura. "That would be me."

"He's a supplier of people. He brings them women, a priest, a doctor. Whatever they need. If you need someone, Chito's the hookup."

So Der Meister had been recruiting has-beens from the counterculture. Part of his messianic appeal was a retirement plan for the country's rock scene. He didn't need the money to squander it on himself, he needed it to support and control a community. Exactly how many people in the region had received his donations?

"Did you pray for Mario Müller at church?" Ricky Ventura asked Ríos.

"Every day," the preacher said solemnly.

Ricky took me by the shoulder. "At six in the afternoon, a bunch of us rock veterans get together. You wouldn't believe these benders. Today we're having turtle eggs. Are you down?"

"Baby Bátiz is coming," Carnitas said with fearful reverence, as if referring to some master of black magic.

"She's still got that booming voice," Ricky said.

At that moment, I understood the best thing about my past was that it had already happened. No wonder Mario hadn't told me about this place. I wouldn't be coming back to the Crafty Bishop. Seeing Ricardo López Ventura was a pleasure precisely because we hadn't seen each other in years.

"I have to go," I said.

"So soon?" Ricky hugged me again. "We'll see you at six."

"Yes," I lied, and turned to Ríos. "Can I tell you something?"

"I want to talk with you, too," he said. The inspector stood and walked me to the door.

Across the street, three girls wearing miniskirts and crop tops were leaning against a car. Maybe they were prostitutes. Maybe they just liked to spend their Sundays leaning on car hoods.

"A hell of a gang, don't you think?" I didn't know if Ríos was referring to the three girls or the broken pillars of the national rock scene we'd left inside. "Leopoldo Támez owes me a favor. I recommended him for a new job. Don't look at me that way, please; he's so incompetent he's completely harmless. I took the opportunity to ask him for something in return—a tidbit he hadn't already told us, something you'll find interesting. Think of this as my Sunday gift. I know who asked him to disable the video equipment."

Ríos stood in shadow under the eaves of a house. He hated the sun.

"Who was it?"

"James Mallett, from London." Ríos glanced up at the sky, as if counting seagulls.

Now I knew who had killed Ginger Oldenville.

Mario, Támez, and Sandra had gone. Roxana Westerwood would soon pack her bags. The Pyramid was emptying out.

It's hard to know when you'll see a person for the final time. My days became a series of last opportunities. I knew that my meeting with Peterson would be a kind of goodbye.

I sat in a chair still warm from the person who'd been there minutes before. The secretary wasn't in. El Gringo had gone to the bathroom. He came back rubbing his temples; his hair was damp and it had clumped into a crest at his brow.

He bolted the door then went over to the little table where he kept his bottles of whiskey. He poured me a shot of Four Roses and refilled his own glass.

"Mallett is doing what he can to save the company's image," he said by way of greeting.

I drank. The liquid burned my throat.

"Why did you do it?" I said.

"What are you talking about?" He leaned back in his seat, intrigued.

I surprised myself, broaching the subject so quickly. Over the years I'd gained Peterson's trust. We talked like friends and swapped personal stories, though we never discussed work. My name was not to be found on the employee-of-the-month certificates that decorated his office, and he didn't treat me like a subordinate.

I could get straight to the point.

"You killed Ginger," I said. My tone was neutral, as if I were merely referring to an act of negligence. "I'm not going to turn you in. I couldn't do that. I just want to know why you did it."

"The law exists, Tony. I don't know why you're bypassing it. If you have proof, then say so." There was nothing challenging in his tone. He treated the subject as a matter of low priority, an interesting topic for speculation. Two friends chatting in the sunny tropics. He took another sip.

"Don't you believe in justice?" he asked. His curiosity seemed genuine. "I like your stories, the hallucinations of colorful lizards, the deliriums of your past. My friends needed war to experience that. You fucked yourself up in peacetime. This country never ceases to amaze me. Mexicans have to screw themselves over to succeed, that's why they're so good at the Special Olympics. I couldn't save my son, Tony, I've told you that a million times. I saw his face in the water: A rosy blur with a speck of white from the cotton swab in his ear. He drowned. Then my wife died. Valid reasons for fucking yourself over."

Maybe he was using this painful story to delay me. It was unlike him to use emotional blackmail, but I'd caught him off-guard. Now I had to press him. Not too much, just enough to make him want to tell me what I needed to know.

"'Solitary responsibilities,'" I said, citing his favorite expression.

He stared at me with an objective curiosity, as if I were describing an important mechanism alien to both of us.

"Támez," I continued, "was the one who disabled the video equipment. Mallett asked him to. Every person did their part. But if those were their designated tasks, then neither one could have fired the speargun. Everyone participates but each individual has to act alone. Have I mastered your theory?"

El Gringo smiled noncommittally. Did it please him not to have wasted his breath? Did he enjoy hearing a description of this admired strategy from someone else's mouth? The tactical resistance of the adversary. Did he suddenly worry he'd said too much? Would he prefer, in the end, to lie, to break a pact of honesty between two people who only met to talk, aware that in every other way, they didn't know each other? It was hard to say. He looked into my eyes, urging me to wrap up my argument.

"Mallett and Támez participated in the final preparations for the killing, but they didn't know what was going to happen. That eliminates them as possible suspects. Only one person can see the whole picture."

"I wasn't at The Pyramid."

"A perfect alibi. Maybe at night you became John Smith or Peter Jones, the guest no one ever saw leaving room 1004. It's easy to disappear inside The Pyramid."

"I attended the divers' funerals. Want to see the stamps on my passport?"

I hadn't considered how Peterson might take care of that detail. It would be easy for someone else to leave the Kukulcán airport with Peterson's passport then return it to him in the States. He was protected by a neat chain of minor offenses.

"Tony, you do know there's such a thing as 'madness by association,' right? There are people out there who believe that everything is connected. Crazy people. For months, you told me about your disjointed memories. Now you want to connect the whole thing. That's not what sobriety is about. There are things that cannot be explained. There are accidents. . . . " His tone was genial, patient.

"You've been trying to finish a story for years, Mike." Using his first name again surprised me more than it did him.

I knew Peterson the way only a stranger could—someone to talk to who was far removed from everything else. He understood that.

As he spoke, Peterson watched the ceiling fan. It was as if he'd entered a mild trance, weighing his words and losing himself inside them, accepting that he might be about to finish the story he'd so often started:

"I'd gotten in line to enlist for Vietnam, but they rejected me. The hardest thing was that they took my friends. One of them got his brains blown out, another died carrying his own intestines. I failed, Tony. That's the honest truth. What does a Gringo do when he fails? He destroys himself. That is, he comes to Mexico. Here, little by little, I got used to not hurting myself. I almost started enjoying life. I'm ashamed to say it, but I've actually been happy; not always—only dogs can be happy all the time—but happy at times, yes."

"You want to stop screwing yourself over?"

"The temptation never goes away. In my country, defeat means tragedy. But here, it means permission to be forgiven for existing. We've talked about a lot of things, *dear* Tony. I'm stunned by all we've told each other. The heat brings strangers together. Speaking to you relaxes me. Your personality is like an anti-anxiety pill. A 'man you can trust'. . . I ask myself whether you might also be a *con man*, someone who inspires trust in order to deceive. Are you deceiving me, Tony?"

"You can't deceive if you're the one doing all the asking. Why did you kill Ginger?"

"You say you can't turn me in. That's very interesting. Why can't you?" He blew out a cloud of smoke.

"I could, but I don't care. Everyone wanted Ginger dead."

"What do you mean, 'everyone?'"

"You, Mario, Támez, Atrium, the DEA, the consulate, the Conchos. . . . Even his family goes along with the story of the gay pact."

"Ríos isn't on that list?"

He flicked a bit of ash off his chest. He was wearing a pale yellow collared shirt made of cheap material. It was transparent, showing the white T-shirt underneath, cut like a basketball jersey. The only luxury he ever indulged in was Cuban tobacco. Now he was whistling the unmistakable opening bars of "Fly Me to the Moon." Mike Peterson was enjoying himself.

We'd gotten along well from the start. I liked his melancholy struggle with the absences that defined his life. It was a quality that dignified him. He'd handled his own fall enviably. I'd squandered mine. He had punished himself in a way that was useful, by helping the hundreds of people who cluttered his office as employees of the month.

"Ríos doesn't want any scandals," I said.

"And what about you? Do you want a scandal?"

I realized I preferred inhaling secondhand smoke to smoking myself. The tobacco fumes were pleasantly luxurious against my skin.

"I want to know the reason. That's all."

"Why?"

"I worked with Ginger. I was fond of him. And I was the only one who didn't want him dead. That intrigues me."

"I see. And Mario, how's he doing? Taking it easy?"

"Putting his things in order. He doesn't have much time left."

Peterson's reply was unexpected:

"He'll expose all the irregularities here at The Pyramid," he said, glancing at his watch as if this prediction might come true at any minute. "He knows what he's doing. He always has."

"Is it good for you if he talks?"

"Like I said, absolute happiness doesn't exist. If the press puts pressure on Atrium, then we'll have to fold. Total bankruptcy. It's the best thing to do with a hotel like this. Mallett is still sure he can straighten things out. Another fanatic. Is it even possible to get six interesting people in a room together without one of them being a fanatic?"

El Gringo seemed to be in the mood for tangents. Now he'd found a new digression: the proliferation of fanaticism.

"Roger Bacon was a better diver than Ginger," I said, trying to get us back on topic. "They killed him because he happened to discover a drug shipment. Then they faked his death at sea."

"Yes, he died before Ginger did. That was Ríos's big discovery. I don't know if such a find can justify his job description, though it certainly justifies his last name. Rivers: a freshwater death. Where are we going with all this, Tony?"

Peterson's humor was getting sharper. Now he was eyeing me with intense curiosity. This prompted me to continue:

"The first murder was committed in secret, the second was meant to be visible. They'd killed Roger, but that didn't stop Ginger. Mario warned him not to, but he went to the consulate, he parted the waters. . . ."

"There was no parting of waters. He spilled the beans, smeared shit everywhere. It was a total fucking mess."

"His death had to be bizarre enough to suggest a pact. Then the first body appeared with a hammock noose tied to its dick."

"That knot was a nice touch," Peterson said, smiling.

"I know it was Mario's idea. He accepted what was going on; that's all he could do. He was always trying to help you. The tattoo in Arabic was what closed the case: nobody wanted that detail to be significant. The autopsy wasn't made known until Ríos found it. By then it was too late: Ginger's death was convenient for everybody. I want to know who fired the shot. Or was it just a case of 'madness by association?'"

Peterson inhaled deeply, savoring the smoke.

"If you ask around," he said, "you'll learn that the leading candidate for governor, the head of the opposition, the Secretary of Tourism, the whores, the bishop—all of them wanted it to happen. That's where the heat was coming from. When the rocks are glowing red and the air is practically roasting your face, it's not so hard to come together for a sacrifice. Just ask the Maya: the best people are always the ones to die."

"But none of them fired the speargun. You planned an eclipse, something very Mayan. A moment of darkness to make preparations. You didn't want Támez following your tracks. The order had to come from London, so nobody would know you were the one calling the shots. How did you do it?"

Peterson smiled with renewed satisfaction.

"I like that you're so interested in me," he said.

"I thought you'd resigned yourself to accepting the hotel for what it was, even though you hated the 'selling fear' part."

"A conformist, is that what I am?"

"No. Someone who accepts things. That's all."

"And what makes a person accept things?"

"How did you get them to make such an unusual request of Támez?"

Peterson's eyes brightened the way they often did during our conversations. I knew he wasn't going to hold back. The pleasure of telling his own story would win out over the consequences. There were other reasons, too, but for Peterson nothing could be better than ordering the facts into a narrative. I was, after all, "the man you can trust." His story would make us accomplices.

"Sometimes there's a reason behind the 'madness by association,'" he conceded, smiling. "I like the tale you're proposing, Tony. Even though it's fiction. But we can explore this if you like. How would one convince Mallett to disable a camera? Let's work it out. First of all, it's easy to persuade the Europeans to get behind cultural projects. Did you know Mallett is a Scientologist?"

"No."

"The Scientologists here organize so-called spiritual recitals. 'Poetry by Candlelight.' I told Mallett that we'd hosted several important members from the Church of Scientology. Which was true. I wanted to do something special for them. They're a very supportive community, and they've helped us a great deal. I wanted to give them a surprise."

"And why would you need to disable the camera?"

"The smoking law prohibits lighting candles in enclosed spaces. In this country, it's easier to cut off your neighbor's balls than to light up in a non-smoking zone. We had to disable the camera so that there wouldn't be any record. A petty crime. *Delito.* It's always fascinated me that the Spanish word for 'crime' should look so much like *delight.*

I'll tell you something else nobody's noticed. We also disabled the smoke detector."

Peterson's tone was no longer speculative. He was starting to confess, enjoying his own audacity.

"Nobody thought to make the connection," he said. "Mallett loved the idea of 'Poetry by Candlelight.' As you know, the recital never happened. Sometimes poetry is suspended for murder."

"Mallett could turn you in."

"I'm not so sure. The Scientologists were real, the printed invitations they received were real, and so were the preparations for the recital. And I wasn't at The Pyramid. There was an eclipse and someone took advantage of it. The Maya were marvelous at that. Think about the mural of the Foliated Cross."

He spoke with ferocious excitement. Peterson was magnificently animated; he looked less like a gambling man and more like a very determined jockey.

"I wanted to do a recital for select hotel guests (I can give you their names) and host it in a place as dramatic as the aquarium, but then Ginger turned up dead. A pity. It's too late to get vindictive: vengeance isn't the same as justice. There's no point rounding up the guilty."

He was right. Nobody was going to bother looking for a criminal who'd done everyone a favor. Even so, I pressed him:

"Killing someone isn't revenge?"

"War exists, Tony. Each of us is waging one. I've taken the risk of living among you. Ambrose Bierce was right when he said, 'To be a Gringo in Mexico—ah, that is euthanasia.' There's a reason he disappeared here."

"Mario was going to fire Ginger."

"He certainly put it off."

"He hated him, but he didn't want to kill him."

"Nobody wanted to kill him. That's the real poetry: everyone hated him, but nobody wanted to put a bullet in him."

"But somebody shot the speargun."

"Yes, and for that you need an actual son of a bitch, a *real player*." Peterson was smiling.

"So what can the *real player* tell me then?"

"I don't know that I'm eligible for that role, Tony. I wouldn't presume. I'm not that kind of cowboy." He looked away. The pride in his voice turned bitter. "You know where Ginger Oldenville trained? The Coast Guard's rescue team. The government paid for his elite training. He belonged to a select corps that are subjected to brutal regimens—they spend hours in ice-filled pools developing resistance to hypothermia, go on rescue missions in Alaska. . . . Roger Bacon was in the corps, too." He spoke as if Oldenville's high-level instruction were a personal affront.

"And this bothers you?"

"He'd been called up. They wanted to recruit him."

"For what?"

"The Iraq War."

El Gringo Peterson ran his hand over his brow, then let his cigar drop. It took him a moment to realize it was still smoldering on the desk. He placed the cigar on a plastic coaster but this produced a chemical smell. Finally, he threw the cigar in the dust bin.

"Ginger's personal life never interested me. Neither did his looks. What's the expression? *Striking good looks!* An Aryan god, the kind beloved by Hitler. The gene pool did a beautiful job with him. But he responded poorly to the actual pool they put him charge of. They train you as a lifeguard in the best rescue corps in the world, and you run away. A *fucking defector*. He didn't go to war. Pacifism can be highly immoral, Tony. That's why Ginger was in Mexico. Nobody checks your papers here. When he went to the consulate, they ran the kinds of background checks you can't perform on Google. That's when we learned who he was. A deserter. Ginger wanted to hand over information about the narcotrafficking in exchange for a pardon. He asked the DEA to make a deal with his report. You want to know what the father of a drowned boy thinks of a lifeguard who's also a deserter? People who think they're that wholesome should adopt puppies."

He paused. He'd gone from self-satisfaction to unexpected rage—now he seemed upset with himself. He pinched his own arm, hard, and took another swig. When he spoke, his voice was barely audible:

"The Maya eliminated anyone who posed a challenge to the gods." He became louder: "Ginger thought he was fighting evil just because he knew what was right. But ingenuity can be very dangerous. If you don't know what you're doing, trying to combat disaster can lead to everybody's ruin. When the shit hits the fan, no one's safe from the flying pieces. Your little friend didn't defend his own country, and he brought us another war. Can there be a worse son of a bitch?"

"Going to war and denouncing criminals are two different things."

"They're two different things to you! I wanted to go to Vietnam. I would've given anything to do that."

"The person who killed him, the *real player*—did he want to go to Vietnam?"

"That's irrelevant. The executioner doesn't exist, not in this case. There's no trace, no footage. That file is closed.

'Res judicata,' *dear* Tony. In Mexico, that's the term they use for whatever's been forgotten."

I'd never seen a hint of vanity in El Gringo Peterson. I didn't expect him to brag about his achievements. He was happy with Oldenville's death but his pride wouldn't let him take credit for it. If he said anything, it would be out of principle—to show he had been an instrument of the collective will, the link that held the chain together.

"I'm not thinking of the guilty party," I said. "That doesn't interest me. I'm thinking about 'solitary responsibilities.' What was yours?"

Peterson rummaged through the dust bin. He fished out his cigar and tried to relight it, but his hands were shaking. He went through two or three matches.

"The no-smoking law doesn't apply to this office?"

"This is the only free zone. It's in my contract. I can smoke as much as I fucking want, even cigars forbidden by the United States embargo. This is no-man's-land."

He looked me in the eye. Behind a veil of smoke, I could see him considering the possibility of having a sole witness. If he kept talking, he might compromise himself. On the other hand, he could defend his actions. I knew he wouldn't keep quiet. He was too enamored with being right.

"You want motives?" He cleared the smoke with a wide sweep of his hand. "Someone who could never purge himself of his pain finally had the chance. A second act, Tony. The *comeback*. This nutcase wanted to screw us over for the sake of the greater good—and, in the meantime, to fix his papers. Someone who believed in good intentions, who was convinced that human beings care about each another and life is a granola commercial. An imbecile, *a fucking asshole!* The Pyramid is not some pediatrics pavilion. We sell fear." He sounded like Mario Müller, his loathsome accomplice. "That's how we survive. Ginger understood nothing; he was a messianic Boy Scout. Well, all Boy Scouts are messianic. The redeemer came face to face with his executioner."

"Didn't you say there was no executioner?"

"There was one, Tony. Destiny, destiny..." Peterson grinned; he seemed disoriented.

It was strange to hear him talk like this. His life had been a gamble against fate—a bet he'd largely lost.

He glanced down at his hand, as if he were remembering something, maybe the tension in the speargun's slings as he shot Ginger Oldenville in the back; this gesture of violence had made it the perfect murder and made Peterson both despicable and exemplary, a sacrifice that was now making him smile.

"I'll tell you one thing: that anonymous *someone* made me very happy. No death could have been better than that. There was never a bastard more deserving of what he got. You know the motives, you can deduce the actions."

Peterson had confessed without a confession. In a manner that was both haphazard and full of exact calculations, he had won his right to peace. He couldn't save his son, but he had eliminated another failed lifeguard. At the age of 65, he could savor the joy of having fulfilled his duty. His broken life, spread across many makeshift rooms, marked by solitude, with a difficult job that didn't interest him and gambling that continued to get him into trouble, had placed him at the center of a complex maze from which he'd set himself this mission.

I thought he was finished talking. But he couldn't help taking the stage one last time.

"Think about what happened, Tony. There was no video. All we have is our imagination. Turn off the lights and project the images. The order coming from London to disable two electrical systems (the video surveillance and the smoke detector). Támez's footsteps in the darkness (a subordinate who prefers simple mechanical failures to the problem of determining motives). Ceballos stalled in the dressing room by an Atrium PR rep interviewing him after hours about winning employee of the month. The guy in charge of the aquarium screwing around with the yoga instructor. . . . Where does this leave us? With a moment of solitude. The stage is set for the responsible party, for someone who cannot fail, someone who sends a message: a spear in the back, the symbol of treachery. You know how they celebrated the news on social networks? I'm guessing you're not on Facebook."

"Correct."

"On the Marine blogs it was *party time*. The traitor would never return to sea."

I noticed a sharp letter-opener on the desk. Someone like El Gringo Peterson, a *real player*, someone with "real responsibilities," would be capable of grabbing a weapon like that and stabbing the executioner. There was one way in which Peterson and Ginger were similar: they had both acted blamelessly, motivated by what was right.

Nobody would ever speak out against El Gringo. The mechanics of sacrifice functioned with precision. The death had benefitted everybody. The Maya couldn't have done it better themselves.

The letter-opener glinted under the halogen lamp. Peterson looked into my eyes with a strange sweetness. Maybe he was trying to figure out what I was capable of. For a moment, his expression showed a fondness beyond the feeling between accomplices. As if I were his soul-mate. Maybe sacrifice is what he longed for—the chance to purge away the rest of his pain. I could help him erase one act of impunity with another.

"This is no-man's-land," he reminded me.

He took the letter-opener and slid it toward me, a slow insinuation. He watched me. The weapon was within my reach, but I chose not to take it.

What I remember most from that final meeting with El Gringo is the odd feeling I had when I left. I walked off down the hall baffled by one undeniable fact: I liked the killer.

My opinion of Peterson didn't change much after I learned of the act that most defined him. Sacrificing Ginger Oldenville was sinister and misguided. He didn't deserve what had happened to him. Still, something was keeping me in the executioner's orbit. I wanted to hate him, but couldn't—at least not entirely. Maybe it moved me to know about his accumulated pain, his solitude, the great patience he'd attained in the fulfillment of his duty. All his maniacal effort prevented me from hating him. What's more, it made me think, with some combination of disgust and panic and inexplicable pleasure, that maybe if I'd lived at The Pyramid a bit longer, if the victim had been somebody else, the motivation slightly different, maybe I, too, could have done something similar.

I never saw Mario Müller again. I did go to his suite one last time and ring his doorbell. No one answered. From inside you could hear an alarm clock going off. I worried he was dead. I found a housekeeper. She made a call on her walkie-talkie and asked for permission to use her master key. I was able to get inside.

His rooms didn't show any signs of occupancy. Nor were there signs of someone having departed. In the closet I found three suitcases in perfect condition; they smelled brand new.

Mario had left without luggage. Above the sink I found his medications, a toothbrush, and a tube of toothpaste with the cap missing. In the porcelain soap tray lay a piece of hair that curled like a tilde.

I turned on the computer at his desk and looked for evidence of him on the Cruci/Fiction homepage. Mario Müller wasn't there. Then I typed in my own name. In a moment of vanity and terror, I had come up with a hypothesis: maybe he had registered as Antonio Góngora to make it easier for me to turn into Mario Müller. That little investigation also proved unsuccessful.

I shut his bedroom door softly, as if to leave the tenant undisturbed.

The palm trees lining the main road by The Pyramid were swaying in the breeze. I inhaled the humid, cottony air of the Caribbean. Mario and I had thought about turning the rhythms of these trees into ambient music. I gazed at them sadly. It was like looking at something that's already part of the past, but hasn't yet receded into memory.

James Mallett had left several messages in my room. I'd come up with various excuses for not accepting his job offer, but in the end I didn't have to use any of them.

Remigio—the gardener missing a hand—stopped me next to a grove of date palms.

"They're looking for you." He pointed to a woman standing ten yards away.

I walked up to a lady wearing a plastic green apron, the kind worn at a greasy spoon.

"I'm here on behalf of the director." She extended a pink hand, polished from use, the hand of someone who cleans for a living. It took me a moment to realize she was talking about the director of the shelter.

"We need to go right away," she added.

"I'll get my things."

"There's no time. Do you have your ID?"

"Yes."

"That'll do." I could see the urgency in her eyes. "I've brought everything you need."

She walked off without waiting for my reply. I struggled to keep up with her. We were heading towards a pick-up truck.

"Forgive me for not telling you my name," she said as she started the engine. "It's better for all of us this way."

Friends of friends, I thought. *Solitary responsibilities.*

I didn't mind leaving Luciana's books behind. I'd already read and reread her underlinings with excessive attention, seeking the advice I hadn't known how to hear at the time.

On the other hand, I did regret not being able to take the collection of sounds that Mario had made for me. There was something of him in that. It would have been a perfect way to remember him with Irene. Now we'd have to start from zero. Another tribute to the Maya, inventors of that strange cipher that, having no weight of its own, gives weight to others.

The truck's transmission grunted with each gear shift. The driver handled it firmly. She barely spoke during the ride, but smiled placidly, as if to imply that happiness needs no reason.

We drove through a small village. The woman pointed to a paint shop at the end of the road.

"Comex," she said.

Farther ahead, we passed a gas station.

"Pemex," she said.

She didn't read out any other signs, but these two company names seemed to burst from her like sneezes. She wasn't allowed to say anything in front of me, but her body insisted on breaking the silence. *Comex, Pemex.*

As we approached the shelter, I felt myself getting anxious about meeting Irene. I knew nothing about how to take care of a little girl. Mario had imposed this assignment on me along with all of his memories.

Driving through that pale green undergrowth, I wondered: was Mario looking out from a helicopter on the turbulent sea below, in his final act as Der Meister? Probably not. Maybe he was dying alone in a room somewhere, dreaming of a different death, that of the sacrificed deity.

I considered whether there might be anyone opposed to the adoption. Our unimaginable enemies also had "friends of friends." Two-Tone was dead, but Laura's husband was still alive. Were we running away from him, or from someone else? There was no way to tell, and it seemed better not to know.

Strangely enough, it felt like Peterson's confession had offered me protection. El Gringo wouldn't let anything happen to the one person who knew the deeper reason behind an act that might otherwise seem ordinary, an act that was easy to lump in with the violence of everyday life. I knew he was "responsible." I understood what he had done. Relaying it would've been useless in a law court.

The secret existed; that was enough. It didn't need to be revealed. *Someone* had heard his confession, and Peterson had given his reasons. In an absurd, violent, proud, and maybe disastrous way, I felt immune from what I knew about him.

El Gringo would be safe, too, while managing the bankruptcy. He'd cooperate with Atrium like a loyal business associate who's been ruined to his own satisfaction—distributing the insurance severance without beefing up his own share (the lion's share). He'd exit the jungle alive. Maybe he'd return to Wallingford, Vermont, with the weariness of someone who's accomplished a dangerous and necessary mission. Above all, necessary. He'd find something close to happiness. A hard-won peace; serenity for an animal who'd always known when to go in for the kill.

The director was waiting for me at the entrance to the shelter.

"I'm Teresa," she said. Only then did I realize that during my last visit she hadn't told me her name.

She took me into her office. Inside, she told me how much she cared about Irene Müller, how smart the girl was, how well she'd turned out.

"Why do all of you trust me?" I said.

"You don't trust yourself?"

"Not really."

"We trust you. We have information. This place is high-security." She spoke efficiently, in the tone of a specialist unwilling to compromise the quality of her data.

She handed me some documents and a vaccination card, then went over Irene's academic record and medical history, all at breakneck speed, as if I had higher powers of retention.

"There's only one piece of advice you need about fatherhood," she added, with benevolent wisdom. "Total improvisation."

Laura came into the room. She didn't say hello, just leaned against the doorway. She was wearing a light dress with a print of large flowers; her hair was drawn back in a clasp. I liked the way she looked, though there was something unsettling about her, like one of those unhinged beauties in a French movie, promising the danger of falling for them. "Love me and I'll have a nervous breakdown."

Maybe in another lifetime Luciana had seen a similar appeal in me. Teresa was giving instructions:

"You'll spend the night in the refugee hangar. A small plane will pick you up tomorrow. Laura knows all there is to know about Irene."

She rose. We walked out of the office, through the electronic door and into a front room with a single table. A girl sat there drawing. Irene.

I went over and sat next to her.

"Do you like to draw?" she said. "Let's see. What animal is this?"

She pointed to one of the figures that looked like a rabbit, though I wasn't sure.

"A dog," I guessed.

"What breed?"

"Rabbit."

Irene laughed softly, revealing her upper teeth and shaking her head a little. A muted laugh, innocent, sort of goofy. Mario Müller's laugh.

"Tony brought you this," the director said, handing Irene a stuffed toy cat.

"What's its name?" Irene asked.

"Yoshio," I said, improvising. "Her family comes from Japan. See her eyes?"

"Yoshio." Irene stroked the cat against her cheek. "And what's your name?"

"Tony, but they call me Mario."

"'Mario' is a nickname for 'Tony'?"

"Sometimes. You can also call me Antonio."

"Aunt Laura, do you like Yoshio?"

"Better than Siguifredo," she said, then turned to me and explained. "Siguifredo was an iguana that lived in the shelter for awhile. He was the only adult male."

"He had bad breath," Irene said. "Once I gave him a Sugus square to make the smell go away, but it didn't work."

I was getting to know my new life, a place where the reptiles ate candy.

Laura Ribas carried her things in a department store shopping bag. Irene had a backpack with donkey ears, based on some cartoon character I didn't recognize.

We went to the truck. The woman with the apron was charged with our belongings. She placed them at the back of the pickup and got behind the wheel, then fell into another hermetic silence. I waited while Laura climbed up slowly onto the seat. I didn't want to see her legs. I didn't want to like what I saw. Not this soon. I didn't want to, because obviously I already did. Far too soon.

Throughout the good years I spent with Luciana, the two of us talked about the couples we knew and which of them we thought might split up. We analyzed "how they were managing," studied their ups and downs, and amused ourselves by designing fears or suspicions or issues they hadn't resolved. We placed bets on which couples would break up, feeling sympathy for the miserable ones or distrust towards the ones who seemed too happy. Thinking about other couples and their cycles of insecurity was a way of convincing ourselves that what we had would be everlasting. We were almost always wrong. Our friends had a knack for falling short of our estimations, or else exceeding them. But even intuiting and anticipating their ruptures kept us together. With the strange immunity of knowing other people's problems, we avoided our own.

That was the only time I had ever been part of a couple. Before then, and after, my life was a confounding mess where I always had fewer women than I wanted but more than I deserved.

Now I was traveling with a woman I didn't know, who remembered the time I'd fainted, and a little girl who'd become "mine" due to her urgent need to be rescued. Our driver was Ms. Plastic Apron and Pink Hands.

Half an hour later, we spotted the sloping roof of the hangar.

"This place can hold four thousand people," our driver said.

A guard opened the front gate and cleared the lane. It looked like he'd been waiting for us. He didn't take out any visitor's log or ask for our IDs. *Friends of friends.* The network was expanding.

Our driver pulled up to the door of the shelter and got out quickly. In the back of the pick-up was a discount store shopping bag. She handed it to me.

"Things for your trip," she said. I opened the bag and

found toothpaste, a disposable razor, some underwear, and a brand-new pair of socks. The essentials for an overnight journey. I'd left The Pyramid with the clothes on my back.

"Travel safe," she said by way of goodbye. She squeezed my hand, then kissed Irene and Laura. She drove off with the same calm swiftness that had brought us there.

The sun was setting. The sky was turning green.

We were the only guests at the hangar. It would be strange to sleep surrounded by four thousand empty cots. There was a kitchenette built into one of the walls, and it came equipped with a hotplate, a refrigerator that made an unnecessary amount of noise, and a cupboard covered in soccer decals.

Laura rummaged through the kitchen drawers and found a box of cereal, which she opened and sniffed. She wrinkled her nose.

I decided to take a walk.

"Don't go too far," warned the guard.

I ventured toward some bushes that were buzzing with insects. For some reason, I started thinking about my father. I thought of his large hands and his particular smell of cologne and raw leather; I thought of the weight of his hand on my chest when I went to sleep, and the way people envied his lightning computations. I thought of the photo of him in the park, where he's smiling with the simple pleasure of offering cotton candy.

We never managed to love him. After he left us, my mother was loved by several men, or maybe it was just one. That vague silhouette, a shadow I used to catch glimpses of from our apartment when I'd wait up till 2 a.m., hating her for getting back so late but feeling relieved she was finally home.

Mario Müller was her adoring puppy, one of the admirers she needed in order to feel loved and desired. When old age started approaching (sooner than she expected, at a time when youth seemed to be getting longer), she quit both her jobs as a hearing specialist, as if hearing fewer compliments meant she shouldn't be hearing anything at all. When she retired, she did so in the same resolute way she cleaned our apartment—a home where we never received any guests. Her decline was gradual and she never cried over it, which was odd for me, a little chilling. Slowly but surely, the Valium became less of a cure than a prison sentence.

Sometimes while waiting up for her, around midnight, I'd start thinking she was dead, and feel tortured by a sense of helplessness. How else could I react to her absence? The next day, when she lit her first cigarette, I felt like asking, "What should I do if you die?" I needed instructions, a phone number, the name of someone with a clear job description, some sort of plan. But I never asked her. I limited myself to waiting up for the telltale sounds: the noise of a car pulling in five flights down; the dry, metallic scrape of the door; the tin slam that assured me my mother hadn't died.

Maybe this is what had predisposed me to a lifetime of insomnia and a sensitivity to ambient sound.

Decades later, Der Meister had invented paternity for me. Here I stood, before the buzzing insects, sweating in the Caribbean air one final time. I imagined rounding up the Müller siblings, the family I'd always wanted to be a part of, and telling them they had a niece.

It was getting dark. The bushes emitted a strong scent, something medicinal. I walked back to the hangar.

A few yards from the spot where we were sleeping, I

heard voices. Irene and Laura were talking. I paused and listened: a few stray words, murmurs of sound. I thought back to Mario Müller's old house, the memory of voices carrying from an adjoining room. While trying to sleep under a thin blanket, I'd hear occasional phrases, as if the air around me was creaking. At home I could make out my mother's footsteps or the ding of a spoon in a cup, but never any dialogue. You needed another person for that. The same thing happened when I lived with Luciana. Only at Mario's house could you hear these conversations about nothing, with no meaning aside from the fact of human breath, impressions of those who were speaking, a large, indistinct company, the greatest happiness of my childhood.

Just before the door, I made out a phrase.

"Look. It's like a fairy tale."

It was Irene. She was pointing at the moon.

There was an enormous moon at the center of the world. Where had I read that? Had Luciana underlined it somewhere? Where did those words exist?

I was scared of entering that room with its four thousand cots. I stayed outside for a while and admired the moon as primitive man might have: as a bumpy film screen, the first cinema in history. I saw amorphous clouds and craters and thought about my father. At another time, fathers had been pulled away by distant entities: a war, a job, another body. A father was a person who at any moment might disappear. For centuries, bodies had intersected so that fathers could run away. Mario had found out too late about his daughter. It was a different time now, perhaps only a brief one, when fathers tended to stick around.

I didn't want to think, but I was thinking. It was because of the moon. Its surface triggered conflicting ideas. A blank screen for those who had no cinema.

I went into the hangar. The curved ceiling had an overwhelming grandeur. It was a place designed for crowds yet to come.

Irene was hugging the stuffed cat I had supposedly given her.

"Is there any Nutella?" she said.

Laura was folding a shirt. I went into the kitchenette and found some Nutella, but not any bread. There were some flour tortillas, the Tía Rosa brand. I smeared one of them with Nutella and gave it to Irene.

"You have four fingers. Like in the Simpsons," she said. "And you're a good cook."

Irene was smart. I hadn't cooked anything; she was teasing me sweetly.

The girl ate hungrily. Laura went up to her when she saw she had finished.

"Your teeth," she said. They were used to communicating with few words. Irene went into the other room where the bathroom was located. It was a relief that she didn't take too long. Laura and I had nothing to say to each other.

"Will you read me a story?" Irene said, curling up on the cot where she'd left the cat. She took a book out of her backpack. *The Worst Woman in the World.*

I read her the story, a tale in which the battle between good and evil made sense. Irene laughed and I noticed she had a few missing teeth. Her mind wasn't inside that hangar; it was elsewhere, in the world of the story.

She closed her eyes, and I stroked her hair.

Soon she was asleep, as if she'd drawn on some special reserves of exhaustion. I wondered if all children had this ability.

The moonlight altered her lips and made her look as if she were tasting something in her dream. What desire or rage or pain or happiness or wild cravings could inspire that mouth? Her lips parted slightly as if she were savoring the night.

I went back into the kitchenette.

"Want a Nutella crepe?" I asked Laura.

"Is that all you know how to make?" She bit her lip.

"Sorry. I say things I don't mean."

Laura sat on a cot, crossed her legs, fiddled with one of her sandals, then took them both off. Again, I noticed her cracked toenails.

The night air was now dense. The sheet metal roof made the humidity feel heavier.

I chewed on a cold tortilla. It was unpleasant but I ate it anyway.

"Did you really meet me when you were little?" I said. "It's very strange."

"Strange enough to be true."

"Did Mario ask you to tell me that?"

"Why would he do that?"

"So there would be a connection between us. He liked doing that, establishing connections. I don't remember you."

"Well, I do. It doesn't matter whether you do or not. You were dead."

"Did you know Mario well?"

"I knew him as a little girl, through my dad. When I got to Kukulcán, he helped me out. I was very lost. Plus, I was a friend of Camila's. He's the one who took me to the shelter. And he was always sending me chocolates, like I was obsessed with them."

"You don't like chocolate?"

"Sure, but that's all he ever sent me. *Laura equals chocolates,* that's how he thought."

"He liked things to be ordered. He grew up in a house that was total chaos. He got away so he could impose order on thousands of rooms."

Our words rose to the ceiling and seemed to linger there. Maybe if there'd been four thousand people around us, the acoustics would have felt more normal. Now it reminded me of the warehouses where Los Extraditables had once played.

"I'm not going to turn into your worst nightmare," Laura continued. "I promise. I'll behave."

She smiled, as if such a promise was impossible.

A bluish glow came in through the window. I burped and smelled the Nutella. Then I went over to Irene's cot. Her breathing was even. Asleep, she seemed strangely trusting, a trust that made me ache. A pain like the damaged nerve in my leg.

"Everything's going to be all right," Laura said.

I took her by the hand. Her fingers felt rough.

"Good night," she said.

She went over to one of the cots and lay down on the blanket, fully dressed.

It took me a long time to fall asleep. Still, for a master insomniac, I slept better than most nights.

I woke up bewildered by the humidity and the buzzing mosquitoes. Laura was making breakfast. I was tangled up absurdly in the blankets, something that always happens when I manage to sleep in the heat.

I went into the kitchenette. Laura was wearing a blouse

that exposed a section of her back with a red scar running right across it.

"The coffee came out horrible," she said.

She was right. I told her so.

"I make other things even worse." She smiled.

An hour later, I heard a motor. The small plane.

The guard came to get us. We took our bags and made our way out to the airstrip, which was shorter than the one at the base.

The plane was sky blue. The paint was peeling: you could see it had once been yellow. I wondered whether we'd make it to Mexico City in such a jalopy. Maybe there would be several stops. The pilot had disembarked and was waving from a distance. The plane was three hundred feet away.

That's when I said something I hadn't said in forty years:

"Let's see who wins!"

We left our bags on the ground.

Irene spread her arms, her body tilted forward. She started running. I'd planned to let her beat me, but this took little effort. Laura ran faster than me, too. The three of us ran with outstretched arms, like planes coming in to land.

"I won!" Irene yelled as she reached out and touched the small aircraft.

I came in third.

"Here's the family!" The pilot welcomed us, like a master of ceremonies. He had a thick mustache, brilliant eyes, white teeth. He exuded energy. The decrepit plane seemed to invigorate him.

He greeted me with a strong handshake and gestured a vague hello to the girls. A respectful person, the old-fashioned kind, who thought that by greeting the head of the household he was saying hello to the rest.

To all appearances, that's what we were: a family. The term didn't seem so far-fetched, not then at least. What do you call those who run so the littlest one can win?

I looked at Laura. She stared back as if she was seeing me in a different light. She tamped down a smile. Something about us was strangely amusing to her, but she didn't want to say it. I didn't want to tell her what I felt either, not yet.

"We have to go back for our things," Laura said, pointing to our bags at the end of the runway.

"You go," Irene said.

Laura started heading in the direction from which we'd come. After a few feet, she stopped, turned back and gave me an inquisitive look.

"I feel dead," I said.

"What, again?" She smiled.

"Always," I said, and went with her.